The Convent's Assassin

Pauline Drouin-Degorgue

Strategic Book Publishing and Rights Co.

Strategic Book Publishing and Rights Co., LLC
USA | Singapore
www.sbpra.net

For information about special discounts for bulk purchases, please
contact Strategic Book Publishing and Rights Co. Special Sales, at
bookorder@sbpra.net.

ISBN: 978-1-946539-22-9

Edited by Heather Mills

Book Design: Suzanne Kelly

To my granddaughter Laurence

Thanks to my editor, Heather Mills

Thanks to Mr. Jacques Beaudoin,
ex Deputy Minister of Security in Québec

Prologue

In the dark hall, one can only see the pale light of a small night lamp. A black silhouette advances slowly, hugging the wall. The hands of the indistinct form are hidden within its garment, until it stops in front of a closed door. Suddenly, one hand appears and turns the doorknob; the other holds a long-pointed object.

In the room, a sleeping body offers its uncovered throat. In a split second, the murdering arm rises and strikes the neck two times. The weapon pierces the throat to the right and to the left. The body convulses for a moment, before surrendering to death. The door recloses, and the shadow slips back into the darkness.

The dead woman is the Mother Guardian of the Convent; Mother Notre-Dame-Des-Pins. She was a mean and cruel woman. Many lives were imprisoned in her hands. They all feared to be destroyed by the avenging woman. She had to die. However, who possessed the courage to overcome fear and administer justice?

Discipline

The young girls passed by the vestry to take a sweater before going outside for the evening recess. They arrived at the pebbled pathways of a large vegetable garden divided into four rectangles, each framed by a row of white stones. In the centre, stood a statue of the Virgin Mary, which was surrounded by a perfect circle of numerous flowers. The path led to a quaint wood. Passing through it, one could catch in the distance a glimpse of a monastery where young men prepared to be monks. Down below on the right, the little village was disappearing behind the rays of the setting sun. To the right, the nearby mountain appeared to be on fire under the descending red dome: the autumn leaves shone in all their colours. The last gentleness of September was everywhere. Touched by all the beauty, Céline watched in silence.

"Hello, your name is Marie-Céline, is it not?"

Céline had not noticed the approach of the little curly brunette. The girl was about her age. Céline was a little surprised by the formal tone of the voice, and she answered sadly.

"No, my real name is Céline."

"Don't worry about that. Here, everyone has a new name. Look at me, my real name is Simone, and I am called Marie-Simone, she sighed."

"How old are you?"

"I'm twelve years old, but please, let's be careful how we talk, or we'll be scolded."

She barely had time to finish her sentence before the terrible voice of Mother Notre-Dame-Des-Pins shouted,

"What are you doing there, you two young disobedient. Don't you know it is strictly forbidden here to speak privately

1

to someone? We walk as a group and we only talk in a group. Is that clear?"

No, things were not clear to Céline. She couldn't understand the reasoning behind all the rules imposed on her. It was as if a stifling yoke had been placed on her shoulders. She had only arrived that morning, but she felt as if a million years had passed since she had left home. It had not been a paradise there, but here, she felt she had descended into hell.

With time, Céline would discover that her mother, in her great wisdom, had chosen for her daughter, the most severe Convent in the country: a place where the young boarders were trained with the intention to make future nuns. There, everything was designed to break the character of the individual, to crush their personality, as to mould everyone according to the sacred Rule of the St-François-d'Assise'Sisters. Humiliations, rebukes, deprivations, nothing was spared in order to tame 'the wild rebels' as the young girls were called by their oppressors. Later, Céline would learn that the name of the place was the Ste Marie des Roses 'Juvenate.

For the moment, Céline was overwhelmed. She didn't say a word till recess was over. By doing so, she hoped to keep the awful woman from yelling at her again. The little girl was relieved when she heard the bell ring to call them inside.

It was the evening study session. The classrooms were located on the second floor. The study room, situated at the end of the hall. There, held thirty desks. Céline was assigned a place. While all the other girls were studying or learning their lessons, she had nothing to do, having arrived that same day. She didn't know what to do until she noticed a bookcase in the back of the room. She rose from her seat and went to select one of the many books which lined its shelves. She loved to read and was soon engaged in a new story. Céline did not notice the approach of Mother Notre-Dame-Des-Pins who forcibly poked her forefinger into the little girl's shoulder as she shouted loudly:

"What are you doing there? Since when do you have permission to read during study time?"

2

"But" … tried to explain Céline.

"And you dare reply impolitely! We will have to put you in your place, and if you do not learn to submit, you will be expelled. I've been very clear on that subject with your mother."

That night, Céline cried silently in her pillow, knowing the worst was yet to come.

The Family

Céline was a child of great vitality. Very young, she had been considered hyperactive. She wanted to see, to touch, to experiment. The price of this gift was her liberty. If she played outside during the day, her mother would tie her in case she became too adventurous. One day, when she was three years old, they had found her standing on the top of her parent's car. How had she climbed up there?

Her home was located near a lake. It was feared that she would want to check the water's temperature. A little further, a heavily travelled street posed a real danger to this impetuous adventurer. As the danger increased, Céline saw her rope tighten. Surprisingly, she showed no frustration towards her situation as she understood that any rebellion would only bring more trouble. Her character adopted a philosophy of self discipline in order to avoid worsening her condition. As the years passed, she calmed down, and accepted her assigned place in the family: To play silently away from her parent's view. If by any chance, she would become excited out of joy and would express her enthusiasm, her father, disappointed that he had not been given a son, was eager to raise his hand against her.

Nevertheless, the father worked hard to correct this betrayal of nature, and a few years later, his wife was pregnant again. She became enormous. She was carrying twins. Céline was elated! She'd have company! She'd never be alone again! She was so anxious for the babies to arrive that she didn't dare express here joy. No one had ever talked to her directly about the upcoming event, but in listening to fragments of conversations, she had finally understood what everybody else already knew.

However, when the yellow ambulance arrived to take her mother away, she did not connect the two events right away. It

4

was the neighbour, with whom she was staying, who told her what was happening. Her mother had gone to the hospital to purchase the babies which she would then bring home.

Céline spent those days away from home dreaming about the wonderful small creatures that would soon be part of her life. One baby would give her great joy, but two meant overflowing abundance.

Céline's ability to adapt was rather short. Anguish overwhelmed her daily. When daylight was fading away and darkness spread its veil upon earth, a heavy weight took hold of her heart, her breath quickened, and her legs grew weak. The child didn't know how to express her distress to anyone. Once, she had tried to receive some comfort from her mother, explaining how she felt. The answer had come like a threatening sword, "You must have done something foolish that you are hiding from us, and that we are about to discover." The child had searched among the vast array of sins she had committed. Which one had caused all this misery? Was it those cookies she had eaten without permission, or her forbidden visit to that kind neighbour, or perhaps it was the little cat she had surreptitiously snuck into her room? The more she pondered, the greater her distress. Céline never again shared her problems with anyone, for she had concluded that her sufferings were deserved, just punishment for a terrible sinner. If no one knew her faults, she could pretend innocence.

The ten days spent with someone who was basically a stranger had been very painful for Céline, especially mealtime since her nervous stomach could not bear any food. The P. family was displeased with the ungrateful child who did not appreciate the delicious meals, given so heartily.

One morning, she was rescued by her father who came and simply said,

"Your mother is no longer in the hospital. You're coming back home."

He was a rather cold mannered man. How could he had been any different towards a child he considered a burden sent by Providence. He resented her. Even more now, that he was the father of two male heirs. Céline was not bothered by her father's attitude, for she was bursting with happiness. As light as a flying bird, she no longer felt that stone weighing inside her. She trotted alongside her father's wide stride. Not a word was said between the two. Céline couldn't care less; she was already conversing with her little brothers.

When she entered the house, her mother, Ernestine, who had already snuggled the two babies into a large crib built by Albert himself, greeted Céline with the command,

"Go fetch me the parcel lying on the floor of my bedroom!"

From this moment, Céline made herself believe she was indispensable to her mother. She became the marathon girl, always aware of her mother's needs. She was running from morning to night to help her, hoping for a little affection in return, but it was useless as Ernestine was never satisfied: Céline was shamefully scolded for the tiniest error, while her hours of devotions went virtually unnoticed. "It's just normal that she helps me a little, I'm snowed under by all the work."

Céline felt very gratified with her new situation. Someone was always asking her to do something. She now had a place in the house. She was very useful since her mature character allowed her to assume responsibilities above her age. For instance, she would give the bottle to one baby while her mother bathed the other one, and then did the same thing for her other brother. She accomplished this task like a competent grown up. Ernestine considered it completely normal, though many, including her own father, believed it to beyond her ability.

Otherwise, the little girl was rewarded greatly for her efforts by her brothers, John and James, who were lovely babies. They soon recognized the warmth and odour of her tiny body. She was the one who could calm their cries, who knew how to make them fall asleep.

One afternoon, when Céline was feeding John and her mother was bathing James, a neighbour, Yvette P, came for an unexpected visit. Puzzled to see Céline feeding her brother, she asked Ernestine:

"Tell me dear, does Céline often help you like that?"

"Yes, she does that several times a day."

"Every day? Are you serious? Every four hours? For both babies?" inquired the woman.

Giving her a look of despise, Ernestine answered, "I already said yes. Why do you ask something so obvious!"

"It is because I thought Céline was only five years old" …

"Yes, she is, and she is old enough to make herself useful… at least a little" ….

"You think that she doesn't do enough?"

"There is always room for improvement and it is not in praising a child that you get results", scolded Ernestine.

"Well, I would not ask my five-year-old Suzanna to take her little sister into her arms, even for five minutes. She could let her fall to the floor." Yvette smiled, trying to inject a little humour into the atmosphere.

"If you would have raised her correctly, instead of letting her do what she wanted… and with whom she wanted," added Ernestine with a touch of wickedness. Yvette felt unwelcomed by this unpleasant woman.

"I think it's time to leave now… I just brought little gifts for the twins…"

"Put them there. I'll open them later. I'm actually overloaded with work," declared Ernestine, putting an end to this annoying visit.

Yvette had promptly left with tears in her eyes, swearing to never come back to this dreadful woman's house.

After Yvette's departure, Ernestine had given her daughter a lingering glance which Céline immediately interpreted as a bit of tenderness. It was more than she had ever hoped to have.

Months went by, and the babies would soon be turning one-year-old. The house was full of joyful laughter. John and James were healthy and happy babies. Céline would sit among their toys enjoying playing with them. She was so happy being with her two little brothers, that she didn't seem to miss the company of children her own age.

Céline had not noticed when John no longer played with them. He would stay in his corner, turning a toy over and over in his hands, showing no interest in his brother or sister. Other times, he would rock back and forth for hours, lost in his own world. Albert was alarmed at the odd behaviour of one of his sons. He swiftly blamed his daughter:

"What did you do to your brother that he won't play with you anymore?"

"We want to play with him, but he doesn't…."

She didn't had time to finish her sentence before a heavy slap from her father silenced her. Albert didn't understand what was happening with his son, and it troubled him. What was wrong with his little John? There must be an explanation or a culprit somewhere.

Céline was an easy target. He was convinced it was her fault. He had never agreed that she'd be allowed so close to his boys. She was too old for them. It was an unhealthy situation. All his worries gathered in a sudden rage against Céline. He grasped her by her clothes and dragged her to her bedroom where he threw her violently to the floor as he screamed, "From now on, I forbid you to play with your little brothers. You have already done them enough harm."

Céline crawled into her wardrobe, closing the door behind her. She stayed there for hours without moving, crushed by her pain, fearing that the tiniest movement on her part would plunge her into a bottomless pit. She wanted to disappear, to not exist anymore.

When Albert went back into the kitchen, he had calmed down a little. He bent down and picked up John. The child began to scream, furiously trying to escape. Ernestine came and pulled the child from his father's arm shouting after him,

"You're so clumsy with children!"

The family was now on alert. John's behaviour had worsened. He didn't seem to hear his name anymore. He was indifferent to his brother's presence. He played alone, but almost never varied his activity. Sometimes, he would stare at a light for hours as if nothing else existed around him. Other times, he'd start running on all fours, all over the place, without anybody being able to stop him. He would bump into an obstacle and hurt himself, but it didn't stop him. It was as if he didn't feel it. His movement carried him like an incontrollable torrent. He was going nowhere. It was as if a spring had burst in his head, winding him up indefinitely. He could go on like this for a whole hour, which seemed an eternity for his parents. If someone tried to stop him by taking him in their arms and talking to him softly, he seemed to double up in pain. One day, he cruelly bit his mother's arm who quickly released him to his own devices.

Céline was finally called to the rescue. She spent a whole afternoon sitting beside the little boy trying to interest him at what she knew used to amuse him. John didn't seem to recognize her anymore. He was alone in his own world. No one was invited into his ivory tower. He couldn't bear being rocked anymore, but he would sway to and fro until he fell down.

A visiting nurse was called to examine the child who refused vehemently her approach. The woman observed John a long time while she asked the anxious parents numerous questions. She appeared very preoccupied, and said at last

"I'm not sure, but it might be a neurological disease. I advise you to consult a specialist."

"He will recover though?" the tearful mother wondered.

"I cannot say," lied the worried nurse. Then, looking at James, who was playing calmly by himself, she asked:

"Are they identical twins?"

"Yes", answered the alarmed mother who seemed to read the nurse's thoughts. "Are you trying to tell me it could happen to his brother too?"

"I never said anything like that!" exclaimed the woman. "I only asked you a question!"

"Don't make fun of me! I understood perfectly what you meant," said the insulted woman.

A few months later, James didn't answer when his name was called. The round of consultations with specialists began as the parents were desperate for answers. They were looking for a magical solution that would put an end to their uncertainty. Finally, the terrible diagnosis fell; the twins suffered from a severe form of autism, a disease without a cure.

Difficulty in the Family

The drama affected each member of the family differently. Albert fell into a deep depression. He behaved like an automaton. He went to work, fulfilled his household obligations, but nothing was done with pleasure, every task was undertaken to avoid thinking too much. He recoiled inside himself, indifferent to everything and to everyone.

Ernestine, for her part, could not think about anything else. She constantly had to face the harsh reality before her. The two boys were just impossible to raise. They wouldn't obey any rule. Nothing she tried seemed to yield any results. Gentleness left them indifferent. They didn't even seem to understand the tender words their mother whispered in their ears. They hated all physical contact. Ernestine's preferred method of coercion failed as well. In fact, any physical aggression provoked incredible rage from the two boys, but they were unable to make a link between the punishment and the forbidden act, which they repeated again and again.

Ernestine was ready to accept disorder, negative attitudes, and even unattainable communication with her sons, but she couldn't tolerate their dirtiness, which utterly disgusted her. She kept telling herself that there were limits to what a human being could bear. Meals were especially trying. As soon as they had a chance, the twins would throw food everywhere, covering their faces, hair and clothes completely. The only solution was for the poor mother to feed them herself, not allowing them any contact with the food. It was a very long and boring task.

Under normal circumstances, this obligation lasts only a couple years. By two, a child is usually able to feed himself. If a mishap occurs, he can express regret because he has learnt that his parents are going to be mad at him. John and James never understood any external intervention. At six, they were still behaving like one-year-old children. Ernestine often thought they could not be that bright. They didn't talk and comprehended absolutely nothing of their parents' language. No need to mention that potty training was impossible to achieve. The mother never stopped changing diapers, washing clothes, and bathing her forever filthy children.

Ernestine only consolation was her regular encounters with other parents who were living the same experience. She felt comforted by them. Sometime, there was even a little hope.

One day, the group began to talk enthusiastically about a therapy centre where certain children had achieved remarkable progress. Ernestine spoke to Albert about it, but they lived in the country, and the hospital was in the city. Ernestine would be away for a whole day, and probably would not be back even for supper. Albert, who didn't want to share his meal alone with Céline, argued that he would like to go by himself to a restaurant.

"It'd be too expensive for the two of us."

The truth was that his daughter's presence bothered him. Ernestine felt strangled by his selfishness:

"Why wouldn't you do your part? I'm doing more than I can bear, and you won't help me even a little?"

"I provide you a living! You should be glad of it. If you had to go out and work!"

"And who would take care of the boys? It's a full-time job, you know!"

And this was the reason it had been decided that Céline would be sent away to boarding school. Anyway, this solution pleased everybody. Since Céline was away at school all day long, her mother could no longer count on her. When she returned home, she tried to do her best, but the twins were now too heavy for her strength since they still had to be handled like babies. Besides, Ernestine had lost all interest in her older daughter, for she was entirely occupied with her crippled sons. Albert, for his part, saw Céline only as another hardship he had to bear. He often wished that things were reversed and that she had been stricken with the disease instead of his precious sons. "Life is so unfair!" he thought." For this man, the superiority of the male sex was indisputable. When God wanted to reward a man, he'd send him a son. The arrival of his two handicapped children forced him to revise his theory. Their birth proved to be a poisoned gift.

Céline had started school with a heavy burden. As much as she had rejoiced at her brothers' birth, their indifference caused her to suffer greatly. They really seemed to have loved their sister when they were babies, but suddenly, they didn't even recognize her. It was as if someone had come during the night and had stolen their souls. Céline couldn't believe it.

Even if everyone in her family tried to hide their pain, at times, Céline had caught a glimpse of hatred in her parents' eyes when they looked at her, as if they thought she was responsible for all their problems.

Unfortunately, she asked herself the same terrible question. Was it possible that her inexperience in taking care of the babies had brought on this terrible sickness? This idea of guilt began to taunt her more and more often. She carried her secret alone. To whom could she have confided her responsibility when she was confronted with the evidence every day?

For Ernestine, the whole world revolved around her. She hardly noticed that others existed, unless it brought her some personal satisfaction. Consequently, her daughter's happiness was unimportant to her. Otherwise, the idea of a boarding school did not displease her at all. Away from all temptation, no one could ever say a word about her daughter, like the gossips she heard about other girls who were said to chase after boys!

One morning after breakfast, Ernestine declared bluntly to Céline that she was being placed in a boarding school. It was not presented as a proposition, but as an order. The institution had already been chosen.

Céline received this news as if a brick had fallen on her head. She had not seen it coming, and it hurt her immensely. She didn't say a word, but went silently to her room. The mother didn't object, glad she had met no resistance: "Good thing done," she told herself, unaware of the agony it had aroused in her daughter's soul. Céline was devastated. Was anyone there to help her? She was drowning!

The family lived on a street where a single row of houses lined each side; nothing had been constructed behind them. In back of Céline's house was a vast wood. It was her personal playground. She had even built herself a little hutch where she would go to read or tell herself adventure stories. Nobody knew this secret hide-away existed. It was her refuge.

That day, she had gone there to be alone and hide her sorrows. She had stayed the whole day without moving, as if she wanted to stop time. Her chosen corner was located in a small clearing, up on a little hill, where one could see the trees down below. The still warm autumn sun had heated the ground all day. Céline had even taken a nap on a heap of leaves, using an old blanket as a pillow. At dusk though, the temperature dropped, and the child was now shivering, but nothing could have made her go back to the place where she was no longer wanted.

She wrapped herself in her blanket and began to dream. Was there a way to escape that Convent? It reminded her of a sad story she had read in her history book about the deportation of the Acadians. She still remembered the date, 1755. A group of French Canadians, who lived in Nova Scotia, possessed land and houses that the English Government wanted. On the charge of insubordination, it was decided they would be removed from their homes. All able men had been imprisoned in the church of Long-Pré to wait for boats that would take them so far that they'd never think of returning.

Céline had replayed this scenario a hundred timed in her head:

Imprisoned in the church, two young men insisted on fighting for their freedom. They wanted to break down the door. Some older men objected, convinced that armed soldiers were waiting for them outside, and that as soon as someone would try to escape, they would immediately be killed. They discussed and fought for hours. Finally, the doors opened, and the French were greeted by a strong contingent of British soldiers who surrounded them and marched them to the waiting ships where they were pushed on board with the points of their bayonets. As the boat left, the prisoners turned their heads toward the shore and saw that their houses had been set on fire. They believed that their women and children were burning inside.

Céline's imagination saw this scene vividly, and she cried her heart out, not understanding that she was only crying over herself. She felt as lost and lonely as these men who had been taken away from their home and brought to an unknown country.

At the little girl's home, it was supper time. The mother, who always needed help while she prepared the meat, called for her daughter. No answer. She went into her room and realized she was not there. She went outside to ask her husband if he had seen her. He told her that he had not seen her get off the school bus that afternoon.

"She didn't go to school then?" said the puzzled mother. I was sure I saw her leave with her school bag this morning."

"Well, you were mistaken", answered Albert unconcerned.

"But where is she?" worried Ernestine

"She is surely not very far. It is not that easy to get rid of bad weeds!" muttered the father.

"I knew you didn't like her, but not that much!" said the surprised mother."

"I would like her if she'd be more lovable," added the man. "She never says a word. She talks as much as a fish."

"I admit she is not very talkative, but I need her right now. She has to come and look after her brothers", argued the mother.

Albert continued his work without adding a word. Ernestine went into the house to prepare supper, rushing to get through her work. When the boys were in bed, the mother made a few phone calls to friends who confirmed that Céline had not been in school all day. At the end of the evening, the tired parents went to bed and slept soundly. The loss of their daughter didn't trouble them at all. She was no longer part of their thoughts. Early the next morning, frozen and hungry, Céline returned.

When Albert saw her, he wanted to spank her as she deserved, but Ernestine stopped him, saying coldly:

"Let her be, she won't be here next week anyway."

This is how Céline learnt that she would be leaving soon.

The Great Disturbance

On a nice September afternoon, the little family whose father, Albert, was recognized as a good father and his wife, Ernestine, a holy mother, suffering deeply from the birth of two crippled children, went to lock up their oldest daughter in a *Cloister*.

The Convent was located about fifty kilometres from their home. It was hidden a little outside a lost village at the foot of a rounded mountain. Travelling down the main street, then, tuning right one would ascend an abrupt slope, and then, it would appear with its flat façade of red bricks. In the center of a circular driveway, there was a statue of the Virgin Mary with her hands open as if throwing down flowers at her feet.

For a week, as Céline looked after the twins, Ernestine was busy packing a trunk with things bought specially for her daughter's departure. She proceeded, checking off a detailed list of undergarments, shoes, nightgowns, bras, towels etc. all identified with their owner's name. It was finally completely filled.

"All this for me!", thought Céline sadly. In reality, she knew it wasn't true. Her mother had not done it for her, but once again was trying to impress others. as the nuns would think everything was perfect. Céline hadn't asked for all that expense! Anyway, she knew everything was only done to keep her away from them. "It's for your own good; you'll thank us later on!" In reality, Céline would curse them for those years of hellish sufferings.

Albert parked the car in front of the main entrance. They went up the steps, the parents in front, Céline behind, and Ernestine rang the bell. A first door opened on a small portal. A little window opened, and an old wrinkled face of a nun appeared, silently staring at them. Promptly, Ernestine announced,

"We are here to bring our daughter. We've already talked to the Mother Superior. She is waiting for us."

Céline noticed her mother was using her grand unctuous voice reserved for special occasions. There was a buzzing sound and the second door opened. The nun came out from her little corner. Her garment was entirely white. She led them to a very small room, furnished only with a few chairs.

"Someone is coming to meet you."

She didn't look at them. Her voice was distant, faint, like that of an automaton. She disappeared immediately. A few minutes later, another woman, smiling, sure of herself, arrived. Her clothes were also entirely white, but with a difference from the other nun. It was a soft woollen dress, instead of the stiff cotton of the first one, and on her forehead, she wore a rigid band holding a woollen veil resting on a white fabric completely covering the head and the neck. Only the face of the woman showed. Céline was to learn later that different clothes indicated different positions within the *Cloister.* Those who wore the soft woollen robes were called *Mothers* and were concerned with intellectual tasks, while those who wore the stiff cotton were called *Sisters* and were assigned the role of a servant.

The Mother Guardian, who was meeting with the parents, was in charge of the girls. She cordially greeted them with an amiable word for Céline. Ernestine chuckled with pleasure. She couldn't resist telling the nun the whole story about the terrible ordeal she was experiencing with her autistic twins, making sure that the nun understood the immense courage needed to overcome such an adversity. Mother Notre-Dame-Des-Pins, the Mother Guardian. was listening compassionately, speaking about Providence and God's will.

Céline watched them closely. She was disgusted, noticing their false smiles and hypocritical bows. What were they so happy about? What were they celebrating? The parents had come to dispose of their merchandise. They had convinced themselves they were doing the best for their daughter, and then washed their hands of the rest.

Céline, wearing a red hat with a green dress under a blue blazer, was a little fair-haired girl with green eyes. She looked terrified. She was about to be abandoned in an unknown country. She understood that she was living her last moments of liberty, that she was to be imprisoned for many years. She had been condemned by a well-known tribunal for a fault she couldn't really identify. In reality, as years passed, she would realize that the main crime she was guilty of was the lack of her parents' love. They couldn't bear her presence any more. She siphoned the air from their house. There was no longer a place for her in their home. In fact, had she ever had one?

The farewells were delivered in confusion. Albert, who had gone with the man in charge of the boiler room to place the trunk in the basement, didn't even say goodbye to his daughter. Ernestine only told Céline,

"We're making a big sacrifice to place you here. Be a good girl and make us proud."

However, Céline only heard the real message which her mother had repeated over and over again for weeks.

"If this boarding school is not severe enough, reform school is waiting for you!"

The little girl didn't understand the meaning of the threat, but every time she heard it, she was paralysed with fear. They were now in the main entry. There were no windows, only many doors.

The Guardian said good-bye to the mother and made a sign for Céline to follow her. A door opened and they entered a dreadful place. When the door closed, Céline realized that something had just broken inside her. The Guardian and the child were now facing the Chapel. The nun bowed before the sacred place, and then she climbed a set of stairs, followed by Céline.

In the dormitory, thirty white beds were perfectly lined. At each place, there was a chair with a small night table. That was all, no curtains, no privacy. On the wall, there was a row of small closets, each hiding a sink. The toilets were near the entrance on the opposite side. The place was completely deserted. On a bed in the middle of the room, there was a neat pile of clothes. The nun showed it to Céline, she pointed to one of the closets and told her to go and change.

Céline obeyed. The uniform consisted of a grey tunic with wide pleats, a white rope at the waist and a little black veil, tied behind her neck, to cover her head. Grey stockings and black shoes completed the outfit. When Céline came out, the nun was waiting for her. At this precise moment, a bell rang and the Guardian said,

"It's time for the Holy Sacrament. I'll take you to the Chapel."

They descended the stairs once again and entered the Holy Place. In the front rows of the Chapel, white forms were entirely covered with huge transparent white veils. These nuns were chanting a sad monotonous melody which they seemed to repeated over and over again.

The woman pointed to a bench at the back and motioned to Céline to sit down. Soon, the door opened and thirty young girls entered. Two by two, they came to the main aisle, knelt down and bowed their head toward the Holy Monstrance. Céline was soon surrounded by girls, almost all older than herself.

At this moment, the priest, wearing the sacramental garments, arrived to preside over the ceremony. In the Chapel, with its high vaulted ceiling, the main altar occupied the whole front. Lovely casement windows adorned the whole walls. On each side, there was a smaller altar. Featuring a meter high a statue was placed above it. On the right, the Virgin Mary stood opposite to St François d'Assise on the left. A small harmonium was painfully blowing out sad and dull hymns, which the audience sang in Latin. Suddenly, a solemn, yet stirring, nearly joyful song, rose into the air: Tantum ergo sacramentum…Céline was carried away by the first burst of life felt in the suffocating atmosphere. The intense smell of incense penetrated the air. It was a magical moment for the child.

When the service was over, the nuns put down their light white veil, as to cover their face and came two by two to lie down on the floor in front of the Holy Monstrance. It was like a ballet of white faceless forms and rustlings silk.

The young girls returned to the ground floor where three halls faced them: on the right, a sign with the word *Cloister* at the front of the central hallway, a door leading to the backyard. The little crowd turned left. At the end, there was a large room with a cold cement floor. Some tables and chairs, a large sink, a few cupboards and three windows decorated the foul-smelling place.

The Mother Guardian put Céline at the head of a table where four other girls had already taken their place. Everybody sat down in an atmosphere of silence which had prevailed since they had left the Chapel. The nun signalled for Céline to stand up and she announced in a loud voice,

"We have a newcomer among us. Her name is Marie-Céline."

Nothing more was said. Astonished, Céline had just heard her name changed, without any warning. She had seen her identity stolen. She wanted to shout, "It is not my name. This woman is mistaken. She must mean someone else." The silence that followed was as heavy as lead. Céline felt threatened, but she kept quiet. She had to remain in this damned place because she instinctively knew that a single protest word would be viewed as scandalous, and her parents would be called to pick up their young insubordinate.

The meal was eaten to the sound of a pious reading, fumbled by a girl who kept her head down on her book the whole supper time. Céline had a lump in her throat and she couldn't eat at all. The place disgusted her. The nun kept observing her. She came slowly to her place and told her bluntly, "Here, everybody has to eat half their portion." For the first time, Céline noticed the two bowls placed in front of her. She obeyed and took a spoonful and put it on her plate. It had a strange and bland taste. By forcing herself to think of something else, she managed to eat a little. When she stood up to put her plate on the pantry, as she had seen the others do, a firm hand pushed her back down, "Did you not understand that you had to eat half of your portion?" The nun quickly filled Céline's plate. She began to eat immediately without complaining. Standing right beside her, the woman watched her closely.

The dishes were washed, while the vegetables were peeled for the next day, as the rosary was recited by another pupil who remained standing. The evening recess was another trying opportunity for Céline to learn the Rules. She quickly learnt the traps to avoid, and the weak links to exploit in order to steal a few moments of joy.

The Encounter

After her first day at the Convent, Céline was exhausted. The whole day, she had pushed away her anguish, but when alone in bed that night, she was overwhelmed by it. More than ever, she felt that she was alone in the world. As the hours passed and she couldn't sleep, her fear grew.

On the wall in front of her, shone the red Exit light. A door opened onto an outside stairwell. Yes, the little girl could escape, but where would she go? Even if her prison had no bars, she did not leave because her guard was inside her. Toward the end of the night, she collapsed and fell into a sleep as deep as a coma. Her whole body refused to accept her present condition, so her soul took refuge in another world.

At five forty- five, a pale lamp flashed in the dark, and a monotonous voice said, *"Jesus, Mary, Joseph, bless our day"*. Céline jumped in her bed and opened one eye to see thirty girls already kneeling besides their beds. Within a few seconds of hearing the call, like programmed robots, all the boarders, who were not allowed to be seen in their flimsy night gowns, had seized their dressing gowns, slipped them on while still in their beds, and then knelt down on the cold floor.

Remembering the previous day scolding, Céline quickly did as the others. The prayer lasted about ten minutes, but it gave the girls a little time to fully wake up. Afterwards, the great rush began because in half an hour everybody had to be dressed, hair done and bed made perfectly, or otherwise, the blankets were pulled off and thrown back on the bed with shouting and scolding from Mother Guardian. This was agonizing for the guilty girl who had to do it again, for it made her late for the rest of the day which added punishment over punishment. It would surely have happened to Céline if the girl in the next bed had not intervened, replacing her blankets properly. She had taken the opportunity when Mother Notre-Dame-Des-Pins turned toward the toilet. The girl worked fast without even looking at Céline. She feared the terrible woman would see her and punish her badly, even if she was only trying to show a little humanity to someone who desperately needed it.

It was that kind of behaviour the Guardian hated most of all: every initiative that did not ascribe to her own moral code. She liked routine done in the same manner, at the same time, by obedient pupils: everything done like a well-oiled clock. Woe the one whose curly hair would be seen peeking out from under her veil or who held her pencil in the wrong way or in the wrong hand!

Sometimes though, everything was going too smoothly and the woman seemed bored. Then, for her own pleasant diversion, she would create a drama for some unsuspecting boarder. She would swoop down, mocking and cursing her, before chasing her away rudely, for one should never be late. This violent woman, probably frustrated by her unemployed libido, released it to the exasperation of the young girls.

After a short prayer in the study room, everyone headed towards the Chapel where they had to be at six-thirty for the morning Mass. At seven thirty, the girls went down for breakfast in the refectory. This was the worst meal for Céline. Depending on the day, it contained plain bread (not toasted), cold baloney, or oily sausages with an astonishing soapy taste. The worst was a bad smelling stew of floating meat, mixed with some carrots and potatoes. Every time she ate, Céline struggled to swallow without tasting the food. This operation was only possible if one held its breath while swallowing. It was a choice between suffocation and coercion.

The dishes done, the pupils went to their assigned cleaning job. Every girl had a special task to accomplish with perfection and punctuality. At a quarter past eight, everything had to be done and inspected by the Guardian. Watch out, the forgotten dust or the hastily cleaned toilet bowl. It could land you in big trouble. Then under public humiliation, the task had to be repeated during recess.

Laughing on the inside, Céline told herself, "I'm lucky to have had my mother's rough training where everything had to be finished before it was even started." The thought of her mother, Ernestine, brought tears to her eyes. The child missed her home, for even if it was not always pleasant, one could breathe there without being berated. This was not the case in this dammed place. The little girl had never been so unhappy in her whole life, and no possible hope or joy could be seen on the horizon.

Fortunately, she passed though the morning hours without any scolding, for she had done her chore perfectly before the bell rang. Céline tried to follow the group who had begun to head to class in different directions, but no one had told her where she had to go. It was as if they had planned to confuse her, so they could then accuse her of not respecting the Rules. Suddenly, a door opened and a young nun grabbed her asking:

"Are you Marie-Céline?"

"Yes, I am", answered the girl without hesitating.

"Well, you're coming with me. I am your new teacher", said the little nun, leading her toward a desk.

Her singing voice was sweet and sensual, her footsteps light. After Céline was seated, she observed this small woman, her soft complexion, her big brown eyes, her long curved eyelashes, Céline, felt immediately under her charm. The child devoured her with her eyes; she drank in all her words and followed her demands diligently, telling herself that she would be the best pupil in the class. Otherwise, looking around, only three other students shared her course, though there were three other girls of a higher grade in the classroom.

The morning passed very fast, and by recess, Céline's mood had completely changed. All the pleasure she had felt during her first lesson had made her forget that she had been so poorly welcomed. She knew now that she would be able to bear everything because she had found a reason to live.

During recess, she talked little, but she had a smile on her face. The Guardian looked at her, surprised of the sudden change. She was mad that her initial rude harassment had not produced the usual results. She told herself, "All was going so perfectly, what happened?", as she recalled the frightened child, she had observed that very morning. "If she goes on like that, she'll escape my control." She immediately suspected the teacher, accusing her of loose discipline. "This Mother E is spoiling all my work!" she muttered. When the bell rang again, the students went back to their classroom. Céline had noticed the evil look the terrible woman had given her. She felt fear rising in her throat, but it disappeared as soon as she returned to class. From this moment, Céline considered her classroom as a secret and soft dwelling place.

Once again after recess, she was greeted by Mother E s' warm smile. Céline told herself that she had not been dreaming. Here in this place, there was someone who could change unhappiness into joy, someone whom she could dream of. She felt less alone.

Céline was a strong child who was accustomed to suffering. She had built herself a set of armour where she could escape when it hurt too much. Reading was one of her favourite ways to forget herself. She would plunge herself into the adventures of the characters with whom she identified. Ernestine had understood the place imagination had in her daughter's mind. In vain, she had tried to tear her away from that world, arguing it was a pastime for rich people, or worst, for lazy ones. For Céline, reading was her last hope from falling into despair.

In the Convent, there existed the same narrow-minded way of thinking, claiming that evil could come from reading the wrong books. As a result, it was forbidden to read during the week. Reading was permitted for only two hours on Sunday, and only from "holy" books, no need to mention that.

In the first letter Céline wrote to her mother, she had said she was very lonely. Ernestine, who was feeling a little guilty, had tried to please her daughter by mailing a book to her. She had not read it herself, but the librarian had assured her that it was a book of great interest and morality. It was a book, written by Alphonse Daudet called Le, Petit Chose. Naturally, the Mother

Guardian had intercepted it, as all the letters were checked by her, but the Mother Superior of the Convent, who knew the book and wanted to please parents, had asked the Guardian to give it to Céline.

The Guardian would hand her the volume every Sunday afternoon, but instructed her to bring it back the same afternoon. Céline just devoured her book during those few hours. She was far from finished when she sadly had to give it back. In a few weeks, she had read it through, but she still went to borrow it every Sunday. One day, the Guardian noticed Céline copying parts of it. Horrified, she pulled the notebook away. Céline had copied the chapter where, Daniel Esseytte, *Le Petit Chose,* had left college after a failed suicide and was taking care of his dying brother, Jacques, who *the implacable galloping consumption was carrying him away on its back.* The woman read the notes attentively and had then put them aside without uttering a word. Céline didn't foresee any good coming out of it. She was right.

On Saturday morning, two full hours were reserved to point out all the mistakes and failings that the boarders had committed during the week, all noted by the Guardian. The event was held in the study room in front of all the girls, their teachers, and some special guests.

This day, Mother Notre-Dame-Des-Pins, the Guardian, had begun with miscellaneous things as a distraction before she attacked; in a severe tone she said "Marie-Céline, would you stand up please! We are going to determine your fate." The child stood up. Her legs were shaking so much that she had to hold onto her desk to prevent herself from falling. Her heart beat so hard that she heard it in her head. The Guardian held her favourite book at arm's length.

"This book is immoral. It is one we have denounced as having a bad influence." She was now looking fiercely at Céline. "And you, you've not only read it, but you are copying it, so you can learn it by heart and share its negative message to others. This is scandalous! You will immediately come in front of the room and confess your crime."

Dying with shame, Céline stood beside the nun.

"Now, you kneel down and ask forgiveness for your immorality."

Crying profusely, Céline apologized, explaining:

"I didn't know it was wrong when I did it."

The Guardian exploded:

"I cannot believe what I am hearing! She is making excuses for herself! She said *she didn't know!* You are making you situation worse, Marie-Céline. You have now disobeyed the Rule that each reprimand must be accepted in silence and with humility." Her voice roared like thunder.

It was too much for Céline! Suddenly, the assault on the little girl's dignity was more than she could bear. She rose up from her humble position and calmly said:

"I'm tired Mother, and me knees hurt. May I return to my place please?"

The woman became white with rage. She opened her mouth to say the terrible words that could settle Céline's fate forever. At this very moment, the Mother Superior, who had been standing unnoticed by the door, but had seen everything, lifted her voice and said,

"Mother Notre-Dame-Des-Pins, would you come with me please?"

Complete silence followed as the woman left the room. Everybody realized that it was now her turn to be judged. When the door closed, another nun took the initiative to take the girls out for recess.

After her glorious victory, Céline felt exhausted. She retreated into her classroom. She was crying with her head on her desk, when she felt a hand on her back, and as softly as a spring breeze, Mother E kissed her cheek. "Come on, everything is over now! Don't lose hope, we'll help you survive." Those kind words encouraged Céline. She was ready to endure more ordeals if someone cared for her like that.

Mother E's real name was Louise de la Durantaye. She was a young woman in her early twenties. Very intelligent, her strong personality did not please the Mother Guardian. Her childhood had not been easy. Her father had died when she was only six years old. Hr mother, unable to get over her pain, had let herself go. She became very sick, and her daughter became her nurse. The doctor diagnosed her with a severe fever, origin unknown. As her condition deteriorated, she was taken to the hospital. One of her friends, Sister Theresa, had taken Louise under her protection. She had even arranged a bed for her beside her mother's. One night, Sister Theresa and Louise were sitting beside the unconscious woman, the nun had spoken very seriously to the little girl,

"Even if you are still very young, you have to understand that your mother is going to die if something is not done for her." Louise had looked at her with wide eyes. Shocked, she couldn't say a word. Finally, she whispered,

"Can we do something to make her recover?"

"I can only pray for her. I can't do anything else to make her well, but you." the woman didn't finish her thought.

"Do you mean I can do something to heal my mum!" exclaimed Louise excitedly. "What is it?"

The nun had hesitated. It was a terrible moment. The child's future was in her hands. She had prayed silently before saying,

"Louise, if you make the promise that you will be a nun when you grown up, your mother will be healed."

The child did not realize the gravity of a commitment that would affect the rest of her life. She only knew she wanted her mother back home. She solemnly swore, "If my mother is cured, I'll be a nun when I'm a big girl." Her mother had recovered.

Peculiar Relationships

The Catholic Church has always preached strict moral standings, often without regards for a person's fundamental emotional needs. The call of nature is not always avoidable. One cannot contradict it indefinitely without expecting consequences. Sometimes, it is through physical aliments that the body expresses its frustration. Other times, mental illness cries out, "Help! I'm suffering too much! I cannot control myself anymore!" Religious Orders frequently reveals souls who suffer from spiritual frenzy or religious mania.

One cannot deny, however, that sometimes, certain restrictive conditions, when imposed on young idealists can forge, in the long term, saintly souls who have overcome the desires of the flesh, and thus, reach peace and serenity. Often, though, it's a life time struggle, and no one will ever know the weaknesses, the numerous failures, the self-deprivations, before achieving any degree of holiness. "The flesh is weak," they preach continuously to pardon their own weakness and that of their fellow men and women

All religious are called to perfection, but very few ever arrived. Here lies the explanation behind the shameful sexual aberrations whose victims and witnesses are still tormented. In essence, sexuality, when lived without the exchange of human affection and respect leads only to perversion and solitude. The aggressor is alone, for he takes, without any consideration or concern. These relationships are often inhumane and destructive.

Otherwise, when two individuals reach the summit of their tenderness, there is one step that is made by itself. The body is then invited to participate in what the soul consummated long ago.

During their first year together, Mother E and Marie-Céline had a very tender and affectionate relationship. Their spirits had blended together under the intellectual atmosphere of the classroom. A great complicity developed between them. For Céline, it filled her social needs since the Convent kept the boarders isolated the outside world. Their lives were contained in a hothouse. Céline, this passionate child, saw her affection transform into adoration for Mother E, whom she soon loved with all her heart.

The situation had evolved slowly. Understanding the child's distress, the nun had tried to lighten Céline's burden by paying attention to her. Little by little, her feeling towards the child had developed without her knowledge. Céline was always near her, taking refuge in her fragrance. She did not say much, afraid to disturb her teacher. As soon as Céline saw Mother E, anywhere in the Convent, she eyed her adoringly. Mother E felt comforted by this affectionate disposition. She knew Céline loved her unconditionally, admired her without any limit, and that she was the centre of her universe. The woman needed this affection which she considered a gift from heaven. She measured the relationship very proper since, she herself, as a teenager, had lived with a nun under similar circumstances.

Imperceptibly, they went a step further. It started one night, after supper, while Mother Guardian was in service at the refectory in the basement.

Céline was in the study room practicing the piano. The place was completely dark except for the little lamp on the piano. The child was playing with ardour when she had heard her name called. She turned her head and recognized the warm voice of the one she loved.

Without a word, the child curled up into the loving arms that welcomed her. The nun held the child on her lap for a long time, and then, softly began to caress her hair, her face, whispering: "My little girl, my very little one, how pretty you are, so nice, so gentle" …

Then, alarmed, Mother E had said:

"Go back to your piano and practice now; your teacher may notice you're not playing any more. Don't forget I love you... always remember that." ...

Céline paced the room, completely shattered. It was the first time in her life that someone had held her like that; the first time, she had felt another body that close to her. She was bombarded by an array of emotions. Above all, she felt an incredible strength, the strength of one who no longer has to share life's burden alone. Céline was overwhelmed by love; she felt she could move mountains for the one she cherished with a renewed vigour. Something new was also happening to her body, as if a knot was twisting in her belly. She felt wet between her legs too... In her innocence, she didn't understand that she had just experienced her first sensation of love.

The piano practice occurred twice a week. At this hour, Mother E had permission to be in her classroom, correcting papers or preparing lessons.

Only a little hall connected the two rooms, and the two lovers were able to satisfy their loving desire for each other. Céline was living only for those few brief moments. Otherwise, Mother E had warned her to be very careful, for a simple mistake could put them in a very problematic situation.

One evening, the caress had lasted longer than usual, and the door had suddenly opened. Mother Épimaque, the piano teacher, had entered abruptly. Faster than a lightening, Céline ran to her piano.

"What are you doing? You're not practicing? I haven't heard a sound for ten minutes! " exclaimed the plump, out of breath woman.

"My music sheet fell under the piano, and I couldn't get it!"

"Why don't you open the light? You would see better", said the woman, wanting it done right away.

"No! It's all right, I've had it now," interrupted Céline, "but since you're here, Mother, would you help me with this sonata's passage. I'm having trouble with."

Céline had succeeded in diverting her piano teacher's attention, for she couldn't resist the request. While the good woman had bent over the instrument, Mother E. had left, taking advantage of the darkness. She hadn't been seen at all. However, the encounters were now too dangerous, and they stopped. The two lovers felt a terrible loss.

In the dormitory, there were two small rooms, each housing a nun, to assure adult supervision during the night. Mother E. occupied the one near the main entrance. Every morning at five o'clock, a nun would come to wake her up. As soon as Céline heard the woman's light footsteps, she woke up too. She knew the time she had to wait before her beloved would come out. This early morning glimpse was a very tiny thing, but in place of physical contact, the relationship now had to be lived from a distance. Later on, in the Chapel, Céline, who already knew where her beloved sat, would fix her eyes on the small silhouette as if trying to maintain a constant connection with her. No need to mention that the classroom was now a privileged place, for a certain intimacy could exist there, even in front of the other pupils.

The relationship between a teacher and her pupils, especially when they have known each other for a long time, is a little like the one of mothers with their children; they look after them, stimulating and scolding when necessary.

Each person had its place in Mother E's group according to their personality. There was Lina, so soft, so nice, but completely lost when it came to grammar or algebra. And there was Jeanne, a little podgy girl, but always laughing, who resolved mathematical problems very easily. The tall Gisèle didn't talk much, preoccupied with her own thoughts. And the little Céline was the teacher's favourite, but no jealousy existed among them, as each felt loved and appreciated by the teacher. Mother E had an affectionate and caring way of guiding her group. The pupils were happy with her. Only in her class could they be themselves without fear.

The Guardian was jealous of the special bond she suspected existed between them. She wanted to prohibit this warm connection. She often came barging in without any warning, hoping to discover some disobedience to the Rule. She was powerless because each teacher was given certain latitude within their own class. More, instinctively, pupils had noticed the animosity between the two women. They didn't trust Mother Notre-Dame-Des-Pins either, and besides, they wanted to protect their teacher. The impromptu visits showed her perfect pupils working hard on their assignments. Nothing could betray the trusted union; even the laughter from playful teasing, which the Guardian heard, but that she could never sanction. She never arrived at the right moment, for everyone calmed down as soon as she opened the door.

That day, frustrated by another wasted visit, the Mother Guardian, motivated by revenge, went directly to the Mother Superior's door to complain about the situation. She came in, and declared angrily:

"Mother E is too relaxed with her pupils. She has no discipline, and I hear their laughter all the way in my office. It is not very professional and may damage my reputation with the Juvenists.".

"Don't forget that their marks on the Provincial exams have been excellent. It was even the first time we received the first prize in French", replied Mother Marie-Des-Saints-Anges, the Superior.

"Yes, I know, the impudent Marie-Céline won it," answered the woman despitefully. "She's a disobedient child, we need to control her."

"Yes, I understand", said the Superior, as she recalled her intervention in the renowned incident of *Alphonse Daudet's* book. She tried to calm the angry woman standing before her by encouraging her educational efforts, which she appreciated. Ignoring the more distasteful details of her excessive interventions.

"Tonight, I'll speak to Mother E. I promise you, things will change", she said firmly.

"I knew you would share my opinion," exulted Mother Notre-Dame-Des-Pins with pleasure. "You understand that it is difficult to build something when your authority is constantly undermined." She added.

The Guardian left very satisfied; "At least, this hypocritical teacher and her pet will be reprimanded as they deserve."

That very evening, to please the Mother Guardian, her valued assistant, Mother Superior invited Mother E to her office. No one knows what was said, but Mother E came out weeping. She had been deeply hurt by her Superior's accusations. The Mother Superior had entirely taken Mother Notre-Dame-Des-Pins' side. Until then, she had always protected Mother E. She admired her courage and her intelligence. However, she had to take measures to balance the two opposing forces.

The day after, Céline, who was always aware of her beloved demeanour, noticed right away that something had happened. Mother E didn't behave as usual. She was distracted as if lost inside herself. Immediately, the child thought it was her fault. Maybe she had hurt her or said something that would keep her away forever...Céline panicked when she observed Mother E. silently crying. Big tears were rolling down her cheeks, which she was trying to hide with her handkerchief.

The pupils were busy writing an exam, but Céline kept her eyes on her teacher. Louise de la Durantaye noticed the child's look and smiled at her. Céline realized that she was not the reason behind the sorrows, someone else was. This thought made her very upset.

For months now, she hadn't had any physical contact with her beloved. Céline longed her body's warmth, but she respected the directives of caution.

Nevertheless, later on that night, Céline, worried and unable to bear her solitude any longer, was very daring... She waited a long time after the lights were closed until the Guardian had finished her many rounds. She even feigned slumber. Toward eleven o'clock, she got up without a sound and went to scratch very gently at the door of Mother E who was a light sleeper. She opened the door part way, and on seeing Céline, she pulled her inside quickly. She led the child to her bed, hugged her, kissed her, and without a word, opened her night gown and offered her breast to Céline, who took it, pressing her body against hers.

An hour passed in perfect happiness for the two lovers, but they had to be reasonable, and the time came for Céline to return to her bed. She left the small alcove discreetly on the tip of her toes. She jumped in terror when she heard the voice of the girl who occupied the first bed who said in a loud voice: "What were you doing for an hour with Mother E? I'm telling everything to Mother Guardian tomorrow morning!"

Sister Marie-Marthe's Unhappy Childhood

Going down the hall which led to the refectory, through a half open door on the right, Céline had noticed a lean little woman. The Sister could be seen stirring over a huge laundry vat, full of dirty clothes. Sometimes, Céline saw her rub, without stopping, filthy menstrual rags. With her head bent over her work, she never seemed to rest. A bad steamy odour came out the laundry room where the nun worked alone from morning to night. This is how Céline discovered that Sisters were the servants of the Mother

Coming out from the refectory, at the other end of the hall, there was another door entitled *Cloister*. It was open only during meal time, for it was where the Sisters would distribute meal plates through a half-opened door. It was the kitchen room. Four Sisters would work there all day long. The youngest, Sister Marie-Marthe, washed the dirty dishes, and went on errands when necessary. She was in the community for a few months only. She was a slim lady of twenty who had lovely delicate features. She had been in Qrébec for her two years of *postulate* where she had taken the holy vows before being transferred to R for her three-year probation, also called the *noviciate*. When a young girl is training to be a nun, five years pass by, before she pronounces her final vows of poverty, chastity and obedience, her last life time commitment.

Sister Marie-Marthe, whose real name was Colette R, was a very special person. For her, the Rule of silence was not a problem. It even seemed to be in her nature. Colette talked very little. She would answer if someone asked her something, but

36

she'd never initiated a conversation. She was like an oyster, opening only on command. Her quiet disposition, added to her strict obedience of the Rule, made her a model nun.

Colette's lips had been sealed long ago when she was but a little girl of three years old. On Sunday while her mother, Leonie, went to church, her father had to look after her. Pretending he wanted to sleep more, Leopold had asked his wife to bring the child into his bed. Glad to escape her household responsibilities, the mother did as her husband requested. She would put the little girl on the bed besides her father, warning her to be quiet, and too obey him for he wanted to sleep,

As soon as the door was closed, the father, who a minute before, seemed to be sleep soundly, woke up suddenly. He'd smile at Colette turning toward her, and then he'd start tickling her on her belly. She'd roar with laughter. For a few minutes, it was pleasant and innocent. Then, the man would turn to serious matters as he realized he had limited time to act. He would completely undress Colette, and then take off his own pyjama, showing an erect penis which always astonished the little girl. He caressed her everywhere before wetting his finger to touch her vulva. At the beginning, Colette was a little surprised with this new play, but she became used to it, and finally liked it. Then, Leopold took his daughter's hand and asked her to hold his penis. She obeyed, but soon had to use her two little hands to hold that "thing" which grew bigger and bigger. Then, her father would say,

"Now we'll play 'making it run', will you?"

Colette felt her father tension increasing. She was a little afraid and didn't dare say a word, but this part of the play didn't please her. However, remembering a painful incident, she knew she couldn't stop the game right there. She had to work hard for a very long time with that capricious thing that wouldn't spit right away. She would go up and down, for what seemed to her forever. She felt relieved when the sperm finally sprang out. Then, the father would warn Colette:

"This is our own secret; you should never talk about it to anyone."

37

Afterwards, Leopold fell into a real sleep, and Colette would go and play with her dolls. The Sundays' plays became routine for the little girl. She didn't realize that this situation was not an ordinary activity between a father and his daughter. For her, it was a normal habit. She was even happy to have her father's attention, for she loved him very much. Those sessions lasted for months without any trouble.

One day, Edmour, her father's brother, came for a visit. He had not seen Colette since her birth. He was astonished to see how big and pretty she was. He invited her to come and seat on his lap. Colette accepted happily. She liked to be petted and admired. As a reward for her nice uncle, she thought to please him by touching his sex that she felt under her. Colette had not predicted the man's reaction. He pulled her off and shouted after his brother:

"Damn pig, you showed her how to do that?"

Before the father could protest, his brother had punched him in the jaw, and Leopold had fallen to the floor. Edmour had left without another word. Leopold stood up, while his wife and three-year old daughter looked at him both astonished. Then, he had left the room. Leonie, the mother, didn't ask any questions, and sent the little girl to her room in a tone which indicated that she believed her daughter was the culprit in this disgraceful incident. The quarrel had greatly frightened Colette. She didn't understand at all what had happened. She felt very upset and guilty. Leonie had easily guessed the reason behind her brother-in-law's reaction. She knew that intercourse had occurred between her husband and her daughter as she had to regularly put lubricate cream on Colette's swollen and painful vulva. She also had knowledge that the little one sometimes complained about a sore on her rectum which bled at times.

Leonie didn't have the strength to react. She feared her husband. She herself had been abused as a child and was convinced that was just the way things were. She tried to heal Colette the best she could without mentioning anything to anyone. In this way, she was a secret accomplice to her husband's wicked deed.

Leonie went to church every Sunday, but she never made a link between the events in her home, which she stubbornly denied, and the sins of impurity the priest passionately denounced up in his pulpit. Every Sunday in summer, the priest preached against those woman and young girls whose provocative garments were a source of temptation, even a sin, for those poor men who couldn't resist the seduction and succumbed to the impulse that was beyond their control.

When Colette started her first year of school, she was still very naïve. What she was doing every Sunday, and even some nights during the week with her father, was just a habit for her. Except for her uncle's unpleasant visit, for which Colette felt entirely responsible, no formal disapproval had ever been sanctioned against Leopold for his behaviour. Colette never talked about it. In class though, her marks were very low. She was considered to be a daydreamer, unable to concentrate on learning.

In the fifties, in Québec, the Catholic Church was present throughout all levels of society. from education to healthcare and its influence even extended to all level of society. In grade one, the main obligation for these little ones was to prepare for their First Communion. This event usually happened during the month of May. However, before receiving the Eucharist, the children had to undergo a massive housecleaning of their six-years-old souls. They were, therefore, initiated to Confession. The parish priest led the children to examine their own conscience. He had already introduced the notion of sin, a concept that was not difficult to understand for children. Everything that their parents prevented them from doing was sin: disobedience, theft, lies. However, the large lewd priest took a particular pleasure in explaining with vivid details the biggest sin of all: *the mortal sin of impurity.*

Colette opened her eyes very wide when she heard him describe all that her father and she were doing regularly. A huge emphasis was placed on the enormity of this sin and on the deep guilt that the offender should feel. More, he threatened of the most appalling punishment for the one who committed it:

the eternal fire of Hell. The little ones were terrified on hearing these horrors.

Colette was deeply distressed. Everything was confused in her head and in her heart. While the man was talking, she was convinced that he could read her mind and knew everything. A terrible doubt entered her thoughts. Had her Dad lied to her? Had he taught her bad things? Who was right? Could she trust her father's affection? And if these things were that bad, could she dare do them again and go to hell?

The priest had said the only way to be forgiven for those horrible crimes was to tell them in Confession, to repent them sufficiently, and to never commit them again. It was the price to pay to purify their souls, and thus, prepared the way to receive Jesus into their hear heart. Furthermore, the priest added, as he glared intensely at the frightened girls, that whenever someone received communion with an impure soul, its sin became unforgivable forever.

Colette went to confess her sins at the Confessional. The priest asked many questions to which Colette tried to answer the best she could. The man didn't seem to realize that he was facing a case of incest. Instead, he vigorously scolded the child, suggesting she was guilty of everything and then imposed on her a severe penance. However, every week Colette would come back to the priest with the same sin. After a certain time, the priest decided that from then on, he would forbid this sinful child to come to Confession and refused to grant her First Communion. Everything was settled, no questions asked. The Parish Priest had spoken.

When Leonie learnt that her daughter was not going to be allowed do her First Communion with the others, she was furious. She came to the school and asked to meet with the Director. The nun had expected this visit and had her arguments ready.

"Colette, your daughter, has a lot of difficulty learning, and for the First

Communion, she must pass her catechism's exam."

"Yes, but this exam hasn't even yet taken place, and you tell Colette that she can't even be there for it?"

"We have very good reasons to think that she will fail that exam."

"It's the first time that I have heard such a foolish reason! You're not even going to give her a chance! You have decided in advance that she won't succeed! You know, Colette has studied a lot, I have quizzed her myself. You'd be surprised…"

The nun looked at her in such a spiteful manner that Leonie stopped arguing. She felt deeply humiliated, but she didn't have the strength to react. The mother gathered her purse and left, holding back her tears.

At the same time that she was standing up for her daughter, the mother saw herself again taking caring of Colette's own private wounds, which she was regularly nursing, and at this moment she understood that because of her daughter' impurity, she could not do her First Communion.

How Colette Became
Sister Marie-Marthe

On this Sunday in May, when all the little girls were in their white dresses, their tulle veils swaying with each step, Colette was not among them. Wearing her everyday clothes, she was seated elsewhere in the church. Under a threat of severe sanctions, she had been ordered to be present at the ceremony. Was it to make her an example to the others, or to humiliate her beyond her limits? No one knows, but on that day, Colette felt overwhelmed with grief as if life had turned fate against her. Standing up as straight as a robot, she followed the ceremony, fighting with all her strength the urge to run away from that place of suffering. The Sister Director, as if she guessed her thoughts, regularly turned her head in Colette's direction to reinforce her will.

At that very moment, Céline felt she belonged to a different race, a damned one. Her heart broke, and despair deceitfully crept in.

As soon as the ceremony was over, when the parents rushed to collect the happy chosen ones, Colette ran towards the woods and hid until nightfall.

When she returned home that evening, it was already dark. Her parents knew very well what had happened that day in church. Leonie had a hard time accepting the humiliation, but she was unable to fight the injustice. Instead, she transferred all the blame onto her daughter, accusing her of bringing the family shame. Colette was received coldly by her mother when she approached her for a little comfort.

"Where were you all day? What did you do? Neighbours told me they saw you running toward the woods after the ceremony.

You're right to be ashamed! If I was in your place…" but she could not finish her sentence before Leopold interrupted her:

"Those priests are the worst kind I've ever seen! I've never been able to stand them. They just hate us. Because I don't go to mass, they have decided to take their revenge by forbidding Colette to do her First Communion. That's what I think!"

Colette took the opportunity of her parents' quarrelling to silently slip into her room, Leopold followed on the pretext of consoling her. When the little girl saw him, she curled up at the end of her bed as if facing an enemy.

"What's the matter with you? You seem very shy today. I'm only coming to talk. Your mother is very hard on you. I'm the only one who gives you any affection."

Sitting down on the edge of the bed, he asked, mincing about, "Are you pushing me away too?"

"I don't want to do those things with you any more! They're dirty tricks…the priest said it."

"And you still trust him after what he did to you? You're hurting me a lot. I, your father, who loves you so much and shows it to you regularly.".

The father could read the distress and solitude in his daughter's eyes. He understood that with a little patience, he would conquer her again.

"Well, if you want nothing to do with me, I'm leaving."

The father left, playing the martyr. Colette was too young to realize that Leopold was emotionally blackmailing her. She was just an unhappy little girl, already condemned by public opinion. When her father tiptoed into her room later that night, she let him caress her.

From that day, Colette's situation at school deteriorated. Up to then, she had not been bullied, but once she had been publicly labelled as *the bad one' who didn't deserve to receive Holy Communion*, she had no more rest. Someone would hurl an insulting word; another would laugh at her, push her down or even steal her school bag. No one ever took her side. Alone to defend herself, Colette hardened and filled with rage. In her pocket, she always carried a geometry compass, whose sharp point was an effective weapon against her adversaries. She used the anonymity of a crowd to attack those who were mean to her. Her target would feel a sharp pain in her arm or bum, but would be unable to identify the culprit. The pupils soon suspected the author behind these acts of aggression, but lacked the evidence to denounce her to the Director. Other times, some of the little girls would wait till class was over to give her a good beating.

Colette almost always foresaw these moments and had a wooden pencil box ready in her school bag. When attacked, she'd have it in hand to face her assailants. As soon as one would come near, she'd receive a knock in the face or on the head. When thrown to the ground, Colette never lost her weapon. She learnt that a good kick in the shins greatly weakened her opponent. Her wooden box in hand, she struck hard, without feeling the clumsy blows of her attackers. She felt immense relief when avenging herself. Ignorant of Mister Laborite's principle of returning aggression instead of enduring it, she, nevertheless, practised it efficiently.

These were turbulent years for Colette, and although she did not succeed in being liked, she was at least feared. She developed an inner strength, afraid of no one or anything. She was not depressed or withdrawn, but felt terribly alone, enduring school till the age of sixteen.

Her aggression also served to stop her father's molestation. The wooden pencil box had easily been put aside by the man, but Colette soon discovered that certain parts of the male anatomy were very sensitive, and that a vigorous blow with her knee would keep Leopold away for hours, with a long-term dissuasive effect.

At eighteen, Colette was more like a porcupine than the gentle little girl, Leonie, the mother, had dreamt of. Every Sunday at church, Leonie prayed for her daughter. One day, she had a revelation which she believed came directly from heaven, as if in answer to her pressing needs. She decided to convince Colette to enter a Convent and become a nun, thus saving both her soul and that of her parents at the same time.

Since she wanted her intervention to be well received, she tried to create a calming atmosphere by inviting Colette for a dinner at a restaurant. As she had never been treated that nicely, Colette was surprised, but she didn't dare refuse. Pretending she wanted to take a relaxing car ride, she drove her daughter outside the city. Having selected an isolated location, Leonie turned off the road where one could barely see a sign marked, Dining Room. Without a word, she signalled Colette to follow. The mother had already made a reservation, mentioning that she wanted a secluded table. The place was almost deserted as they were escorted to the back of the room.

"Tonight, I'm treating you to a delicious meal. Choose what pleases you."

"For heaven sake! Did you win the lottery?" said Colette to disguise her feelings at such a nice offer.

"No, but is there something that forbids a mother from spoiling her daughter a little bit?"

"Hum, let me question your good intentions. In eighteen years, I have never received this kind of treatment, why today?" wondered Colette dubiously

"Because I want to have a serious discussion with you," answered the mother

"Well, what did I do this time? What wrong are you blaming me for? You could have done it at home. You've never been ashamed before" said the girl defensively.

"Why are you getting mad so quickly?" said Leonie, trying to calm her daughter.

"You don't want to scold me? You're sure of that?" Insisted Colette.

"I want to talk to you about your future"

"About my future? Only that?" teased Colette.

"Well, yes, is it not important?"

"It depends on your point of view", answered Colette suspiciously.

"Try to control yourself, please. I just want we talk together about some questions I think are important," added Leonie, putting her hands softly on her daughter's.

Leonie had never demonstrated this kind of attention towards Colette. This gentleness, this tenderness was all suspect to the young girl.

"All right, I give up. I'll try to listen and understand what you want so very much to tell me."

"I would like to know how you envisage yourself in the future?"

"I've never really thought about it, but one thing is sure, I don't want to be like you, to marry and have children. Never! No way!"

"I understand. You've never been really happy at home. I've always known it, but I didn't know how to change thing." Leonie sighed, trying to excuse herself. "But what I fear in hearing you, is that you'll finish your life alone? That's not a life!" exclaimed the mother.

Leonie had come straight to the problem. Colette suffered terribly from the solitude she had created around herself. She tried not to think of it, but she deeply envied all the young girls her age, going out with their friends. However, in this little city, she was stigmatized. Her reputation was finished, and everyone avoided her.

"I think, you'll have to change your surroundings to find some happiness," said Leonie thoughtfully.

"It's true, here I'm burnt out. Everybody knows me, and everybody hates me."

Colette had already made this observation, but she never dwelled into it deeply because she didn't have a solution. It was the first time in her life that her mother had spoken calmly to her like a friend. She even seemed to understand her pain. Colette felt her wall of resistance melt away as tears rolled on her cheeks. Leonie was also deeply moved and tried to lighten the mood.

"Let's not cry like children," she told Colette, wiping away her own tears. "Instead, let me tell you an idea I have for you that would secure your future and assure that you are never alone," said the mother mysteriously.

"Now, you're talking about miracles, and you are not making sense! What are you talking about? Just be honest!" said Colette, suddenly becoming very dubious.

"Up to now, your life had been like Hell. Isn't it time to have a taste of Paradise?"

"Does such a place exist on earth?

"Yes, it does".

"Oh! Yes! Where?"

"In a Convent."

"In a Convent!" exclaimed Colette." Do you really believe that the school's Nuns will accept me into their community? They know me too well and have hated me for a long time!"

"I've heard about a Missionary Community in the city of Québec that is looking for young girls like you."

"Oh! Yes? And you think they'd accept me just like that, without knowing who I am?"

"They'll learn to know you" assured the mother. "Up to now, nobody ever gave you the chance to show the best part of you. I've taken care of you since you were little, and I know you're a good girl, but that life has been unfair to you. You've had to be tough to defend yourself from all those who attacked you, from all parts, and in every possible way." said the mother, giving her a look that Colette understood all too well.

"Oh! Mummy! Why didn't you talk to me like this before? I'd never thought you could understand me so well! I'm so touched. You'd never believe it!" sobbed the young girl.

Leonie just took her daughter's hands in hers. She knew she had completely won Colette over to her plans. She was personally convinced that Colette had to go away because her reputation was completely lost in the little city where she had grown up.

Leonie also realized that she and Leopold, her husband, had completely ruined their daughter's life and in a way that was irreparable. Colette had been soiled by her father. Her mother, a silent accomplice, had accepted her being sacrificed. Colette hated herself; she was convinced of her guilt. There was not a day when she didn't think about disappearing from the earth. She had played with the idea of suicide from the moment she had understood that she was but a trinket in her father's hands. She had turned that self-hatred against all those around her whom she thought felt the same way. All of a sudden, she realized that during all this time, her mother had never ceased loving her. Her, the villain, her, the damned one. An infinite tranquility descended on her. She wanted to believe that all was not lost, that somewhere there existed a place where she could forget all this filthiness, and become purified and respected by all.

Nicolas and Colette Discover Each Other

Some months later, Colette entered a Convent where she was warmly welcomed. Her docile and obedient attitude pleased the Postulants' Mistress.

Right away, she was in her good graces. The young woman was willing to accept every manual task demanded of her. The lower rank of Sister didn't humiliate her at all. As a Postulant, she tried to accomplish everything with perfection. She achieved personal satisfaction and even received congratulations from the authorities.

This young girl, who had always been pushed aside by everyone, was now accepted by her colleagues and respected by her superiors. Colette was building herself a new identity; she was now honourable. Her self- esteem was improving. For the first time in her life, she was happy. However, this quest was centred on herself, consuming all her energy. She was totally unable to socialise with the others girls. Her long history of rejection prevented her from trusting others. Anyone who tried to be friendly with her was kept at a distance because she doubted their good intentions. On the outside, the young woman seemed calm and quiet, but inside, her soul was a burning volcano, always on the verge of exploding.

The first two years of religious life passed relatively smoothly, and her vocation was recognized. As a result, Colette climbed another rung in the hierarchy and advanced to the level of Novice. A ceremony was held to celebrate the occasion, and her parents were invited to witness their daughter take the veil and receive her religious name.

After the service, Colette met with Leonie and Leopold, who were visually moved to see Colette coming toward them in her white clothes. "She looks like an angel" said the mother who walked all around her daughter in admiration, not daring to touch her. Leopold felt very ill at ease and couldn't even look at her. Remorse had made its way into his conscience. He wished that nothing had ever happened to soil the relationship between them and he would have like to gather her in his arms, without any hesitation, with all the tenderness of a parent, but he was convinced she held such resentment against him that he couldn't even go near her. Colette had read his thoughts and made a very generous gesture. She opened her arms to the one who had degraded her for years and gave him an affectionate embrace. Leopold had to wipe away a tear rolling down his cheek. Leonie was glowing.

Colette had her revenge that day when she took the new name of Sister Marie-Marthe. Now she was to wear forever the white dress she had been denied when she was six-year old and refused her First Communion. She couldn't help but ask her mother;

"Did you tell the parish priest I was in a Convent?"

"Yes, he was so surprised that he nearly got strangled in his roumain collar" said Leonie laughing.

"Roman collar mum, not roumain", corrected Colette.

"Anyway, call it as you like, he didn't believe it", added the mother. "I've told everyone I know! I'm telling you; people don't look at me in the same way now. Some person even crosses the street to come and talk to me. The mother of little Michaud, you remember that man chaser, she came to inquire me if I thought she should do the same for her daughter?"

"What did you answer?" asked Colette laughing.

"I told her it was God's Will and that someone had to deserve it!" added Leonie maliciously.

The two women chatted, happy to be together. Beside them, Leopold was looking straight ahead in silence. Inside his head a tempest was brewing: "Did Colette forget what he had done to her? Had she really forgiven him, or was she only pretending?"

This uncertainty haunted his mind more than all the reproaches she could have given him.

He argued that they had to leave, making the excuse that he wanted to travel during the daytime. Sister Marie-Marthe was not bothered by this at all, for she was no longer a part of them. Her new family was here, in the Convent.

Some time later, she was transferred to R where kitchen helpers were needed. She was very pleased with her new surroundings. With her white costume, she was now a real part of a religious community. Sister Marie-Marthe had all that she had wished for. She thought her happiness couldn't be greater. At least she believed it up to that spring day…

Kitchen duties were not physically tiring, and Colette was not at all repulsed by the dirty dishes she had to wash all day long. Cleaning the pots and pans allowed her time to think. Her other task was to run errands when something unexpectedly happened in the kitchen.

This particular day, the electricity had failed. The nuns were in the middle of preparing dinner, so it had to be repaired quickly. Colette was asked to go downstairs because all the electric boxes were in the basement, and it was the boiler room man's responsibility. Colette was sent to ask him if he could fix the problem right away, since it was urgent. She had never been there before and was a little frightened to do so alone. The nun showed her the door leading to the furnace room. She just had to go down the stairs, and she would find the man there, she was told. Sister Marie-Marthe would have liked someone to come with her, but looking around, she noticed that everyone seemed very busy.

In reality, it was an unpleasant mission for a Cloistered woman to meet people *from the outside world* as they called anyone who did not belong to the religious community. *Especially a man,* they thought. For these women, who lived among themselves for years, an encounter with the other sex was so unfamiliar and frightening, it was almost repulsive. Reluctantly, Sister Marie-Marthe did as ordered.

The stairs were dark and narrow. The only light came from a faint glow far away. Tightly holding onto the banister,

Colette descended carefully. Then, she followed the light toward what seemed like an extra long hallway. She found herself in a vast room where a huge noisy furnace who occupied the entire centre. No one seemed to be around. Sister Marie-Marthe went around the obstacle, and at last saw a man sitting in front of the fire eating a sandwich. When he raised his eyes to her, Colette nearly fainted. He was a young man in his early twenties whom she found very handsome. His nice face was adorned with beautiful blue eyes, "as blue as the sky", she would later remember. His nose was straight and his lips full.

His mouth turned into a little amusing smile when he looked at the young startled nun standing before him, obviously lost and frightened. It must be mentioned that he was used to the older nuns who came to discuss technical problems or salary conditions with him, but the sight of this young woman, around twenty, had surprised him. Coming back to reality, he asked politely:

"Can I do something for you, Sister?".

"Well, there's no electricity in the kitchen, and as we are preparing dinner, we have a problem. They asked me to come and see if you could do something to fix it" she answered without stopping, as if reciting a lesson learnt by heart.

"Maybe something overheated, and the breaker jumped" said the man calmly, while he rose up from his chair. He was tall and slim, and Colette looked like a little girl next to him. "We have to look at the central electrical board" he added.

Without thinking, Colette followed him. The man had the assured pace of someone who knows what he is doing. He opened a wide metallic plate where dozens of commands were located. He pushed one of them and turned toward Colette saying:

"Now, you have to go back to the kitchen and ask if the electricity has returned. If that's the case, you'll have to come again and tell me, so I'll know the problem is settled. If it isn't, I'll have to start the generator, at least for a few hours, until I locate the problem." His voice was low and warm.

Colette turned to head towards the stairs, but being in a strange place, she no longer knew where she was heading. The man noticed her trouble and smiled at her:

"You're not going in the right direction. Do you want me to guide you?"

"Yes, please," said the confused little nun.

"Come on, follow me. It is very dark in here," he added apologetically.

In her disarray, when turning around, Colette tripped on her skirts and fell down. Hearing an unusual noise, the man turned his head and saw Colette on the ground. He rushed to help her.

"Did you hurt yourself?" he inquired, helping her to her feet.

"No, it's all right," responded Colette very shyly.

"It is too dark in here. Give me your hand and let met lead you. I wouldn't want you to fall again!"

The man led the young girl to the stairs. One could see nothing, but a black hole. Familiar to the place, the man put Colette's hand on the banister and told her:

"Don't move! Wait for me, I'll get some light." Although very troubled and a little afraid, she obeyed. Some seconds later, the man came back shining a flashlight at the white form standing still at the base of the stairs. Then, he directed the light up the stairs, and Colette quickly went up. In the kitchen. She was informed that everything had returned to normal. She explained that she had been asked to go back and tell the man that everything was alright.

"You may go and tell him that everything has get back to normal."

Sister Marie-Marthe went down the stairs again. The place was fully lilted now as the young man was waiting patiently for her with his flashlight. Colette took each step slowly until she was standing right beside him. Then, she said with a pleasant smile.

"You accomplished a miracle. The lights are back on up there," she announced joyfully.

"Thank you! You are very nice and have administered your task successfully as well," replied the young man who was charmed by Colette's gentleness. For him, it was a welcomed change from the nastiness of the other nuns who looked down at him with disdain.

"Are you new here", he asked hastily.

"Yes, I've just come from Québec", answered Colette, looking directly into his eyes.

"Froom now on, will you be the one to come down when something is wrong in the kitchen?"

"Yes, I'm in charge of the errands." Colette could hardly hide her pleasure in speaking with him. "I think we'll see each other now and then," she said hesitatingly.

"Now I am going to hope for further breakdowns to have the pleasure of seeing you again!" Nicolas stopped, realizing how inappropriate his words had been.

Colette looked at him and was very troubled as well.

"Well, thank you again and until next time," she muttered.

She climbed the stairs quickly, holding up her skirts with her two hands, with the light following behind till she reached the top.

Back in the kitchen, Sister Marie-Marthe went directly to the sink, her eyes lowered, afraid that someone would notice the feelings that had taken hold of her from her head to her feet.

In the basement, Nicolas had gone back to his chair. He was disconcerted as well. He didn't understand what was happening to him. Why was this young nun upsetting him so much? In his mind, he visualized the so small silhouette, lost in her long white robe. He reminded her dark eyes where he had read so much distress. When he had helped her up, she had felt as light as a child in his hands. He could still recall the feeling of her body against his, and it disturbed him.

Nicolas was twenty-two years old. He lived in the village with his mother, a widow, and his uncle who had moved in to help his sister after her husband had died. His father had worked at the Convent. Since he was young, Nicolas had visited this place. Every day during the summer, at noon, his mother had sent him to bring his father's lunch. He would come on his bike, and while his father was eating, he would wander around.

He was curious about everything, asking a hundred questions. Philibert, his father, had answered the best he could, happy to see his son was interested in a trade he had practised whole heartily for years.

Then, one day, Philibert passed away. A stroke had struck him down at forty-four years of age. Nicolas was eighteen at the time. He had suggested to the Mother Superior that he take his father's place. The nun hesitated hiring such a young man, but his mother had pleaded his case, explaining that he was now her sole support. The Mother Superior had agreed on the condition that he would follow an engineering course because a diploma was needed to be in charge of a steam producing installation such as theirs. Nicolas had inscribed himself in a correspondence course which allowed him to practice as a beginner. He had qualified for his fourth class and was now studying for the third. The Convent supplied the required work experience.

The young man had taken his new role as head of the family very seriously. He was proud to provide his mother with a better living than she had had with his father. His leisure time was spent repairing and maintaining the family home. The rest of the time, he studied. Going out with young men his own age was not part of his life. He had become a man before really enjoying his youth.

Romance Between Colette and Nicolas

olette believed firmly in her religious calling. Since her arrival at the Convent, her life had been transformed. She thought she had completely changed after her conversion. She was not the same person, at least that's what she liked to think. This new way of life, its Rules, its secured surrounding, led her to believe that she was protected from all the difficulties she had encountered outside these walls.

In her childhood, her life had been utterly destroyed by her parents. She had lived through humiliations, torments and rejection. As a teenager, she had suffered from low self-esteem, but here in the Convent, she was rebuilding her confidence. She felt as if she had been "born again". Peace and serenity lived within her soul. Colette imagined that she had finally arrived at her destination.

Sister Marie-Marthe would have liked to dwell in this tranquility forever. Colette ignored the fact that life is a long battle and that souls are measured by their capacity to overcome obstacles. A new destiny was waiting around the corner. The young woman had not been born for an easy existence, but rather had been reserved for the first line of fire on the battlefield.

Her encounter with Nicolas had been a shock, for she didn't believe in love. It had appeared in her life too soon and as a coarse mockery of its greatness. The young woman had never known the softness of a warm sharing love. The very pleasure of friendship had also escaped her too. Up to that moment, her soul had only been nourished by a solitude void of any affection.

That day, a young man, as gorgeous as a god, had welcomed her as a friend. Colette was deeply distressed, filled with uncontrollable and powerful emotions. It was as if time had stopped when Nicolas's blue eyes had looked at her. She was remembering every detail, his well-designed lips opening to reveal straight white teeth, his eyebrows perched high on his large forehead, his tall height, his strong hands which had lifted her up like a feather when she had fallen. She still felt the warmth of his body against hers. Nevertheless, it was his gentleness which had truly conquered her. "Now I am going to hope for further breakdowns to have the pleasure of seeing you again." She replayed those words in her mind like a piece of music and felt a passionate warming all over her body.

Sister Marie-Marthe dreamt of Nicolas for a whole month. While praying, his face was now intermingled with that of Jesus. Colette neglected to confess this to the priest, who would have extinguished her fantasies, telling her how wrong they were. He would have been right since Colette had fallen the spell of "love at first sight" The religious man would have warned her against this terrible disease that burned inside her like fire. Instinctively, Colette knew all this, but what was happening to her was so extraordinarily wonderful that she couldn't consider losing it.

Up to that day, Colette's emotional life had been like an empty pit. Even if she was only twenty, the young girl was like those old disenchanted women, who feel betrayed by their own bodies and no longer believe in the promises of love. However, they had tasted its fruits with eagerness for years before arriving at this sad conclusion. This was not the case for Sister Marie-Marthe. Colette's body had already been dirtied, but her heart had never known the tenderness of love. It was simply not possible for her to push away her dreams for love.

Nicolas had also fallen under the charm of this young woman. However, his practical mind immediately forbade him to hope for some sequel to this brief encounter. He was, therefore, very surprised to see the young nun as he sat dreaming in front of the big furnace.

"Hi," said Colette who sat down on a chair near his. She kept looking into the fire without saying a word. Nicolas didn't dare break the silence between them, for he knew it was as fragile as porcelain which could break into a thousand pieces by a single word. Then, the young woman began to talk very fast without looking at him. Like a child fascinated by water and ignoring its danger, after weeks of hesitating, Colette, torn by solitude, had decided to gamble everything, even at the risk of being mocked or pushed away. Anything seemed better than this incertitude.

"I know it's ridiculous. I shouldn't be here, but I needed so much to talk to you. Before I met you, I didn't know what solitude meant. Since the day I first saw you, I can't stop thinking about you. It's crazy, don't you think? I'm so ashamed to be here, telling you my feelings. It's so improper."

Nicolas was stunned. Lightening striking his feet wouldn't have surprised him more. This young girl had come because she had feelings for him! He was moved by her declaration and didn't want to take the time to think. He silenced an inner voice warning him to be careful.

Colette was quiet once more. Nicolas had to respond. Instinctively, he knew he had to act and right away. A young wounded animal may approach a man, but it doesn't stay long before retreating into the darkness of the forest. Nicolas took Colette's hand and held it in his. They remained like that for a long time, without saying a word. What could he tell her? That this adventure was foolish? That everything was against them? Is this the way one behaves at twenty? This is how wonderful the young are! Lovers don't know, they don't ask questions, they just listen to their heart which speaks louder than the wisdom of those who know too much.

Colette could feel the warmth of this man's hand. It strengthened her softly to know that Nicolas had accepted her foolishness.

"What's your name?" asked Colette. Tell me about yourself!

"My name is Nicolas. I'm twenty-two. I live with my mother and support her because my father is dead. I don't have anyone in my life, and I spend all my time working. That's all. And you, how did you become a nun in this Convent?"

"I'm not yet a real nun. I'm only a Novice. I still have three more years before taking my final vows."

"If I understand correctly, they give you three years to think it over before making the big decision."

"You're right! But before leaving, I want you to tell me something. Do you judge me badly because I came here to see you?"

"How can I judge you? After you left that day, if it had been possible, I would have tried to see you again. But can you picture me coming up into the *Cloister* and asking: Could I see the pleasant little nun you sent to the boiler room the day the lights went off? She was very nice with me and I want to talk to her some more, and maybe take her to a movie."

The two young people laughed heartily. Suddenly, Colette rose to leave. Nicolas held onto her hand stood up and took her into his arms. They embraced each other for a few minutes before the young nun ran to escape. Nicolas had been faster and was waiting for her at the bottom of the stairs with his flashlight. When she was in front of him, he just asked:

"When will you be back?"

"I don't know, it's hard, I don't want to be found out," said Colette mysteriously,

"Listen, you know I'm always here. I'll just wait for you. It will be when you are ready…. But please, not in a month! I miss you already!"

The young nun nodded and ran upstairs. Nicolas went back to his chair. He was happy. Like Colette, he was in love for the first time. A great joy had come into his heart. He felt as light as if he was on a little cloud. The familiar things around seemed to be looking at him kindly and life itself seemed brighter.

The Bible says: "Having created man, God said: He should not be alone… let's give him a woman"

This search for companionship is written in the very cells of the body. As soon as it wakes to life, a baby cries out for someone's presence. If he cannot find it, he'll die. An only child suffers from solitude. He seeks out friends. At school, friendships play a very important role in a child's social development, and the worse fate, for the unfortunate ones, is not knowing the joy of having a friend who waits for him to come and play. By far, teenagers are the ones who need an attentive ear from their peers. Their vulnerability is so great that solitude is almost unbearable. They are like a crustacean without its shell. The only way to regain their strength is by the support of friends.

Colette had passed through these difficulties, but an ardent thirst of love had accumulated in her as a fire builds up inside a volcano. Suddenly, like a gift from Heaven, (or from Hell?) she loved, and she was loved. Her heart couldn't ignore this call from nature.

When she returned to the recreation's room which she had left under the pretext of feeling ill, Colette was already trying to find another reason to see her beloved, and soon.

During the following months, Colette went back often to see Nicolas. The two lovers were in a hurry. They didn't talk much, trying to communicate with their caresses. They felt an ardent desire to have more time together. The quick encounters just increased that desire.

One day, Colette asked Nicolas:

"Would it be possible for you to spend a whole night here?"

"Why are you asking me that?" answered the young man.

"Because we could be together for a longer time," uttered Colette, looking at him intensely.

"Yes, it would be possible. I just have to pretend I'm worrying about a problem with the furnace, and that I have to stay and watch, in case... My mother would understand very well, as my father often used to do so."

"We should determine a precise night though," said Colette, thoughtfully.

"Yes, it would be better if we don't want to miss our rendezvous."

"O.K., let's say next Sunday, decided Sister Marie-Marthe." I'll go to bed with the others, and at eleven o'clock, I'll come here to see you."

"It is perfect for me, too. I'll have my supper with my mom and be with her part of the evening, and then I'll pretend I'm worrying about something. Since I don't work on Sundays, she'll understand, and I'll be here, right on time."

"Will you bring a camping cot, please? It could be useful…"

"Yes…surely." answered Nicolas, doubtful of the young woman's intentions.

Next Sunday, at ten thirty, Nicolas was already there, waiting for Colette. When he saw her, he noticed she wasn't wearing her usual clothes. She had on a much lighter nightgown. Her hair was worn loose under a small veil, she had thrown a woollen cape over her shoulders. Nicolas kissed her tenderly. Then, he undid the veil holding her hair. Colette placed her cape on a chair. The dim light showed her body's shadow through the robe. Nicolas came nearer and began caressing her all over. She shivered under his male hands. Suddenly, he gathered the light form and brought her to the bed where he laid down beside her.

That night, for the first time in her life, Colette gave her body with love.

From then on, every Sunday, the woman came to meet the one she now loved more than everything in the world,

Colette slept in the linen room located a half floor higher than the Juvenists' dormitory on the third floor. When she was going down, she just had to take the long staircase that led into the basement.

The Guardian, Mother Notre-Dame-Des-Pins slept on the second floor near the stairs. Her room served as both her office and her bedroom.

One night, Colette was running down for her rendezvous when she suddenly faced the terrible woman. The young nun was not under her authority, but she knew her reputation. In front of the questioning face, Colette whispered:

"I think I forgot my beads in the kitchen"

As she continued on her way, Colette felt the Guardian's eyes burning into her back. The woman would wait for her right there, Colette thought. When she came back up, she hastily said, out of breath:

"It was not there; I hope I didn't lose it." Then, Colette went back in her bed where she waited a whole hour to be certain that the nun was sound asleep.

When Colette finally came to Nicolas, he was worrying. The two lovers were lying tenderly intermingled in each other arms when they heard a dreadfully frightening voice above their heads,

"You finally found your rosary, Sister Marie-Marthe?"

The Guardian aggressively pulled off the blankets, revealing their nakedness,

"Now young man, you just scram away from here quickly, and by the way, you can look for another job. As for you, Sister, go back to your bed and tomorrow, Mother Superior shall meet with you about your future."

Mother Notre-Dame-Des-Pins gathered the man's clothes on the ground, she opened the door and threw them outside. When Nicolas had gone, the Guardian locked the door from inside, and then escorted Sister Mare-Marthe to her attic.

The morning after, the Sister who came to wake up Mother Notre-Dame-Des-Pins, found her soaking in her blood. She was dead, murdered, her two jugulars sliced. Sister Therese-de-Lima rushed out of the room shouting her lungs out:

"Help! Mother Des-Pins has been killed! Help! There's blood everywhere! Help!"

The Convent in Turmoil

The news spread though the Convent like wildfire. The absolute silence observed by these cloistered nuns was broken. Death, this dreadful visitor, had provoked the violation of the Rule. An incredible fright seized these women. "There is a murderer in our walls! Maybe he is still there! Will he strike again? Who will be his next victim?"

The Superior, Mother Marie-Des-Saints-Anges, who was under the shock herself, had to keep the calm in her Convent. She had to be like a good captain on the bow of the ship in a tempest. Those noisy women, speaking all at the same time, one crying, the other praying out loud, were like chickens in a henhouse. They had to be controlled. The Superior sent them to the Chapel. Was there a better dwelling than a place of prayer to terminate the commotion?

The boarders were not yet aware of the drama. When they arrived at the Chapel, they were a little surprised to see the nuns whispering among themselves. They had never seen that! Everyone waited in vain for the Chaplain to come and celebrate the Mass, but he was very occupied that morning…

Mother Superior waited till he arrived at five fifty before making a decision. She didn't have the courage to go and see her dead Sister. When the Chaplain, Father Jean, learned the news, he became as white as a sheet. Mother Marie-Des-Saint-Anges was afraid he was going to faint. He leaned against the wall, and she set a chair for him. He just crawled into it without a word. A few minutes later though, he regained his self control and asked:

"Did anyone move the body?"

"Not yet, I haven't even seen it! I thought we should call the police first, what do you think?"

"You are absolutely right; we shouldn't touch anything! But I would like to see her, please."

The man seemed stunned. His voice sounded as if coming out of a dream.

"Yes, Father Chaplain."

The Superior was astonished. She didn't understand the reason behind the request, but as she was already overcome by the situation, she didn't inquire further. What bothered her most though was the impudicity of the demand. These cloistered women had never shared their intimacy with any man, and now, Mother-Notre-Dame-des- Pins, in her dressing gown, had to show to one of them. More, as she was the victim of a gruesome crim\.

However, what Mother Marie-Des-Saints-Anges didn't understand yet was that the dead body no longer belonged to the community, as it was soon to be delivered into the hands of the police, the doctors and even to the journalists.

Father Jean was part of the community of the Clerics de Saint Viateur, whose monastery was located on the mountain about half a kilometre from the Convent. The man had been the Convent's Chaplain for many years now. The Bishop had made an arrangement which allowed him to come daily to celebrate the Offices twice a day. His quarters included the Chapel, the Sacristy, and a little room in the parlour where a Sister served him a light meal two times a day. He had entered the *Cloister* itself only two times previously to administer the Last Sacrament to a dying nun.

"Will you wait for me a moment while I go to the Sacristy," said the priest. He came back with his stole, a vase of Holy Water and an aspergillum. The Superior led him though the deserted Convent to Mother Notre-Dame-Des-Pins' room. They both stopped on the doorstep.

The woman's body was resting on her back with the legs opened in an indecent pose. Her head was tilted back showing her neck entirely covered in dark blood. It had spread onto the white robe and had fallen to the floor where a pool had formed from which branched little streams. Starting in the doorway, the priest recited the prayers for the dead, "Absolvo te peccatum, in nomine Patri et Filii et Spiritu Sancti Amen," and then he sprinkled the Holy Water onto the body as he traced the sign of the cross.

Mother Marie-Des-Saints-Anges admired the Chaplain's calm and appreciated his religious initiative. In her panic, she had forgotten this primordial ritual of the last absolution of the dead. She noticed that the nun's body was not yet in rigor mortis, as she would recall later. It was fifteen minutes past six.

After the short ceremony was over, the Superior, completely distraught by the scene she had just witnessed, returned to her office. She sat down and for a few minutes was immobilized by an agonizing lethargy. She barely had the strength to pull out of it, but she knew she had to call the police as soon as possible.

During this time, in the Chapel, Germaine, an older Juvenist, was preparing the little speech she was going to tell the Mother Guardian when the right moment will come. In the dormitory, the night before, she had seen the little Marie-Céline coming out of Mother E's room. Her bed was the first beside the nun's room. At a certain moment during the night, she had woken up, believing she had heard voices. At first, she had been frightened, but after listening more closely, she realized the sound was coming from the adjoining room. She hadn't gone back to sleep, but watched to see what was going to happen. She was rewarded when the door opened to let pass a slim silhouette she easily recognized, and she had threatened loudly;

"I'm going to tell the Mother Guardian".

Those words had come naturally to her lips. It was the normal reaction according to the moral education given at this institution. As in every totalitarian government, disclosure was greatly encouraged. It was taught as a virtue. Germaine was proud of the recognition that was soon to be bestowed on her. At the same time, it was an opportunity for a little revenge, for she too was enamored with Mother E who had always ignored her advances.

Germaine was a stout girl from the country. Her parents were farmers, and their podgy red-faced girl was their pride.

Instinctively, the teenager sensed that her body possessed neither the grace, nor her face the beauty of Marie-Céline, a small and lovely blonde.

Soon, outside in the Convent's entrance, one could see a police car, its red light flashing in the grayish dawn. Two Policeman came out of the car, almost at the same time. With quick strides, they mounted the stairs. The first rang the bell impetuously while the other violently knocked at the door, shouting:

"Police! Open up!"

The Mother Superior, herself, came to open the door. The older Policeman asked harshly,

"Is this where a murder has been committed?"

"Yes, I'm the one who called you. Come in, I'll show you," said Mother Marie-Des-Saints-Anges in a controlled voice.

The two men followed her up to the Mother Guardian's room. They stopped at the doorway without entering. They looked intensively at the body for a moment, and then appeared to consider the situation. They had to make the right decision. Then, the senior Officer told the other: "Stay here. Make sure nobody comes near the body. I'll go to the car and call the Criminal Investigators."

About thirty minutes later, two other cars were parked in front of the Convent. In one was the head Detective, and in the other, a Forensic technician, his camera in hand. The two men were from the Provincial Police. They were both led to the scene of the crime. The two Patrolmen were waiting for them. After a brief greeting, the Detective said,

"Only one of you needs to stay here, the other may return to his regular duties."

There was a short discussion and then, one of them said, "Have a good day, Sir", as he left to go down to the main entrance.

The two Investigators approached the body cautiously. The one with the camera walked to the window, examining it meticulously. When he came back to the dead body, his fellow Officer stood back. The technician took many frames, and declared:

"She was struck at her throat," he said pensively.

'Yes, the jugular seemed to have been cut on each side," added the Officer.

"The body is not yet completely rigid. The death is relatively recent," added the photographer.

"Hardly two hours," recited the other Detective, repeating the Conventional lesson.

"It's seven o'clock. It is an important fact to note. There is no evidence of a struggle. The murderer knew where he was going. The deceased was probably sound asleep," concluded Officer Leduc.

The Officer wrote all the details in a small note book. Suddenly, the Technician said:

"I've looked at the window. It has bars on the outside and was locked from the inside. Neither shows evidence of tampering. No one entered from there. Anyway, we're on the second floor. The murderer could only have come from inside the house," assessed the Technician with confidence. Then, he began sketching the room on a big white sheet. The bed and the religious woman occupied the center of the drawing. Afterwards, he slipped on gloves to search the room for evidence.

"How long is this going to take?" asked the prime Officer.

"At least an hour," answered the technician.

"In that case, I'll go down to take notes and begin the interviews." Then, turning toward Mother Marie-Des-Saints-Anges, who was standing a little way in the corridor, he asked, "Sister, is there a quiet place where I could ask you a few questions."

The Mother Superior took him back towards the main entrance where she indicated a small room beside the large central parlor. There, seated at the little table where the Chaplain took his meals, Mr. Leduc, the Detective, opened a large notebook in which several white sheets were held in place by a paperclip.

"Sister, are you the person in charge?" he asked.

"Yes, I am the Mother Superior of the Convent," she answered in a firm voice.

"Are you ready to make your statement?"

The woman hesitated, uncertain how to answer. The Detective's voice seemed accusatory as if he was addressing a culprit. She feared putting herself in a disadvantaged position.

The man understood and softened his voice to reassure her:

"You have nothing to be afraid of, it's only a formality.'

"I'm not a little girl, Sir! I know perfectly well that this is a very serious matter, and that every word I say will be noted, and eventually will be used in court," declared Mother Marie-Des-Saints-Anges with authority.

"You are right to say that we are faced with a grave crime, but I want you to know, that at this stage in the investigation, no accusations have been made. We're only at the preliminary stage, and your testimony, as a person in charge, is essential." The Investigator was now speaking in a deferent tone to this woman whose authority had impressed him.

"With your permission, we'll continue. If I understood correctly, you are the highest authority in this house."

"Yes, I am the Superior, Mother Marie-Des-Saints-Anges."

"How long have you been in charge of this community?"

"For about fifteen years."

"And the deceased?"

"For less than a year," she was returning from a mission in Cameroon.

"Now, can you tell what happened?"

"Well, at five o'clock, the Sister, who is responsible for waking up Mother Notre-Dame-Des-Pins, went to knock at her door, the same as she does every morning. When she didn't receive the usual answer, she opened the door softly and called a little louder. As nothing moved in the room, she entered and saw what you saw a few minutes ago," told the nun with emotion.

"Who is this nun? Can I meet her?"

"Sister Thérèse-de-Lima is actually in the Chapel. Do you want me to go and bring her?"

"Not right away. Let's finish our conversation first. What did this person do afterwards?"

"She can tell you better than me. All I know is that I heard her terrible cries."

"Was this person addressing someone in particular?"

"No, she was shouting while running. She was repeating the same sentence as she dashed toward my office: Help! Mother Notre-Dame-Des-Pins has been murdered! There's blood everywhere! Help!"

"What were you doing at that moment?"

"I was already awake. I was meditating."

"Are you always awake before the other nuns?"

"In fact, I am the one who gives the signal that begins the process of waking up the whole Convent. So yes, I am the first one to begin the day."

In spite of her anxiety, the woman seemed calmed and confident.

The Investigator was surprised by the certitude of her answers. He went on with his questionings.

"How many people live here?"

"Sixty nuns and thirty Juvenists," specified the Superior.

"Who are the ones you call Juvenists?"

"They are young girls from twelve to eighteen years old, who, while pursuing their studies, are preparing to become nuns."

"But where is everyone? The Convent seems to be empty."

"By now, everybody is in the Chapel for the celebration of Mass."

"Who celebrates the Mass?"

"Father Jean, our Chaplain."

"Does he live in here?"

"No, he comes from a nearby monastery."

"At what time was he in this morning?"

"At five fifty, as usual."

"Is he celebrating mass right now? Otherwise, I'd like to see him and ask him a few questions."

"I'll go to the Sacristy if you want. If he is there, he isn't yet in the Chapel, and I'll ask him to come to see you."

In a few minutes, Mother Marie-Des-Saints-Anges returned, accompanied by the Chaplain.

"Sir, here is Father Jean. May I leave?"

"No, Sister, please stay, I still have a few questions to ask."

What the Detective failed to mention is that he wanted to observe the relationship between the two people who occupied positions of authority in the Convent. Mother Superior sat down beside Father Jean, both of whom were facing the Investigator.

The police Officer, Mr. Leduc, took a moment to look at the two people sitting in front of him. Both were in their fifties, the same generation in fact. The woman was tall and slim; her blue eyes highlighted her pale figure. She was elegant in spite of her religious attire. She came from a wealthy family in Québec city. Her brother was a Bishop. She was very proud to invite him a few times a year to the Convent.

Besides her, the Chaplain was small and podgy with brown curly hair. As soon as he had come in, the Policeman had been struck by the priest's effeminate manners. Curious, Mr. Leduc wanted to verify his first impression. He asked him to identify himself.

"I am Father Jean of the Cleric de St-Viateur's Congregation. I am also the Chaplain of this house."

The man spoke with in a high-pitched tone, moving his hands with affectation.

The Officer tried not to laugh, so exaggerated were the man's mannerism. He couldn't help thinking of his fellow police Officers who would have exclaimed: "Another 'poof' again!" The Investigator proceeded with his inquiry,

"And you, Father, how long have you been in this house?"

"I am the Chaplain of this Convent for fifteen years."

"Do you come here every day?"

"Yes, two times a day, every day."

"Do you have your own key to enter, or are you obliged to ring every time?"

"...Hem, I..." the priest didn't seem to know what to answer. The Inspector became impatient

"I'm asking you again: Do you have a key to come into the Convent?"

The Mother Superior came to his help;

"For many years, Father Chaplain rang the door. A year ago, our Sister in charge of the door felt ill, and she had to leave and go to rest in her room. Receiving no answer, Father Chaplain had to go back home, and the whole community was deprived of the Mass that day. Afterwards, we gave him a key, so that such an incident would not happen again. This is an exception. Otherwise, no one is supposed to be in possession of the key to the Convent."

The Investigator seemed very interested in this story. He was writing everything down. Looking obviously uncomfortable, the Chaplain's face had turned red as if he was guilty. The Investigator looked intently at him in silence. Father Jean mumbled:

"Listen. I have done nothing to be ashamed of. Mother Marie-Des-Saints-Anges and I both know that our Rules do not allow us this slight transgression," said the priest nervously. "However, between the letter of the law and common sense, there is a place for one's own judgment. If, for one reason or another, I cannot get in here, how can I minister to this Convent?"

The man sweated profusely, trying to explain himself. The Investigator judged it was enough, but he put a little note beside the priest's name. He suddenly rose and asked;

"I have to make a call, is there a telephone I can use, Sister?"

"Yes, in my office. Will there be other questionings today?"

"I don't know. It will depend on the Coroner's advice. I have to call him" immediately to tell him about the whole affair. I also have to call the morgue. They probably will come and get the body this afternoon."

"Will the body come back here for the funeral?" worried Mother Marie-Des-Saints-Anges?

"Yes, certainly, after the autopsy. I'm not sure if it'll be suitable to show her though, she may be damaged," answered the Officer.

71

"She is so now," said the Superior with sadness.

"Father, this will be all for today. You can go," said the Detective leaving the room. "Sister, would you show me the way, please."

The Superior's office was in the *Cloister*. She had forgotten that detail as no lay person can enter this reserved place. She, hence, led the policeman to the entrance where there was a telephone in the little room beside the main door. Mister Leduc noticed the change in direction, but he didn't say a word.

The Investigator went to use the telephone, but before shutting the door, he said to the Superior:

"Sister, I would like to meet the person who came to wake up the...dead Sister." He didn't know how to refer to her. "But leave me a little time to put my notes in order. Let's say in about half an hour."

"You want to meet Sister Rose-de-Lima who came to wake up Mother Notre-Dame-Des-Pins?" précised Mother Marie-Des-Saints-Anges.

"Yes, that's it," answered the police Officer.

He was becoming frustrated at the complexity of this religious vocabulary. He realized that he would have to learn their religious name, their function as well as their civil name because for legal purposes only the latter was valid.

On the other end of the line, the Coroner claimed that he had to review the crime scene himself. He also mentioned that he would arrange for the morgue to collect the body. The police Officer, André Leduc, explained to his superior how to get to R's Convent. Mr. Ryan said he would be there that very afternoon.

"I'll work on my notes, I'll question this nun, and then, I'll have lunch in the village around noon," the Inspector told himself for encouragement. He was beginning to comprehend the complexity of the case. "It is as if everything is a secret here," thought Mr. Leduc. In reality, it was the first time he had entered a Convent. He knew neither its code, nor its Rules. He continuously had to interpret every action, every word which he saw or heard.

The Investigator returned to the room, where he had begun his interrogations. A nun was already waiting for him. She stood up when she saw him, keeping her eyes lowered. She was a stout woman in her late forties, a farmer's girl thought the Officer.

"Good morning, Sister, please sit. What is your name?"

"Sister Thérèse-de-Lima," answered a rough and muffled voice. It had the tone of someone, used to silence, whose vocal cords had atrophied with time.

"I was told that you discovered the dead body. Would you tell me how everything happened?"

"My duty is to wake the nuns who sleep on the Juvenate's side of the house. Usually, I begin in the attic. Three Sisters sleep in the linen room there. At the children's dormitory, on the third floor, there are two. Mother Notre-Dame-Des-Pins is the last one on my list, on the second floor. Everyone is familiar with my routine. I come every morning at the same time. I just knock lightly and recite the awaking prayer, and they answer right away."

The woman spoke in a monotonous tone, without any intonation. With her eyes down, her face void of any expression. Only her lips moved.

"What happened when you arrived at the dead woman's door?"

"I knocked as usual, reciting the prayer. I didn't hear any answer. I began again, a little louder, still nothing. Then, I took the liberty to open the door. Nothing moved in the place. I went in a little with my flashlight, and I saw the blood…" The nun's voice was calm, without any emotion.

"What did you do after that?"

"I went to tell Mother Superior," answered the nun undisturbed.

The Investigator was just dumbfounded on hearing this deposition. The Superior had spoken of a hysterical woman, who was screaming her lungs out. On the contrary, this woman in front of him was a complete sang-froid. He couldn't even imagine her losing her temper. "Religious people are a mystery to me. I really cannot understand them", he kept telling himself. "It would be easier to move arouse a stone than this nun."

"What did the Superior say when you gave her your report?"

"She sent us all to the Chapel."

"What are your other duties in the Convent? "

"I'm in charge of the garden and the henhouse."

"For how long have you live here in R?"

"For five years."

"Do you like it here?"

"It's my life!"

For the first time, she lifted her eyes towards the Officer. The man read a furious determination in her face. He noticed her low forehead and strong jaw. The Detective thought that she looked more like a man than a woman, and that the Chaplain was more feminine than her. "Indeed, hormones are just crazy in here," thought the man, laughing on the inside.

"It'll be all for today, Sister."

The tall woman stood up and left without saying good-bye. The Superior entered right after, and the Investigator had the impression she must have been listening at the door to know so soon that the meeting was over. She asked:

"Do you wish to share your meal with Father Chaplain? It'll be served in about an hour." It was ten thirty on the Officer's watch. He answered quickly.

"No, thank you Sister, but I prefer to go outside. Is there a restaurant in the village?"

"Yes, I think meals are served at the hotel."

"And where is this hotel?"

"Down the hill, on your right."

"Thank you, Sister, I'll be away for about an hour, from noon to one o'clock. May I hope that I won't have to wait too long for someone to open the door when I return?"

"Don't worry, the Sister will be there, and I told her to let you come in and out as you wish."

"Thank you, Sister, for your collaboration."

Mr. Leduc, police Investigator, put his interrogation book in order with great care and went out, happy to breathe fresh air and avoid spending an hour with the Chaplain. "There is a time for work and another for rest," he thought, while his conscience whispered that he could have learnt more if he had spent an hour with the priest.

When he returned, the Mother Superior was waiting for him. She told him that another man was already there. She also informed him that she was waiting for his return before allowing this man to visit the body. "Since he didn't wear a uniform, and I wondered what he was here for?"

"He didn't tell you he was the Coroner?"

"He did, but there are so many people running about here, I preferred to wait for you to confirm his identity."

Mr. Leduc was pleased with the confidence Mother Marie-Des-Saint-Anges showed toward him, but at the same time, he feared the aggressive temperament of the Coroner Ryan. This man was the incarnation of perfection when he was administering his duty. Even if he was there, for many years, every inquest was accomplished with the same zeal as if it was the first.

In the parlor, the Investigator found an angry man.

"I was not allowed to go near the body. Imagine that religious woman doubting my identity!"

"Welcome Mr. Ryan, said Mr. Leduc, holding out his hand. I'm glad to meet you. This affair seems very complicated. I feel reassured to know you're in charge. I'll lead you to the scene of the crime myself."

Mr. Leduc had spoken with great politeness as if he hadn't noticed the rude and angry man who had ignored his hand and had not even bothered to return his greeting.

The Coroner followed him without a word and went directly into the room of the crime. The Investigator stayed outside. He addressed the Sergeant, who was posted there since early morning,

"Is someone coming to take your place?"

"I don't know, I don't think so, Sir," answered the man who was visibly tired.

"And you didn't eat yet?" asked the Officer.

"No sir",

The Investigator knew he had failed taking care of his subordinates.

"Well, go downstairs and ask to see the Sister Superior. Tell her, on my behalf, to give you something to eat since you've been on watch without any rest for a long time."

"Thank you, Sir, said the man gratefully." The young man thought to himself: "Inspector Leduc is a good man. His reputation is merited!"

During this time, the Coroner had called from the room. On hearing his voice, the Officer ran.

"At what time did the Convent call for police?" asked Coroner Ryan

"Around a quarter after six, answered the Inspector.

"At what time did you arrive?"

"After they arrived here, the patrolmen called us at six thirty, and we arrived at seven o'clock."

"How was "rigor mortis"?"

"It had scarcely started as we noted."

"Who was the other person?"

"He was the scene crime Technician. We arrived almost at the same time."

Mister Leduc knew the fearsome Coroner wanted to check if everything had been done perfectly.

"Well, everything seems to be under control. I'll call the morgue, so they'll come and get the body for autopsy. The Forensic Surgeon have been advised. He'll take care of the body as soon as it arrives. Can you take me to the main door?"

Inspector Leduc was ill at ease. He knew the dead body was never to be left unwatched, and he had just sent away the policeman who had been posted for that purpose.

"Hem… excuse me, I can't."

"May I know why?" said a dry voice.

"Because I've just sent away the sergeant who was here since the morning. He went to get some food and rest a little. I'm taking his place for a few minutes."

The Coroner looked at him with a despising look. These weak ways of settling things disgusted him deeply. He was hard on himself and expected everybody to act the same way.

"Well, if you're happy playing the role of a watchman, it's up to you. Feel free to demote yourself, but just keep hoping a bad report won't make it permanent."

And on these malicious words, M. Ryan had left.

Mother Superior Takes Control of Her Convent

other Marie-Des-Saints-Anges had settled her problem by sending everyone to the Chapel. It was a temporary solution though, and she was very aware of that. She had to think of something else. The nuns knew everything, the children nothing. Not for now anyway… the Superior wanted to tell them later on much later on… However, she realized that she could count on the indiscretion from some foolish nun who would let things slip through her lips. It would panic the Juvenists. She wanted to avoid this scenario at any cost! But, how could she?

At eight-thirty, while Inspector Leduc was conducting his investigation, Mother Marie-Des-Saints-Anges took the opportunity to visit the Chapel. Everyone had been waiting for the Mass to be celebrated for over than an hour. She felt the impatience of the crowd. She stood in front and announced in a neutral tone:

"There will be a few changes in our daily schedule. Father Chaplain is not available to say the Mass now, and Mother Guardian is very sick, so you won't be seeing her today. In order to let her rest, we'll not work on the classrooms floor today. So, listen to me: There will be no household work after breakfast today. Instead, you will be given a few minutes to go to your classroom, or to the dormitory, so you collect everything needed for the rest of the day. You will not be allowed to return there for any reason. Am I making myself clear? For to-day, your lessons will be held in the refectory. For everything else, you will follow your regular program. Mother Pauline-du-Saint-

Sacrement will replace Mother Notre-Dame-Des-Pins today. If there's something important, ask her."

Then, the Mother Superior addressed the congregation of nuns:

"As for you, Sisters and Mothers, I count on you to accomplish all your regular duties in accordance with the obligatory silence of the Rule."

These women, who just a short time ago had disobeyed this Rule, understood the hidden message perfectly.

"Since there will be no Mass today, and we are already late for our usual schedule, everyone will go directly to the morning breakfast."

Silence was the cornerstone in this Convent, so the Mother Superior hoped the secret would hold... "At least till the end of the day," she tried to reassure herself. "Then, the dead body will have been removed away from here, far from the children's view at least."

She could easily imagine the drama if one of the children saw the horrible scene. Mother Marie-Des-Saints-Anges was a very intelligent woman. She was also a courageous one. She had been in mission in China for years. Imprisoned with other nuns, she had suffered the horrors of a concentration camp. Without regards for their religious status, they had been mingled with the other women. The strange nuns were not one of them. They would often be used as a scapegoat by the Chinese women who had laughed at them, pushed them and sometimes even beat them. They had returned home at the end of the war. The nuns had been strongly affected by this experience. Some of them had never overcome the trauma. Mother Marie-Des-Saints-Anges had not succumbed to her sufferings because of her exceptional strength of character. And, it was once again her willpower which would allow her to survive this terrible ordeal.

As the directives had been clearly explained, things went smoothly up to the moment when the young girls arrived on the classroom floor. There, they saw the policeman in his uniform standing in front of Mother Notre-Dame-Des-Pins's closed door. Strangers had never been allowed inside the Convent. The

Juvenists were stunned, asking themselves hundred questions that they didn't have the right to ask. Their curiosity was so strong that some of them stayed there, mouth opened, staring at the man. They seemed hypnotized by this vision. Mother Marie-Pauline, noticing the situation, and she said loudly:

"Come on, go ahead, you've got things to get for your school day. Also, don't forget, if you have articles to fetch in the dormitory, do it now as it will be your only chance for the whole day! "

These words called the inquisitive girls back to order. As well-disciplined children, they obeyed silently. Each teacher took a corner of the refectory with their students. No one really had the heart to teach. All the teachers, as in every emergency case, assigned a composition to their pupils on the pretext of being unable to be efficient without a blackboard or any of their usual tools. It was about nine-forty-five when Germaine asked to go to the washroom. Her secret was tormenting her. She was burning to tell it to someone. She had thought that if Mother Guardian was not available, she could tell everything to Mother Superior. She edged her way to the parlor. She planned to ask the Sister who was guarding the doo to find the Mother Superior pretending to have something very important to tell her.

When Germaine arrived, Mr. Leduc, Police Investigator, was sitting at a round table in a small room off the parlor. He was writing down the morning's main events. He had finished his conversation with Sister Rose-de-Lima, and his door was opened. The Officer saw the young girl. She looked uncertain. The Investigator called her:

"Are you looking for someone, Miss?"

Germaine jumped and smothered her cry with her hand. She was frightened as she hadn't "

"I've come to meet with Mother Superior", said the young girl shyly.

"Is she expecting you?"

"Not really, I had planned to ask Sister Olive, the door keeper, to go an find her for me."

"Is it the usual way of proceeding when you want to meet with the Mother Superior?"

"No, we never ask to meet Mother Superior as Mother Guardian is always there to answer our questions," explained Germaine with difficulty in front of this man who wanted to know everything.

"You must have something very important to tell her, to disturb her like this!"

Germaine became speechless. At this very moment, Mother Marie-Des-Saints-Anges, the Mother Superior, came out of the *Cloister.* She looked at the Juvenist with surprise and reproof. A boarder here! So near her secret! The woman was greatly irritated. She could hardly dissimulate her fury and asked bluntly;

"What are you doing here? Are you not supposed to be in class with the others? Who gave you permission to come here?"

"I have very important things to tell you…" hesitated the girl.

"About what?" shouted the nun

"It's more about whom…."

"What's your mystery? Will you speak at last!"

Anger is a bad counselor; Mother Superior learnt when she heard what was said in front of the Investigator whose ears were wide open.

"Last night, I surprised Marie-Céline who was coming out of Mother E's room. They were making noise for a whole an hour which kept me from sleeping."

Mother Superior whitened under the shock. She realized the blunder she had just made, publicizing such an intimate secret. She would have liked to verify the truth before proclaiming it from the rooftops. However, it was too late now, the evil was done. The poor messenger was rudely sent back to her business without a single word of gratitude that she had hoped for so desperately.

"Would you come here one moment please, Sister? said the Investigator to Mother Marie-Des-Saints-Anges. Would you close the door too, please?"

The Mother Superior obeyed, feeling very uncomfortable.

"What about this nightly rendezvous? Who are these two individuals?" asked the police Officer. Facing her silence, he added "You know Sister, every event may be very important to our investigation."

"Are you implying there could be a link between Mother Notre-Dame-Des-Pins's death, and what this poor girl has just related!" said the Superior with indignation.

"I did not say anything like that! replied the Detective. However, we have to verify every uncommon event which happened on the night the murder was committed," said the man with authority. "I'm asking you now, to identify these individuals."

"A Juvenist, Marie-Céline, and her teacher, Mother Elizabeth" answered the nun reluctantly.

"Could you ask them to come here this afternoon without any delay," insisted Mr. Leduc.

"At what time would you like to see them?"

"Just after the Coroner's visit. Since I know him, he'll be here soon after dinner. Until then, I would ask you not to say a word about the reason of their summons here."

Mother Marie-Des-Saints-Anges forced herself to obey Mr. Leduc's orders. For many years now, she made all the decisions, obliging people to comply with her wishes. Now, she had to summit to a police Officer when her own Convent's reputation was in danger! However, she also knew the man would quickly discern if she tried to intervene. She would then lose her credibility which she so badly needed in such a delicate situation.

The woman was deeply troubled. What had really happened between this Juvenist and her teacher? Was it a sexual encounter? Was it the first time? And this Germaine, had she told everything? Could she have invented it all to be the center of attention? The nun had witnessed this kind of thing before, where perfectly innocent people had been unfairly accused. Mother Marie-Des-Saints-Anges didn't know what to think!

The two young women were sitting together while waiting for the police Investigator to return from watching over the dead body.

Coroner Ryan's rude words had irritated Mr. Leduc. Moreover, he was infuriated when he noticed the two witnesses had enough time to confer together before being questioning. He didn't greet them, but only gestured for the young girl to follow him.

Marie-Céline was completely devastated. She went into the Detective's office still under the shock of Mother E's revelation that the Mother Guardian had been murdered. Her lover didn't have to explain that under such circumstances they were suspects in her death as both of them would not have appreciated Mother Guardian knowing about their relationship. Furthermore, they were certain that Germaine had already denounced them as she had threatened to do. This girl was a real traitor who could not be trusted or relied on. The two witnesses had had time to design a common strategy to face the Officer.

Marie-Céline was only thirteen years old, but she had gone to a school of a hard woman whom she had learnt to resist. If she hadn't stood firm against her mother's exactions, Céline wouldn't have survived.

At this crucial moment, she strengthened her will against the man. She suspected him of wanting to hurt Mother E. She swore to herself never to betray the one she loved more than her life.

"Hi, Miss Marie-Céline, how old are you? asked the man with a sweetened voice".

"I'm thirteen," answered the child, a little surprised to be called by her name.

"Do you love Mother E a lot?" The man didn't prepare the ground as he usually did for an adult.

"She's my school teacher," she said dryly.

"Yes, this I know, but one can appreciate a teacher without loving her in a particular way," insisted Mr. Leduc.

"What do you mean? I don't understand your question at all!" Céline said with the candor of a well-rehearsed innocence.

"I mean to love someone, to want to kiss her, to touch her, to be in her arms."

"You have strange ideas, Sir. Things like that never happen in a Convent, you know!" Céline seemed truly sincere.

"Will you tell me then, what you were doing in a nun's room in the middle of the night?" asked Mr. Leduc impatiently.

"I had a sore belly. I went to ask Mother E for some medicine."

"And it took an hour in her room?"

"An hour! Who told you that? A few minutes, yes, not more," declared Céline

"Another student came to tell us that you had prevented her from sleeping for part of the night!"

"Oh! that big Germaine already came! When I left Mother E's room, she woke up saying while half asleep: "I'll tell Mother Guardian" I didn't believe she would come to tell such a lie!"

The police Officer realized he was losing the game against a thirteen-year-old child. She had the nerve not seen on many hardened criminals. What he didn't know was that she was fighting for a sentiment more powerful than any court in this world. Céline was also convinced that she could resist the greatest torture without saying a word. Mr. Leduc understood it too. He didn't insist and decided to strike harder on the other witness.

The Interrogation of Mother E

r. André Leduc of the criminal squad was not conducting his first inquest. He had already known many complex and difficult hours of work, but this day in November 195… was to be classified among the worst in his memory. It's like he was facing a wall and that he couldn't see farther!

All had started with a very early phone call when Mr. Leduc was still enjoying his last hour of sleep before dawn in the warmth of his bed. Then, he had rushed toward this strange Convent where a crapulous murder had been committed on a religious person in her own bed. Moreover, the man felt confused among those women who were hiding heavy secrets under their white veils. Added to this, were his superior's critical remarks, whose nastiness equaled his manic determination. No, for sure, the police Investigator's humor was very dark when Mother E entered his office.

"Sit down, Sister," said the Detective dryly. "As you know, we received information against you."

This accusatory remark was meant to destabilize the witness. The Detective was looking hard at the religious woman in order to scrutinize her reactions. Mother E stood without flinching. Her usual happy smiling face was at the moment like marble. Alike little Céline, she knew what she was risking, and that at the slightest weakness, a scandal could explode, expelling both of them from the Convent.

When leaving the Investigator's office, Céline had turned her back on the Officer. She had then taken the opportunity to look straight into her lover's eyes and tactfully made a sign of victory with her thumb raised high, while her arms remaining completely still. The man hadn't notice, but her accomplice had understood the message: the child had won over the police Officer. This simple gesture had revived Mother E's courage. This little girl had possibly just saved her life. She had to succeed as well.

"What do you have to say?" insisted the Investigator.

"May I know first, what I'm accused of?" answered the nun, standing tranquil in front of the police Officer.

"You're accused of having sexual relations with a child, "answered Mr. Leduc coldly.

"What evidence do you have?" replied the nun calmly.

"A student, sleeping just beside your room, heard everything."

"Could you tell me exactly what she heard? As for myself, the only noise that disturbed the quiet of the night was when Marie-Céline knocked at my door, asking for an aspirin to relieve her sore belly. I heard nothing else."

"And this visit lasted an hour?" insinuated, the Officer.

"No, just a few minutes."

"On the contrary, the person said she heard sounds for a long time, about an hour."

"How can you believe someone, half asleep, in complete darkness, talking about time?

The young woman had raised her voice, just enough to ensure her credibility and bring doubt to the Officer's mind. Mr. Leduc was furious. He had lost the first round. He decided to attack another way.

"You know that a murder was committed here last night. The victim was the same person to whom everything was to be told." The man's voice was now an accusation.

"Did you kill Mother Notre-Dame-Des-Pins?"

The young nun thought: "He doesn't know anything; he's just trying to trick me. I shall not fall into his trap."

When she was a young woman, Louise de la Durantaye was very interested about judicial investigations. She followed trials in the newspaper; she had learnt that the Investigators must have very solid evidence before accusing someone. She understood that Inspector Leduc had none, but that he was trying to obtain some. She didn't want to give him that gift.

"No Sir, and it is impossible for me to add anything else," said Mother E drily before turning quiet.

"The interview is over. But I assure you, we'll see each other again!" added the Officer with a knowing look, and he went on "We're certain, the murderer came from inside the Convent, and that he knew the house very well....Also, you had strong motives to wish this woman dead, for she would certainly have denounced you....following a witness very serious accusation."

The nun departed with dignity; her exterior very calm. Inside, her head was on fire. She had been very frightened. She was still a Novice and her perpetual vows were scheduled only in two years. In the meantime, the community was not obliged to keep her. Furthermore, her expulsion would mean that she had broken her vow about her mother's life. She was still alive. If something should happen to her, the young woman knew she couldn't forgive herself. She thought she had fooled this Inspector, but who knows?

Mr. Leduc, criminal squad Officer, was on the verge of a nervous breakdown. He was extremely discontented about the day, for despite all his efforts, he hadn't succeeded in controlling the situation. He had then decided to go home. He was satisfied though because the morgue had come to retrieve the body during the afternoon, and the road Sergeant had been relieved from his duty.

He was heading towards his car when a taxi entered the driveway. He could distinguish the presence of two individuals inside the vehicle. To be quite sure, he decided to verify their identity. He posted himself on the first step of the stairs and waited for them. A nun led the way while the other carried the luggage. The two wore a black veil and a gray cape which completely covered their clothes. In the Investigator's mind, they couldn't be from the same community whose members were entirely dressed in white. Who were these visitors? When the first traveler arrived at the stairs, Mr. Leduc stopped her from going up by putting his two arms on the banisters. The woman seemed surprised at first, but then she exploded:

"How dare you keep me from entering my own house!" Her voice was impetuous and full of rage.

"Listen, Sister, serious events have happened here, and a police Command is necessary. You have to identify yourself if you want to enter the Convent," explained Mr. Leduc calmly.

"I am the Mother Provincial of this community", answered the nun with authority.

"As your garments are not like the one of the other nuns in this house, I wish to check with the doorkeeper."

"Your insolence is going to cost you a heavy price young man", menaced the nun, red with anger

The police Officer was not intimidated at all. He went to the main door and rang. The doorkeeper's nun recognized him and immediately opened the door. He came in followed by the nun who was shouting angrily.

"What's going on here? Now, you open the door for a stranger, and you leave your Mother Provincial outside?"

The nun was beside herself while the poor doorkeeper kept excusing herself, calling her respectfully: "Mother Provincial" thus confirming her identity. In front of that dangerously irate woman, Mr. Leduc, now convinced, just vanished with prudence.

"You go and call Mother Marie-Des-Saints-Anges," she ordered the petrified nun.

She quickly disappeared. When Mother Superior arrived, the Provincial had completely changed her humor. She amiably greeted Mother Marie-Des-Saints-Anges and wanted to know everything immediately. The Superior helped the nun take of her mantle off and told her:

"Come to my office, we'll be more at ease to talk," said the Superior, dragging the Provincial toward the *Cloister*. A light lunch was waiting for her. She devoured everything with a good appetite. When she had finished, she declared:

"Now, tell me everything!"

The Mother Provincial, who was seated in front of the Superior, was a small pudgy woman with a rather tanned skin. She was from Italy and had kept her accent as well as her hot-tempered manners. She was aware of her superiority and didn't tolerate anyone who ignored it. She could bear her fellow sisters, but she openly hated all that was masculine. She liked to despise them. Mother Marie-Des-Saints-Anges knew her well, and she always tried to soften the quick temper of her Superior. Her name was Mother De-La-Purification.

The Superior started to recount all that had happened. She started at the moment the body was discovered by Sister Thérèse-de-Lima, followed by the arrival of the police and their questions which had lasted the whole day. The Superior didn't reveal Germaine's denunciation, keeping those details for later on, and only if needed. As soon as Mother Marie-Des-Saints-Anges had finished her story, the Mother Provincial had exclaimed:

"I know who the murderer is! I've always distrusted him, but now I know he is a dangerous man!"

"I'm astonished by what you have just said, Mother Provincial! I don't know whom you're talking about. Explain yourself, for heaven sake!"

"How innocent you are, poor you! What you've told me is a horror which only a man can commit! Are there many men coming into this house?"

"I hope you're not talking about Father Chaplain, good Father Jean? He wouldn't hurt a fly," said Mother Superior with indignation.

"He wouldn't hurt a fly, but he sexually molested his mass servant and his friend last summer!" exclaimed the Provincial triumphantly.

"Woo! What are you telling me? I've never heard these horrible things you're mentioning!" exclaimed the Superior.

Mother De-La-Purification got closer and started: "Last summer, Father Jean received an inheritance from his parents when they died. It was a country house by a river. His poverty vow kept him from keeping it. It became the property of the community. Otherwise, the brothers already possessed a big country house. So, Father Jean was asked to prepare it for sale. He was allowed to take the community's car and settle everything. He obeyed, and for this trip, asked his little mass servant to come with him. The child, with his parents' permission, arrived with a little friend who wanted to go with them. They were supposed to be away for the day. However, they returned only the day after. The parents were furious. They called Mother Notre-Dame-Des-Pins who told me."

The Superior was mad. She said with reproach:

"Why did you hide this information from me? I've never heard a word of this. I am the Superior of this house as far as I know!"

The Provincial knew she was in fault. She didn't answer and continued.

"Mother Guardian and I waited till today: We had to decide if we were to tell everything to his Community or give him over to the Bishop's authority."

Mother Marie-Des-Saints-Anges was shattered at this piece of news. She felt a great friendship towards Father Jean. They had worked together for years. She knew him as a responsible man, who had helped her on many occasions. She decided she was to defend him.

"Why are you convinced that inappropriate things happened to those children?"

"Come on, Sister, don't be that childlike! A man alone with two little boys! And for a whole night! Dirty things certainly happened, even if they all denied it," she added maliciously,

"Were the children questioned?" persisted the Superior.

"Sure, they have been, but they defended their great friend! They were in collusion with him. Don't forget they too will be men."

"Does Father Jean know all you have against him?" Mother Marie-Des-Saints-Anges wanted to know.

"He certainly does! We took pleasure in tormenting him, letting him wonder what we were going to do. However, everything had already been decided for a long time. We wanted him to worry before we struck the final shot," said the Provincial proudly.

"Poor man," muttered the Superior. She remembered now how she had noted distress in his eyes as if he wanted to tell her something

"Did Father Jean think I was acting with you?"

"No, he even wanted to tell you everything, pretending that you alone would be on his side. We formally forbade him to act against our will."

"And now, you claim that he killed Mother Notre-Dame-Des-Pins?"

"He had an excellent motive, as to prevent us from denouncing him, and the fact that he is a *man*. In my opinion, these evidences alone are sufficient to confirm the charge." concluded the woman firmly.

"And you are going to tell this story to Inspector Leduc tomorrow morning, I suppose worried the Superior.

"Who are you talking about? Who is this man?" said the Provincial aggressively

"He is the Officer in charge of the inquest. He came here early this morning; he inspected the scene of the crime. He also called the Coroner and the morgue. He spent the rest of the day questioning people."

"Is he going to be here a long time?" worried the Provincial

"I'm afraid he'll stay until he has found the culprit."

"In that case, he'll leave soon because I'll go myself and tell him the murderer's name," said the woman with assurance.

The Accusations of Mother Provincial

The day after, early in the morning, Mother De-La-Purification, Provincial, was standing in front of the little room used by Inspector Leduc to conduct his interrogations. She was the first person he saw on his arrival. The Officer understood the day was going to be a rough one, for this shrewish woman was real poison. He was not wrong. He saluted her coldly, went into his office, sat down, and started consulting his notes. He kept her waiting on purpose as to let her know he was in charge of the inquest.

For her part, Mother Provincial, used to being honored and entertained with consideration everywhere she passed, now cursed this dumb Pceman who was so impolite with her. She didn't have any other choice though. If she wanted to denounce Father Jean, she had to lodge her complaint against him to this man, even if she had to wait for hours.

When he thought his authority had been well established, Mr. Leduc stood up, walked to the doorway and said:

"Do you want to talk to me, Sister?"

"Yes. Sir, it seems obvious, no?" Her tone was dry and authoritarian.

"I'll meet with you, then. However, my schedule is loaded, so you'll have to be brief," answered the police Officer coldly.

"I don't have to be in a hurry, Sir. When I leave you, your inquest will be over because I'm bringing you the assassin's name."

Mr. Leduc was rather skeptical on hearing this declaration. His twenty years of experience, as a police Officer, had taught him to be very cautious. So, he didn't seem impressed, but just kept staring at the nun, one of his eyebrows raised high like an interrogation mark. He declared with authority.

"I hope for your sake, your evidence is indubitable, and that you're absolutely sure of your testimony before accusing anyone. I hope you realize the responsibility you're taking on. Someone's own life is hanging on your tongue, if I may say."

The Mother Provincial found these words disconcerting. She had expected the Investigator to eagerly question her, inviting her to give more details, happy to have resolved the problem. On the contrary, he seemed to distrust her testimony before even listening to her. She could hardly contain her furious impatience as her hot-tempered character plunged her into a great state of wrath.

"Do you want to solve the murder or not?" she asked the Detective furiously.

"Make your deposition, Madam. I'm listening."

The Officer Leduc had used the word, *Madam*, on purpose. It was irreproachable, but it lacked the respect usually accorded to the woman's religious station. The Officer was declaring war against the woman who wanted to take control of the investigation if she was given the slightest chance. He tried to softened the atmosphere. So, he asked calmly:

"Please talk Sister, I'm listening.

"The murderer of Mother Notre-Dame-Des-Pins is the Chaplain of this house, Father Jean," said Mother De-La-Purification with an air of supremacy.

"Oh! yes? What are the reasons behind your accusation, Sister," said the man surprised?

"The facts happened last summer. Father Jean had gone to his country house with two children, and one of them was our little Mass servant. In spite of the parents' recommendations, he kept them to spend the night… You understand what I mean, insinuated the nun with a knowing look. The parents complained to Mother Notre-Dame-Des-Pins, who told me everything. This very day we were to denounce him to the Bishop and Mother Guardian is murdered."

"Naturally, the Chaplain knew what you were planning to do?"

"Certainly, and he's been very uncomfortable since that moment," added the wwoman with satisfaction. "That's why I'm sure, as to avoid being brought in front of an ecclesiastic court, he preferred to savagely eliminate Mother Notre-Dame-Des-Pins," affirmed the Provincial obstinately.

The police Officer didn't utter a word. He bent his head to one side and scratched his ear while gazing into space. He appeared to be deep in thought. The nun was exulting. She was convinced she had persuaded Mr. Leduc with the pertinence of her deductions. In her eyes, her assessment was irrefutable. The Police were going to arrest Father Jean immediately.

On the contrary, the Detective started a cross examination about *her own* testimony.

"Did the parents lodge a complaint to the Police against father Jean if, as you aaffirm, their children had been attacked by this priest?"

"But they complained to *Us*!"

Ah! The word had been launched! The ecclesiastical *Us* had pointed its nose at last! observed the irritated Inspector. He knew very well those religious abuses of authority that pretended to be above laws in taking possession of controversial cases, manipulating them, amplifying them, dissimulating them or just strangling them as it suited their needs.

How many Policemen, convinced of the guilt of someone protected by Church, had been told by his superiors to abandon an investigation after an Episcopal phone call. The frustrated Detective had often said mockingly: "Oh! It's Divine Justice which continues the inquest," though he knew too well that religious injustice would triumph once again.

"Sister, you seem to forget that we live in a country where a civil government enforces the law. We're no longer in the Middle Age where the *Inquisition* led its own inquests. In this specific case of ours, if a moral violation was made against their children, the parents must file a complaint to the Police, not to a Sister, neither to a Bishop!"

Mother Provincial was obfuscated to hear such disrespectful language from this man. He didn't only question the Bishop's authority, but he dared to doubt the impartiality of the Church. What blasphemy!

"Did you question those children, about what happened during the night spent away from their home?" asked Mr. Leduc patiently, realizing that he might have pushed a little too far by placing secular justice above religious one.

"We questioned them. They didn't dare admit the truth, but we are sure they acted in collaboration with the Chaplain."

"You said the parents had complained. What did they complain about exactly?"

"The children were supposed to be home by the end of the day. Late at night, when they still hadn't returned, the parents called Mother Guardian to ask for an explanation."

"Did the nun know something that could reassure them?"

"She had no answer to give them."

"How did everything finally end?"

"The day after, Father Jean came back with the two little boys. He pretended a thick fog had prevented him from driving the night before, and that without a telephone, as he swore, he couldn't call."

"Did the parents say that their children confided in them about the sexual abuse?"

"Certainly not, I just told you that they all agreed to lie."

"And you, Sister, were you there to confirm with certainty that the abuse occurred?" insisted Inspector Leduc.

"Why should I have seen them? I know it! It's enough!" State Mother De-La-Purification with the arrogance of someone who hold the truth in its hands.

"Your evidence wouldn't hold up for long in front of a judge," said the Inspector.

"Am I to understand that you don't believe me? That you won't accuse Father Jean for the murder of our Mother Guardian?" questioned the furious woman.

"Calm yourself, Sister, I didn't say anything like that. You'll agree though that I have to convene with this person, so he may give his own version of the facts."

"I just gave you the version. I am the Mother Provincial of all the religious houses in this country. My word is certainly more valuable than the one of an obscure Chaplain of a minor religious Order!"

"You seem to forget, Reverend Sister, that the man you've accused risks the death penalty. Don't you think he should be allowed to defend himself since he was present during the night in question!"

"Do as you like, but your disrespectful attitude offends me a great deal. I can guarantee that you'll be hearing from me soon!" The nun left without any salutation.

"What a vixen!" muttered Mr. Leduc when she had left.

During this time, Mother Marie-Des-Saints-Anges, Superior of the Convent had made a decision. She was going to call the Bishop as soon as possible. She had to inform him about the terrible incident which had befallen the Convent: the murder of Mother Notre-Dame-Des-Pins, but she also wanted to try and save her friend, Father Jean. She dialed the Bishop's number.

"May I talk to Monsignor Bishop N?"

"Who is calling please? "asked an unpleasant voice.

"It is the Mother Marie-Des-Saints-Anges, Superior of the Juvenate of R. It's a very important matter," she added, not wanting to wait indefinitely.

"One moment please, I'll see if his Excellence is free." The tone had softened.

"Hello! It's you, Mother Marie-Des-Saints-Anges? How are you?" inquired the Bishop cheerfully.

"Not very well indeed, we're going through a terrible time."

"You're worrying me, Sister. Has someone died?"

"Yes, but it is worse than that!"

"Come on! Explain yourself, what can be worse than death?"

"Mother Notre-Dame-Des-Pins has been murdered!"

"What are you telling me! When did it happen?"

"Yesterday morning when we awoke at five o'clock."

"Are you quite sure of your conclusion? I mean about the murder?"

"Someone had cut her jugular. She was covered with blood," précised the non.

"My Lord, it's horrible!" said the Bishop quite emotional... "And after this discovery, what did you do?"

"We called the police," answered the Superior with a feeble voice.

"You did that! You've acted too quickly, Sister", said the Bishop reproachfully. "You should have called us before. Now, it's too late as everything had begun, and we're facing civil justice being imposed on us", scolded the far away voice.

"I did what I thought was best...." apologized the nun.

"Hell is paved with good intentions, Sister. Now that the damage is done, we will have to bear the consequences. Did anyone call the newspapers?"

"I can assure you; we did nothing of the kind. However, I cannot promise that the judiciary police had the same discretion."

"You are to inquire about it right now! And no, you're not! I'll do it myself. This news must be kept quiet at any cost!"

"There is something else," Monsignor, hesitated the nun

"Not more bad news, I hope!"

"Yes, alas..."

"What is it now?"

"Mother Provincial is here. She thinks Father Jean, our Chaplain, is the murderer."

"What! She is completely crazy! I hope she didn't talk to anyone else about her brilliant theory!" The man was now shouting so loudly through the telephone that the nun had to hold the receptor at distance to avoid splitting her eardrums.

"Yes, right now she is in the process of telling the police Investigator who is installed in our parlor."

"Don't do anything more, Mother! I'm sending you a priest immediately! He is a Canon trained for this kind of situation. You've done enough stupid things! Now, you keep quiet! You don't move! You don't talk to anyone till Father R comes to your place. You'll follow his orders to the letter." The voice was harsh, and the cutting tone suppressed any response. His Eminency had already hung up.

Mother Superior had been rebuffed, but she was glad, for she had tried to do something to save her friend.

On her side, Mother Provincial had come away empty handed from her interview with the Investigator. She was, otherwise, planning a revenge of her own against this insolent Policeman. She saw Mother Marie-Des-Saints-Anges with a tormented look on her face.

"What's the matter with you? You look as if something is wrong?"

"I called the Bishop to tell him the bad news. Monsignor is sending us Father R. to supervise the situation. He also ordered us not to even breathe till his delegate arrives."

"Oh! I see. His Excellency doesn't trust us! He wants to insure his male power over our house. We'll show him who the master is!"

Mother Marie-Des-Saints-Anges was frightened by the excessiveness of the Provincial's character and looked around to assure herself that no one had heard.

"Mother, may I remind you that, even if we have a certain level of independence as regards to our internal functioning, our community remains under the authority of the first Prelate of the diocese, the Bishop."

"Alas! I know it! We'll have to bear this intruder and be polite with him, and especially submit to his orders," said the nun raising her eyes toward heaven.

Father Jean Has To Explain

In spite of everything, Mother Provincial's visit had greatly puzzled the police Investigator, Mr. Leduc. He had to know more. He decided to meet with the Chaplain. "If I am lucky, the priest has finished his Mass, but hasn't left the Convent yet," thought the Officer. He knocked at the doorkeeper's post and opened her door half way.

"I'm sorry to disturb you, Sister, but could you go and check if Father Jean is still here?"

"Father Jean is in the sacristy. I didn't see him come out," replied the nun shyly.

"Could you go and tell him I wish to talk with him please, Sister". The nun rushed from her guardroom and ran to the door written *Cloister*. The police Officer understood that the woman had orders to always be present at the entrance, but at the same time, she had to answer to all the Detective's demands. "Poor soul! What a dilemma!"

Mr. Leduc tried to imagine the meaning behind such a life of self-sacrifice. He was deep in his thoughts when the nun came hastily and said: "Father Jean is going to be here in a few minutes."

"Thank you, Sister, you are very kind!" said the man with warmth.

The woman didn't move for a minute, and then, keeping her eyes lowered, she moved her head almost imperceptibly as if to say "thank you". Maybe her lips smiled faintly, but Mr. Leduc couldn't be sure. This humble attitude, full of modesty, impressed the Officer. He couldn't help thinking of the Mother Provincial proudly claiming her superiority in his office an hour ago. "Without any doubts, I have still a lot to learn about these women!" he realized.

Father Jean arrived, looking worried.

"You asked to meet with me?"

"Yes, Father Chaplain, would you come in, and sit down."

Father Jean, with a little hop in his step, came in and sat on the edge of the chair, crossing his hands on his knees. He tried to dissimulate his trouble, declaring in a detached tone:

"What can I do for you?"

"If you allow me, I'll formulate it in another way? What can you do to help us in our inquiry?"

The chaplain lifted his questioning eyes. He didn't see the difference between the two questions, but the Inspector noticed terror in his eyes.

"Listen, Father, I'll come straight to the point. This morning, somebody came and deposited a plea against you."

"Against me! For heaven sake! Who did that?"

"I don't have to tell you that, but I can assure you, they're very serious accusations."

"What are they?" said the priest in a feeble voice.

"Hem, his conscience is more loaded than I thought", noticed the policeman silently. Then he added looking in the priest's eyes: 'The question is about morality…. with young boys," said the police Inspector.

In an instant, Father Jean became very agitated. He started to fidget in his chair, moving his hands nervously as he sighed repeatedly. All of a sudden, he screamed:

"I'm innocent! I'm innocent! You cannot put me in jail! I am a priest! You do not have any jurisdiction over me! I want to see my Bishop!"

"Don't panic, Father; I only wanted to verify some details on the affair. Could you confirm that you were away at your country house last summer with two young boys?"

"Yes, but their parents agreed to it. I didn't kidnap those children. They wanted to come with me." The priest was becoming more and more nervous.

"That is not the question, Father. The problem begins when you went against the parents' wishes, and kept the children to sleep at your place, taking them back, only the day after. The parents were worried, and they called Mother Guardian to know if she knew how to get in contact with you."

"Now, listen to my version of the facts," interrupted the priest in a voice he was trying to keep calm. "We had left only in the beginning of the afternoon as one of the boys had a ball practice in the morning. We had to wait for him. It took two hours to get there. I had a lot of things to do, so the house would be ready for sale. The boys were a great help to me. Then, we went to eat at a restaurant. It was already nine o'clock when we left the place. We were on our way home when a thick fog arose. It became very hazardous to drive in such conditions. I didn't want to put our lives in danger, so I drove back to the summerhouse with a lot difficulty. I couldn't see a foot in front of the car. Once safe, I thought of the parents. Alas! There wasn't a telephone in the house, and it was out of question to go back on the roads to look for one. So, we slept there and very early the next morning, we came back home. I met with the parents and explained everything to them. They seemed to understand. I didn't hear anything else about the matter till a few weeks later when Mother Provincial visited our house. She asked to meet me, along with Mother Guardian, to talk about the incident. I told them everything, and they seemed satisfied with my answers."

"Did they threaten to tell everything to the Bishop?"

"Absolutely not! said the man startled. Why would they have done that? They seemed convinced that I had told them the truth."

The police Officer was perplexed. Though visibly nervous, this man seemed otherwise sincere, but Officer Leduc, an Investigator for many years, had learnt the meaning of the proverb which says, "Everyone may be guilty as long as the contrary hasn't been proved." Moreover, he wasn't entirely convinced that Father Jean was telling the whole truth, as if the man was hiding something else...

"Your version of the facts seems plausible, Father. However, you'll understand that I have to meet with the children and their parents to complete my investigation."

"I understand," answered the priest whose chin had started to tremble. The Investigator thought: "Oh no! Not that! No tears, please!" Mr. Leduc rose up quickly to avoid hearing the sad and personal secrets he didn't really want to shar. The Investigator held out his hand.

"Good-bye, Sir, and thank you for your cooperation".

The main doorbell rang. The Sister opened to a cassock, hanging loosely around a little thin man. He was the Canon sent by the Bishop. He took off his fur hat to reveal an almost completely bald head except for a tuft around the nape of his neck. Weasel eyes, a quick and elusive glance, a mouth with no lips, he looked like an animal on the watch. He gave his coat to the doorkeeper and asked to speak with the Mother Superior, Mother Marie-Des-Saints-Anges. A few minutes later, Mother Provincial appeared in front of him.

"Mother Superior, I'm the Bishop's Commissioner, said the man with an obsequious politeness."

"I am Mother De-La-Purification, Provincial of all the Convents in the whole country," précised the woman with haughtiness.

"I'm sorry for my mistake, Reverend Sister. It is unforgivable. Even if I've never had the pleasure of meeting you, Sister, I should have recognized your high status, Sister Provincial."

The more the man humbled himself, the more his wise strategy was apparent. Someone observing the scene could have detected the irony hiding behind those sweet words. The Provincial only saw a servile man whom she would make short work of. She was convinced there was nothing to fear with such a weakling.

"Would you like to see Mother Marie-Des-Saints-Anges, our Superior?" asked the woman condescendingly.

"No, thank you, I just wanted to tell her I had arrived. It is already done, isn't it Sister? said the man mockingly. Now, I wish to meet the police Investigator. Would you please lead me to him?" said the man with authority.

Mother Provincial was dumbfounded. In a few seconds, the Priest had completely changed his manners. At first, she had seen him as someone who would be at her feet, but a short time later, he was giving her orders. Too surprised to react, she answered furiously, thinking she had been tricked:

"Ask the doorkeeper! She is the one who talks with this man."

"Goodbye, Reverend Mother. Until I'll have the pleasure to see you again!" he said with a touch of sarcasm.

The Sister in charge of the door led Father R to Inspector Leduc.

"How do you do, Sir! I'm Canon R send by His Excellency," he said, holding out his hand to the policeman.

The Investigator acted as if he hadn't noticed it. Suddenly, he was very angry. He knew this amiable gesture was from an enemy, trying to appease his adversary. He was highly repulsed by this religious intrusion in his inquest. He could guess in advance the game that would follow, where each of them would look out for his own interest, ignoring or even cheating the other. Mr. Leduc was reminded of his perpetual complaint: "Will this fight between Church and State ever come to an end? What an immature society we are? What a government of puppets do we have that continually tolerates this kind of interference?" Inspector Leduc was highly frustrated.

This inquest, which was already a challenge for the Inspector, was in danger of turning into an agonizing ordeal as a result of this split in authority.

Without a word being said, Canon R had understood the man's reluctance. He tried to calm him.

"Listen, Sir, I'm not coming here to take your place. You represent human laws and justice. I'm only here to guarantee the respect of the individuals involved."

"Do you pretend that up to now, I have not treated everyone with all the consideration they deserved?" argued the Inspector angrily.

"I never thought anything like that, Sir! Sincerely, I have to tell you that I wasn't sent here to check up on you, but rather to ensure the protection of one of our Brothers and to calm the Sisters."

Mr. Leduc became more relaxed as he realized he had thought wrong. He could remember Mother Provincial violently accusing Father Jean, right here, only a few hours ago. It clearly occurred to him that this woman was dangerous! But how could the Bishop have learnt these things so rapidly? The police Officer tried to rectify his attitude toward the priest sent by the diocese.

"Would you sit down please, Sir? I beg your pardon for my outburst, but you must understand that, as a lay person, this inquest in a Convent is a very complicated situation for me."

"I understand you perfectly, said the Bishop's representative. Where are you in your investigation?"

With this clever discourse, the priest had just postponed a conflict with his adversary.

"I don't really have any leads yet. But there are interesting things, I have noticed though." Answered the Officer.

"Did you meet with Father Jean?" asked Father R suddenly.

"Yes, this morning".

"Do you think he could be a suspect?"

"It's hard to say. At first glance, he seems to be sincere, but in our job, we have to check twice before coming to any conclusion."

"What do you mean?"

"I have the intention of inviting the children and their parents here, to give their version of the facts. This verification is a very important step in my inquiry."

"If their testimony is overwhelmingly against Father Jean, would you consider him a potential suspect in the murder of the deceased?"

"Yes, eventually."

"Listen, I don't want to interfere in your work, but I have to tell you that I qquestioned those people last summer, when we first heard of this matter. I can assure you that everything corresponded with Father Jean's statements."

"I thank you very much for this information, said the police Officer. However, you must understand that if I want to do my work properly, I have to see to these things myself."

"Oh! Do as you please, Sir."

The Canon was not pleased with the Investigator's conclusions. He believed he had succeeded in distracting his vigilance. He had just reinforced it. The first round was a tie. Each opponent had been as clever as the other.

The parents and their little boys were called for the next day.

The Canon Confesses

anon R was a man of exceptional intelligence. However, he suffered from a serious inferiority complex. His father had believed in raising his children with military discipline. His son was a dreamer, so, his educator had tried to suppress his imagination. If his son's personality tried to establish itself, his father would immediately humiliate him to put him back into his place. At school, he had to achieve high marks. When his report card was good, the father paid little attention to it, but he would shriek in outrage if the results were less than expected.

For the rest of his life, Father R had fought a long interior battle. He attempted to overcome the shameful image of himself, but he was unable to resist its power. That's why he had always chosen the Eminence Gris's role for a Superior: The priest would attempt the impossible for the Bishop without ever claiming any personal ambition.

For the Bishop of the Diocese of Valleyfield, this priest of the Augustine Order was the perfect person to have at his side. He had appointed him Canon because of his knowledge of religious laws. As the spiritual leader of his churches, His Eminency had to keep the Church's reputation above any suspicion. His favorite Canon was sent on the most delicate missions. Due to his cleverness and his subtle maneuverings, he had always succeeded in preserving the Church's reputation under the most difficult circumstances.

But this awful incident was poisoned. The presence of the Police, who had been called before the Bishop, and was therefore in charge of the affair, would considerably complicate the Canon's responsibility. Otherwise, the worst part was that a religious man seemed to be involved in this sordid murder affair. In a situation of this kind, his role was to put a gag on the rumors and to hush up any scandal before it started, and most of all to save the Church's reputation. Here, someone else had the better position. The dices were loaded.

The Canon, who was a sly fox, knew how to extricate himself out of a complicated situation. The Investigator could meet with all the witnesses he wanted. No matter, Father R resolved to conduct his own inquisition. The Canon decided to implement an obligatory Confession for everyone in the Convent.

He asked the doorkeeper Sister to find the Mother Superior and insist that the Bishop's messenger requested her presence. He could imagine the angry Provincial, spurred by curiosity and irritated not to have been invited first. Father R was practicing his favorite tactic, "divide to conquer."

Entering the room, Mother Marie-Des-Saints-Anges greeted the Canon respectfully and said with sincere gentleness:

"How are you, Father? I don't think I have had the pleasure of meeting you. I am the Superior of this Convent."

"Good afternoon, Sister, I'm very glad to meet you too even though I would have preferred other circumstances..."

"Yes, indeed, we're passing through a terrible ordeal, but if you knew how comforting it is to have you with us. We are part of the same spiritual family, and it reassures us to have your protection."

The priest was charmed by the gentleness of this refined lady. He couldn't help compare her cordial welcome to the one of a certain Mother Provincial.

"Mother, I asked to see you, for I know you'll succeed in convincing your people, as I wish to hear all of them in Confession, today."

"All of them?" the nun précised.

"Yes, Sister, all," he said, looking her straight in the eyes. "Except Mother Provincial!" he added with irony.

Politeness refrained the Superior from telling him what she thought. She understood perfectly that the priest was trying to obtain information through the secrecy of the Confession. She disapproved this action, judging it inappropriate.

The Canon had perceived Mother Superior's reluctance. He knew his idea could be misinterpreted. He wanted to elaborate:

"Listen, Sister, I don't intend to violate the Confession's confidentiality, but we have to stay a step ahead of the police. You have to understand that in case of a scandal, if we do not act quickly enough, the Church could be disgraced, and your Convent's name rather tarnished in the same way".

"I understand your point of view, Father Canon, and I have total confidence in you. More, it is going to be rather easy to grant your request, since we come to the celebration of the First Friday of the month this week, and as we always give attention to preparing our souls on this occasion, the timing for a good Confession is perfect."

"How easy it is to work with you, Sister. You understand things so well…"

Mother Marie-Des-Saints-Anges blushed with pleasure. She was not used to praise. A little shy with her reaction, she excused herself and left like a little girl. The Canon thought: "I think I've found an ally in this Sister, and I'll need it to confront the terrible Mother Provincial."

He was not mistaken, Mother De-La-Purification, Provincial, was impatiently waiting for Mother Superior's return.

"Why did he want to meet you?" she asked hastily.

"He wants to hear everyone in Confession," answered the nun, ill at ease.

"What was your response?"

"Did I have a choice? Is there a way to oppose the Bishop's Canon?" Anyway, he didn't ask for my permission. He presented it as a decision already taken.

"We expected it would happen this way! Those men, all of them in fact, as soon as they enter a house, they want to have complete control whether we like it or not! Personally, I would have totally objected to this man. How can he use of the Confession to conduct his little inquiry! But you, with your submission in front of masculine power, you accepted as always!" reproached Mother Provincial.

Mother Superior didn't want to argue with Mother Provincial's reprimand. She knew she had done right, and that it was the best decision to take. Besides, she was the one who would have to bear the consequences of her relationship with the Bishop after the Provincial had left, going from place to place, always received as a queen. Mother Marie-Des-Saints-Anges also understood that the Provincial's bad mood was in part related to the fact that she hadn't received the usual honor bestowed on her during her visits. *The dead woman has taken over everything.*

Mother Superior had another task to accomplish. It was not an easy one either. Moreover, it ran counter to her most cherished principle she had to lie to them. In fact, she should tell the Juvenists about Mother Guardian's death while cheating the*m*. It was out of the question that the parents know that such an odious crime was committed in their own Convent. They might come and take their daughters away! "God knows the discretion required to avoid the gossips!" she thought.

In assembling the children, she thought: "I'll kill two birds with one stone; I'll tell them of the death as well as for the Confession."

When she met the Juvenists in the large study room, she noticed an unusual overexcited climate. She understood that the rumors had already started to circulate. What has been said? What did they know exactly? She wanted to check.

When everyone was seated, Mother Superior addressed a young girl in front of her and asked;

"Marie-Claire, have you heard something concerning Mother Guardian?"

"Yes, they say horrible things, Mother" said the girl spluttering.

"Oh! Yes?" questioned the nun. "What are those terrible things you have heard?"

"They say… but I'm not saying it myself, I'm only repeating what I heard," hesitated the child, trying to appease the Superior.

"Marie-Claire, I beg you to tell me. I know you're not guilty of anything. This is such malicious tittle-tattle! Tell me what you have heard, and I promise I shall not be angry at you afterwards."

Encouraged by these good words, the little one said in a faint voice,

"They say Mother Guardian has been stabbed to death. There was blood everywhere, they say." She was now shouting her head off.

"Well, I see some people have a lot of imagination," grumbled the nun.

Marie-Claire had put her head on her desk and was now crying loudly.

"I'm not scolding you. Marie-Claire, calm yourself."

Her sobs were increasing, threatening to panic the whole group.

"Marie-Louise, would you take your sister to the bathroom? A little fresh water will do her good."

Then, the woman talked quietly with extraordinary softness. She knew she was holding the Convent's destiny in her hand. She had to convince them.

"Juvenists, pay attention to what I'm going to tell you. I see that false rumors have been running in our house. It is time to put things back to order. Let me tell you the whole truth about this affair: Mother Notre-Dame-Des-Pins hemorrhaged during the night. She vomited a lot of blood… and she died. It is not a question of murder; it is a question of a disease. It is very different, isn't it?"

Mother Superior paused, then her face hardened, and her voice sounded menacing. "Now, I'll tell you something very important. From now on, it is strictly forbidden to talk about this death under any circumstance! Do you hear me? If someone starts to converse about it, I order you to come see me and report her immediately. The culprit will be sent home right away. Is it clear? Now, you must cleanse yourselves of all the lies that you have invented or chatted about. The Canon, sent by the Bishop, will hear your Confessions to prepare for the *First* Friday of the month."

The priest, wearing his surplice and his stole on his shoulder, was seated in the Confessional.

It was a big wooden box divided into sections, allowing three persons to be in at the same time. The central part had its door in front and was the priest's compartment. The penitents could flee by the doors located on either side. Inside, two small sliding panels permitted the priest to open the right or the left-hand side accordingly. A wire mesh separated the priest from the penitent. The confessor listened while the sinners confessed:

"Father, forgive me for I have sinned…"

And the enumeration of faults would begin. Often, one would start with innocent little things, so to try hiding a bigger sin among the avalanche of venial ones, but the half asleep confessor, more or less asphyxiated by the people's bad breath, had a sixth sense which would wake him up as soon as a mortal sin was mentioned, and then a series of tight questioning would begin: What was it? How was it done? How many times? With whom? and so on… then, followed a pardon formula, an act of contrition, and finally, the absolution for the delivering pardon. The penitence would end the session. This process could last for hours, and even if only small sins were told, the priest would remain there in a state of lethargy the entire time.

The Canon finished with the Juvenists in two hours. He took a brief coffee break to fight his drowsiness before confronting the Sisters.

Canon R had learnt nothing of interest from the children. Even Marie-Céline had judged it better to keep religion away from her great love, convinced that the priest wouldn't share her point of view on the question. The nuns had nothing very interesting to tell as well, and the priest was asking himself if he was not wasting his time. He thought that maybe the idea was not as bright as he had first imagined.

Colette, consumed with remorse, was among the last. She started bluntly:

"Father, I confess to having had sexual relations."

"Do you mean complete sexual intercourse?" asked the confessor frenzied with curiosity, convinced he had caught a big fish.

"Yes, Father."

"With whom? my child."

"With a man, Father."

"How many times?"

"Once a week for three months."

"When was the last time?"

"Last Sunday".

"On the eve of Mother Guardian's death?"

The priest heard soft cries. There was a long silence. The Canon didn't want to rush the young woman, but he sensed, at the same time, that he had to know more.

"Were you leaving the Convent to meet with this man?"

"No, I went down to the furnace room."

"Did someone know about your…love?"

"Yes, Mother Guardian surprised us."

"And then, what happened?"

"She threw Nicolas outside, locking the door behind him. I got dressed during that time, and then she escorted me up to my bed."

"Did you come and kill her during the night?"

"No, Father I did not."

"Did you lead this man to her so he could kill her?"

"No, Father, I didn't do that."

"What is your name Sister?"

"My name is Sister Marie-Marthe."

"Now recite your contrition act, promising to never see this man again. Otherwise, I cannot give you absolution.".

"I'll never see that man again."

"Absolvo te pecdatum…" Colette left the Confessional.

The Farewell of Colette Known as Sister Marie-Marthe

Colette had hesitated a long time before going to confess. Since that fatal Sunday night, a terrible anguish had engulfed her. That night, Mother Guardian's surprising interruption, had absolutely terrified her. Mother Notre-Dame-Des-Pins represented the religious authority that had come to sanction her bad behavior and reveal the ignominy of her shameful conduct for someone desiring to be the spouse of Christ. It also meant the end of Colette's dreams of monastic life. As soon as she was discovered, she knew her religious garments would be stripped from her and that she would be thrown onto the street right away. She imagined her disgraceful return to her family, the bitter disappointment of her mother, the mocking remarks from her father, and especially, the gossip: the people who talk behind your back, who turn their heads as you pass by, their terrible eyes judging and condemning you at the same time.

The young girl had been torn apart between her desire to fulfill her religious vocation and the intensity of her love for Nicolas. She understood that this unexpected visit from Mother Guardian had broken all her dreams. Not only would she be chased away from the Convent, she would also never see Nicolas again. *She was now- has she not always been- an unwanted damned soul on earth.*

For two days, Colette's mind was totally occupied by the enormity of her fault. She had confessed it to the Canon, asking him to bear the burden in her place. She had disposed of her sin like a bag of smelly garbage. Now, there was an empty void inside her. Despair, like a poisoned river, had wormed its way into all the fibers of her being.

A long-ago image from a familiar memory revisited her. Colette was six-years-old. It was the day when she had not been among the other Communicants, all dressed in white. After the ceremony, she had run to hide in the woods, and there, she had had a vision: She was on the bank of a lake. Far away, on a little round island, there was the form of a woman sitting on a rock. She was entirely covered by her black veils. Suddenly, a hand had come out and appeared to have a life of its own. It was talking to the child: "What are you doing here, Colette? Do you not understand that you have no right being here? You've stolen your existence. You are a nuisance on the earth. You're a burden to others, for you bring them only unhappiness. How long are you going to poison the earth by your presence? Come with me! Don't be afraid! All will be over if you accept to come near me. Come Colette, Come!" And as the hand kept insisting. Colette had understood that this black woman calling her was *Death.*

And today, this filthy joy brought by the vision had come again, haunting her. A bitter relief took root in her. She was not totally imprisoned for there was an emergency exit. One just had to have the courage to open the door which leads into nothingness.

Toward the end of the afternoon, she had succeeded in creeping down to the furnace room. She wanted to see Nicolas for one last time. She turned towards the huge boiler, focusing on the far away light as she had done so many times before.

An old man was sitting on Nicolas's chair. He looked at her surprised:

"Are you looking for someone, Sister?"

"Hem, no, yes, in fact. I thought I would find Nicolas here", answered the troubled young girl.

"You mean Nicolas S? He doesn't work here, anymore. I'll be taking his place from now on", said the man proudly.

Colette thought she was going to *faint;* her legs didn't support her anymore. A sudden burst of pride allowed her to regain her composure. Without adding a word, she turned on her heels and headed back towards the stairs. She ran to washroom to be alone. There, she cried her heart out: Nicolas was not there; he would never be there again. He would never hold her tenderly in his manly arms and reassure her. He would never again whisper sweet words in her ears. He would never cover her with his warm body. All of this was over. She felt as if she had lost half of herself.

Life was fleeing from Colette like running water flowing through her fingers. She didn't try to bring it back. She rose up as if in a hurry. Sister Marie-Marthe washed her face, took a deep breath to calm down and left the bathroom to make her way towards Mother Superior's office.

....

When the nuns' Confessions were over, Canon R had knelt down in the Chapel and prayed for a long time. He was distressed by what he had just heard. He was not scandalized. He was not judging either of those young people. In fact, he understood them. In his twenties, he had lived a great amorous adventure; her name was Helena. She had the beauty of those flowers which last only a day. They had promised each other to always stay together. Death had decided otherwise and had carried away its finest creature at the end of the summer. He had cried so much. He wanted to be with her wherever she was. He couldn't live without her.

He had recovered, but his heart had remained closed to any other love. He had become a priest, consecrating his soul to his work, safe from any emotional suffering. And today, without any warning, because a young girl had cried about love in her Confession, everything had risen to the surface like an impetuous spring he couldn't control. He hadn't forgotten Helena, he still loved her. The man was deeply troubled. He had scarcely seen Sister Marie-Marthe's face, but he had the impression Helena was there, coming back to talk to him one last time.

However, he knew that his duty toward his Bishop was to discover the potential culprits who were probably closely tied to the murder of Mother Notre-Dame-Des-Pins. Canon R shook off his trouble, and came back to reality. He saw everything clearly.

The nun had surprised those young people while they were making love. She had threatened them and was going to denounce them. They had much to fear from that merciless informer. Their future together was going to be destroyed by the nun. They had killed her to keep her from talking. Now the only thing left to determine was if they had acted together, one opening the door for the other, or if the murderer had acted alone.

Looking at the problem objectively, Father R thought the solution was a gift from heaven. Moreover, it would be easy to claim that the young man had acted alone, and after accusing him send the young girl back to her family. Everything was settled, leaving the Church untouched from this sordid affair! The Canon was proud of himself. Once again, he had succeeded in cutting the Gordian knot of a desperate situation, It remained now to manage everything, without offending anybody...

The priest decided to talk about his suspicions to Mother Superior first. He asked to meet with her. She arrived, sensing the Canon had discovered something through his Confessions.

"Good afternoon, Sister, can we find someplace with a bit of privacy? I have something important to discuss with you."

The Superior led him to a small parlor and closed the door. Father R started:

"I can see by the look of reproach in your eyes that you think badly of me. You are convinced that I'm going to betray the privacy of Confession. Well, be assured, I'll not do it. I just wanted to talk about this young man who looks after the furnace."

"You mean Nicolas S? He doesn't work for us anymore. We've replaced him with a much more mature man. He just started this afternoon."

"Can you explain to me how it all happened?"

"Monday morning, the young man phoned to tell us that he would no longer be working for us, because he had found a better job elsewhere. We were very annoyed, for it happened at the same time as Mother Guardian's death. For us, it was another problem to solve. We looked elsewhere and found Mr. Ovide Ladouceur."

The Canon looked at the nun intensely, hoping she would connect the two events without him having to saying anything else, but she didn't seem understand at all, for she explained.

"We have a steam system. That's why, to be in accordance with the law, we have to have someone in charge of the furnace."

At this moment, Sister Marie-Marthe, looking distraught, knocked at the door of the tiny parlor, calling for Mother Marie-Des-Saints-Anges. The Canon jumped as he recognized her voice.

"Mother Superior, may I speak to you a moment before you go and answer. It is very important!" The priest's demand seemed very serious. The nun understood and answered Colette through the slightly opened door

"I'll be with you in a moment, I'll just finish my meeting, it won't be long," said the Superior kindly as she could detect the young woman's distress.

When she came back, the Canon said hastily:

"I have to know all the comings and goings of this nun, Sister. It's of the highest importance."

The man's voice was both imperious and imploring. Mother Marie-Des-Saints-Anges didn't understand, but she obeyed.

"I won't do anything without talking to you. Is that right?" said the woman before leaving.

"Yes, Mother Superior, thank you," said the Canon, satisfied.

"Well, Sister Marie-Marthe, what can I do for you? You're so pale! And you've been crying? Are you sick?" worried Mother Marie-Des-Saints-Anges.

"I would like to call my parents with your permission, Mother."

Mother Superior's first instinct was to answer that it was not possible, as the Rule forbade it, but she remembered her promises to the Canon, so she said to the girl.

"Could you wait a minute, please? I'll come and give you my answer right away."

Mother Marie-Des-Saints-Anges came back to the little parlor, carefully closed the door, and said quickly to the priest;

"She asked to call her parents."

"What did you answer?"

"Nothing yet, but, according to the Rule, I should say no."

"Forget the Rule for today. They're more important things to settle," said the priest impatiently. "Is it possible to listen to this conversation on another telephone?"

"Yes, certainly, it's normal to do so when a call is suspicious".

"All right, how do we proceed then?"

"There's another telephone in the next room, and from it you can hear everything. You pick up the receiver a few seconds after she has begun her conversation. Be careful not to breathe loudly, though, if you don't want her to detect your presence on the line."

"I understand. Go and give Sister Marie-Marthe permission to make her call. When it is safe, come and get me."

"All right, Father."

And this is what the Bishop's informer heard at the end of that afternoon.

"Mommy, it's me, Colette, do you recognize me?"

"For sure, darling. How are you? You're not sick, I hope?"

"No, mom, I just wanted to talk with you for a little while. I miss you! I wanted to tell you that I love you, and I thank you for all you've done for me. I don't want to talk to dad, but tell him the same, and that I'm not angry at him anymore. I've been trying to forget! I have to leave now because we don't have permission to talk long. Bye mom, don't forget I love you!"

After her call, Sister Marie-Marthe came out, thanked the Superior and disappeared through another door. Mother Marie-Des-Saints-Anges would have liked to talk to her a little more, but she was afraid the Canon would come out of his hiding place, putting her in a delicate position. She went to open his door.

"Yes, Father, did you learn any big secrets from our little Sister Marie-Marthe?"

"Hem, no, she's just been talking with her mother."

"You see, there was no need for any drama."

"You were right, Mother. However, please advise me if you notice anything unusual with this Sister."

The bell rang, announcing the Holy Sacrament Service. The nun left after nodding to Canon R.

During that time, Colette had gone to her room located in the attic. It was very dark. Only a small lamp shone in the dark. Colette stayed a long time seated on the edge of her bed. She was restless; she felt an urge to act, a need to do something. At the same time, she was paralyzed by a heavy torpor. All of a sudden, she appeared: The woman in black was standing on the right at the end of the room. A veil was still hiding her face. Her hand soon appeared. It showed Colette the iron support for the curtains which separated the beds. Then, the hand started to talk:

"It's time Colette, you cannot continue. Your road stops here. All your problems are going to be solved. You've done enough damage. You've lost your honor! You have to disappear! Do you hear me? You have to vanish from the surface of the earth. You don't deserve to live. You took that right without any permission. You have to give back what you've usurped.

Take off your St Francis's rope from around your waist. Climb on the chair. Tie the rope around the bar. Make a slipknot you remember how? Put your head into the knot! Push the chair now and come to see me. I am the Great Comforter. Come to me, Colette, come…

An hour later, when the Office was over, Mother Marie-Des-Saints-Anges was worried, for she had not seen Sister Marie-Marthe at the Chapel. She asked two Sisters to look everywhere in the house for her. In the attic, they found a body, all dressed in white, hanging at the end of a rope.

How the Bishop's Representative Became an Informer

The terrible news had rapidly spread. On discovering Colette's body, one of the nuns had become hysterical. Her cries had resounded loudly throughout the Convent: "Sister Marie-Marthe is dead! She is dead! She hanged herself!"

This time, the Juvenists couldn't be spared. They were petrified with fear as Mother's Guardian's death was still present in their minds.

Death had once again unfolded its heavy burden over the whole community. Each of them felt threatened. All their past fears were rising to the surface. One wished to leave this damned place, to run away as far as possible. Panic was settling in everyone's mind. In a desperate attempt to save the situation, Mother Superior ordered all members of the house to gather in the Chapel.

Mother Marie-Des-Saints-Anges, herself, felt utterly overwhelmed by remorse and guilt. Sister Marie-Marthe had come to her before ending her life. What had she done to help this desperate soul? She had plotted with the Canon to deceive her during her farewell call to her parents. She couldn't forgive her insensibility. She felt miserable. She saw herself as an odious woman. A familiar temptation was crushing her soul once again. She knew it well. She had been fighting it since she was young. She had first met it while a teenager. It hadn't left her since; its name was Despair: It questioned the absurdity of the human's existence. It said: "What if this life of suffering of griefs, all those miseries, the tears and the silence from above; what if those prayers, were nothing more than a coarse comedy?

And if we suddenly discovered that the path, we are on is only a false trail, that our existence had no real significance like a flower which fades, and then is thrown in the refuse. What If God doesn't exist?…"

In the darkness of the Chapel, lighted by a single lamp in the sanctuary whose red flame was trembling, Mother Superior's voice rose strong and grave:

"O Lord, why do you overwhelm us with such terrible struggles? Our hearts are afflicted by a sense of desertion. We ask your forgiveness. We implore you to keep the temptation of Despair far away from us. Please, look at our sufferings. Do no forsake us in our time of hardship. Let heaven open for the two people who left us this week. May they be our emissaries to calm your wrath against us. Relieve our sorrow. Do not let the Devil continues his destructive path."

And in a pleading voice, she recited the prayer of the Holy Gospel:

"Our Father who art in heaven, hallowed be thy name, thy kingdom come, thy will be done on earth as it is in heaven. Gives us this day our daily bread, forgive us our trespasses as we forgive those who trespassed against us, and lead us not into temptation, but deliver us from evil. Amen."

A great peace descended on the assembly. After a long moment of silence, everyone left calmly to resume their tasks.

The Chapel was now, almost completely deserted. Alone in his Confessional, the Canon was weeping. He now understood the significance of the premonition he had received during Sister Marie-Marthe's confession. He had felt Helena's presence. She had come to warn him that death was hovering over this young woman and that he could save her. But how had he answered this call? In his pitiful egotism, he had returned to his inquest. Not for a minute had he imagined the drama this young girl was living. In his scheming, he had even arranged Colette's destiny. "If the girl is sent back to her family, the problem will be settled." He tried to recall the exact words of his thoughts, to reproach himself even more. How could he have been so despicable?

The saving of souls had been his sacerdotal engagement, the ultimate goal of his vocation. What had he done with his ideal? He had become an informer in the service of the Bishop. He was the right-hand man of Episcopal Justice! What irony! While he was pursuing his reach and congratulating himself, a young woman, who had confided in him, was killing herself!

The next morning, at five thirty, when the first nuns entered the Chapel, the priest was still in his Confessional. Weakened by sorrow, he had dozed off.

Psalms, rising in damp morning dawn, had woken him. He left the place without making a sound.

He wanted to go away from the Convent to have a little relief. He was hoping a hot coffee would help him recover from a trying night. He parked his car near the hotel. On entering, he was noticed immediately by Inspector Leduc who rose to greet him.

"Good morning, Father, would you come and join me. I'm having my breakfast at a table over there?"

"For sure, Inspector Leduc, I've been wanting to speak to you.!"

"Come and have a seat, you look awful this morning. Is there another problem over there?"

The priest sat down and looked around the restaurant. The place was nearly deserted except for a man reading his newspapers at the other end and the waitress who was busy preparing food, pretty far from their table. Canon R leaned towards the Detective and murmured in a low voice.

"Yesterday, at the end of the afternoon, a young nun hanged herself. When she was discovered, it was too late…"

"That's horrible! It's incredible! Why didn't you call me?"

"We've been trying, but you were not home!"

"It's true; my wife dragged me to the theater."

"What would you like for breakfast, Father?"

The waitress had arrived while Mr. Leduc was still recovering from the shock. Canon R had seen her coming and had lowered his head, moving his index finger slightly to warn the Officer. Mr. Leduc had understood in time.

"I'm not hungry, Miss. I'll only have a coffee, please."

"You have to eat, Father Canon, insisted Inspector Leduc. Miss, bring him a continental breakfast, and I'll have the usual."

"All right, Sir."

"What did you order for me?"

"It's an expression which means buttered toast and jam."

"It'll be perfect; I thank you for your kindness. It's true, I'll need strength to get through this day." said the priest pensively.

The two men remained silent for the rest of the meal. Each was lost in his own thoughts. When they finally went outside, Inspector Leduc said to the priest:

"I would like to see you in my office for the first interview of the day. I think we have things to tell each other! Don't you agree, Father?"

"I intend to make meeting you my first priority. I'll be there as soon as possible."

A short time later, they were facing each other, but they were no longer two confronting adversaries, nor two authorities fighting for power, they were simply two men weighed down by tragic events. During his night of insomnia, the priest had understood many things. He didn't desire power anymore. He had decided to let the Inspector have carte blanche. He would collaborate willingly, but only from a secondary position. The Investigator opened the dialogue:

"Is it possible that your own personal inquest led to the result you mentioned a little while ago?"

"Yes, that's true, you're right. I thought I was only doing my duty, but I realize I'm the one who provoked this new tragedy."

"Explain yourself. I really don't understand anything of what you're saying." said Mr. Leduc puzzled."

"Yesterday, I ordered everyone to Confession."

"Hem! It was not a bad idea except that you were treading on my path!" exclaimed the Inspector.

"You're right, I wanted to find the culprit before you," admitted the priest with humility. "However, I assure you it was only to protect the Church…"

"Surely, but did you succeed at least?"

"Maybe... you'll judge yourself. Let me tell you all I know. For the rest, I leave everything in your hands unless you specifically ask for my help."

First of all, Father R. explained that the death of Sister Marie-Marthe had liberated him from the Confession's confidentiality. Then, he told all he had learnt from the young woman. Throughout the narration, the Investigator's eyes were wide open. He told himself that as a result of the Canon's interference, the puzzle that had seemed impossible to solve at the start of the inquiry was beginning to take shape. Inspector Leduc was very satisfied. He warmly thanked the priest for his precious collaboration. The Canon seemed indifferent, lost in his thoughts. The Inspector tried to reassure him:

"Don't think I'm mad at you, Father. On the contrary, you've saved me many days of work. I now have a trail to follow. It's more than I could hope for."

"I'm glad to have helped you, but I am handing in my resignation as an Investigator. I've caused enough damage."

Mr. Leduc realized that Father Canon felt guilty about the young nun's death. The Investigator respected the priest's pain and didn't add another word on the matter, but asked lightheartedly,

"I think we'll have to look into our principal suspect, don't you agree?"

"I think everything is in good hands. Now I am going to go and rest a bit. I didn't sleep last night, and I am not thinking clearly," said the priest, rising to leave.

"Have a good day, Father Canon, and thank you again!"

The Inspector was cheerful: "Here I come, Mister Guilty!"

Inspector Leduc asked for the Mother Superior. He had her confirm Nicolas's identity, his exact address as well as the date of his dismissal.

Otherwise, Mother Marie-De-Saints-Anges, was totally confused. Why was the Bishop's Envoy and the police Inspector both so interested in this young man? How did he fit into the story? She could no longer help restrain herself, and she began to question the Investigator. As if it was a common everyday occurrence, Mr. Leduc recounted the liaison between Sister Mare-Marthe and Nicolas S. He added the surprised arrival of Mother Notre-Dame-Des-Pins catching the two lovebirds in action.

Mother Marie-Des-Saints-Anges had been Superior in this house for many years. She had witnessed many things in her life. However, in less than a week, she had seen more horrors than ever before. Moreover, the Superior was deeply shocked by the Inspector's words. She thought he was vulgar to talk about those things like he did, even if she had to admit he was just relating what had happened here, in her Convent, under her Rule! All of a sudden, she couldn't bear to listen anymore. She thought her nerves were going to snap. And the Mother Provincial who was going to hear all of this. "What a mess!" She sighed at last,

"Will that be all for now, Inspector?"

"Yes, Sister. I thank you for your cooperation. One more thing, I have to make a call. Could I use the phone?"

"Certainly, go to the entrance. The nun will show you."

The nun went back to her office. She knew Mother Provincial was watching near her door, curious to hear about recent developments. However, the Superior had decided to tell her the details a little at a time.

Inspector Leduc called the Coroner to explain the latest developments and ask for an arrest warrant against Nicolas S. Then, he contacted his colleagues from the road patrol and requested they be ready to make a special visit to the residence of Nicolas S.

Since the previous Sunday, Nicola was hiding away in his home. After Mother Notre-Dame-Des-Pins had thrown him outside, the young man had tried only once to come back to his place of work. On Monday morning, he had returned to the Convent at seven o'clock as he had done for the past four years. When he had placed his key into the lock, it had not opened as it was still bolted from the inside. Concluding that he was no longer welcomed, he hadn't insisted further and returned home. He felt terribly guilty, knowing he had abused the nuns' confidence and was unworthy of working for them anymore. He told himself that he was freeing Colette from the chain he had placed on her. In short, he was leaving a job which had been his joy and his pride for many years. He was ashamed of himself and didn't want to wait until officially dismissed. He called Mother Superior to tell her he was quitting, pretending that something more interesting had been found elsewhere.

Surprisingly, all the drama at the Convent had remained almost unnoticed by the local population. Of course, the immediate neighbors had seen the Police cars coming and going from the Convent, but they knew nothing more. No journalist had succeeded in worming their way into the troubling events happening there. This situation would not last. The arrival of the patrol car at Nicolas's residence and his arrest in handcuffs delivered another part of the sordid affair to the whole population.

Mother Provincial Does It Again

Mother De-La-Purification, once known as Lauretta P, was a hardheaded woman. Emotions were not her strong point. Maybe, she had felt them, a long time ago, when she was a young girl, but she had strangled them ever since. In fact, she had channeled them into two avenues; pride and anger. She carried out this polarization of her character with much success.

The Motherhouse of her religious community was in Rome. The founder was an Italian woman whose numerous houses were now scattered all around the world. The Convent of R in Canada was but a small far away house.

Lauretta P was born from a wealthy patrician family of Rome. On account of her origins, she was soon convinced of her superiority over ordinary people. After successful studies and a painful love affair, she decided to enter a Convent as the great romantic ideal commanded. As a result of her family's name, she had been received wholeheartedly into the Motherhouse of the Franciscan Missionary of Marie.

After becoming Mother De-La-Purification, she had soon climbed the ladder of the religious hierarchy to become Mother Superior in a small monastery in the south of Italy where she very quickly became bored to death. Having an adventurous spirit, she wanted to travel and see the world. She had talked about it to Mother General with whom she had an excellent relationship. The answer was soon delivered and Mother De-La-Purification was named Mother Provincial of Canada. Lauretta P. had gladly accepted. Her port of registry was in Québec, but in reality, the entire country was her territory. Her mission was to insure the proper operation of every Convent in Canada. She was a kind of General Inspector.

It goes without saying that everywhere she went, everything was always perfect. As soon as an upcoming visit was announced, months in advance, each community tried to hide any problem, sweeping them under the rug to present an impeccable façade. Great preparation went into these visits. Hymns were practiced to honor her. Children recited compliments praising her. Even the regular menus were changed. The Sister in charge of the henhouse would take her sharp knife to impale big white chickens which were suspended by their feet to drain out their blood. It was the way to assure a firm and flavored flesh. The Juvenists knew poultry was simmering because its delicious aroma filled the whole house. However, they would only have a taste of it from a soup or a sauce made from the leftovers.

Mother Provincial was accountable to no one, and this life as a queen pleased her. However, in every good situation, there's a less agreeable side: traveling from one place to another by buses or trains can be very tiresome, and the nuns who accompanied her suffered from her bad mood.

The Mother Provincial was not shy in insulting train conductors, calling the bus drivers names, criticizing them for the least tardiness, or the smallest inconvenience, so frequent in the life of a nomad. She worked off her frustration on everything and everyone at hand with flamboyancy and without any remorse, convinced it was her right: the one of a sovereign to whom all is permitted.

In contrast, Mother Marie-Des-Saints-Anges, Superior, was a pacifist who hated conflict. She knew the Provincial's character and did everything to manage her. However, she was a woman of great sensitivity, and the events of the last week had particularly upset her. The facts, concerning the behavior of Sister Marie-Marthe, which she had just heard from the mouth of the Inspector, had finished her off. Her morale was at its lowest point. It was at this moment that Mother Provincial chose to pass judgment on her while she was sitting at her desk overwhelmed with anguish and exhaustion.

"Mother, I have to talk to you. I don't know if you realize that your Convent has become a scandal for the whole

Congregation! When I'll tell everything to Mother General, can you imagine her reaction? She may very well dissolve your community and definitely close your Convent!"

Mother Marie-Des-Saints-Anges looked at the woman standing in front of her and she reacted: two people had died within a few days, she had just learnt about an affair between a nun and a man working for them, and this woman was talking about scandal and punishment? Did she think that death, despair, and shame were nothing compared to gossip? How hardhearted was this woman! How insensitive was her soul!

For the first time in her life, Mother Marie-Des-Saints-Anges deeply hated the proud and egoist stranger who was her Provincial.

"Mother, your heart is closed. Do you ever feel compassion for anyone? Don't you think the ordeal we're going through is sufficient without you adding blame?"

Then Mother Marie Des-Saints-Anges' voice changed, her tone hardened and became menacing.

"Now, listen to me, I am going to tell you something you may be interested to know. Last month, when all the Superiors in the country met with the Bishop of Québec, we talked about you."

"Oh! Yes?" exclaimed the Provincial, "What was said?"

"We've let him know that we would greatly appreciate a change in authority. We mentioned your fits of anger, your lack of compassion, your inability to find solutions to problems that you should resolve. In short, the performance of your function was given a very low score. Observing your attitude towards the present problems we're facing now; I can't help but realize how right we were."

The Provincial was consternated. It was the first time in her life she was criticized. She saw herself as an extraordinary nun, loved by all.

"You are speaking out of frustration, my dear, for you are completely wrong! Everywhere I go, I am honored as you will never be in your life!"

"We fear you Mother, but we don't love you! We hide problems because we know you would aggravate them by your tactless attitude! We are only human, traveling through this valley of tears. Sometimes, evil forces bending on our destruction may test us, and in these moments, we need the help and support of our Superiors. But for you, life is a continuous celebration where, without concern for anyone, you go from place to place always looking for praise. That's why we wish to have a responsible and mature person for a Mother Provincial."

Mother Marie-Des-Saints-Anges had spoken without raising her voice. She was not angry. She was just so weary that she was unable to play her part in the comedy any more. She had said out loud what everyone else thought in silence.

Mother De-La Purification was in a state of fury. She hadn't listened to the Mother Superior's complaints; she had only understood that someone was questioning her perfect conduct. She was opening her mouth to utter the worst insults, to threaten the greatest punishments, when the entrance bell rang. She peeped outside to see a police car and a young man in handcuffs walking between two Policemen who were heading towards the Convent's main door.

"Come over here and see, Mother. Who is the young man with the Police?"

"He was our furnace man;" she answered after a short glance though the window.

"He is no longer employed here?"

"No, we laid him off this week."

"Why are they bringing him here? Is it related to Mother Notre-Dame-Des-Pins's murder?"

"Yes, maybe…"

"What are you still hiding from me, Mother? I have the right to know everything about this affair!"

"He had sexual relations with Sister Marie-Marthe. Mother Guardian had surprised them on the eve of her death."

When she heard those words, the Mother Provincial stood frozen, mouth open, for a few seconds. Then, as if an interior spring had exploded inside her body, she turned on her heels and rushed like a flash towards the main door. She arrived at the same time Nicolas was coming in with his hands tied. The nun darted at him and slapped his face with all her strength before anyone could react. The young man didn't reply, but simply lowered his head. Mother Superior, who was following the terrible woman, had tried to stop her. Now, she feared this ungracious action had just worsened the situation.

Standing in the doorway, Inspector Leduc had hidden a smile on seeing the Provincial in action. Using his authoritarian police voice, he shouted out:

"Sister, cease this violent behavior immediately, or I will arrest you for assault!"

"You, mind your own business! This man is guilty of destroying the harmony of this house and acted under the influence of an Evil Spirit. He is a rapist, a murderer, and you want me to respect him?" she vociferated.

"I would like that you let me do my work, and that you return to yours. Your place is not here, Sister, do you hear me?"

And the Investigator's voice began to sound menacing.

"I wouldn't want to be obliged to remove you from the premises because you are interfering with justice!"

"That's absurd! To kick me out of my own house!"

She didn't have time to add anything more. On a sign from Mr. Leduc, the two Officers, two giants, came toward her. She ran away from them while screaming:

"You'll hear from me! I know people in high places!"

As soon as Mother De-La-Purification had left, a peaceful silence lightened the atmosphere. Inspector Leduc directed Nicolas into his office for interrogation. When he was in front of him, the Inspector said:

"Nicolas S, you've been detained as an important witness in the murder of Mother Notre-Dame-Des-Pins. I am going to ask you some questions. All your answers could be held against you in the case of an actual trial. Do you want to call a lawyer?"

These words fell on Nicolas like a hard blow. Mother Des-Pins, as he used to call her, had been killed! Moreover, he was accused of having killed her! Unable to utter a word, Nicolas was in a state of dismay. He could no longer hear anything, because one thought was playing in his head like a carousel.

"I'm accused of Mother Des-Pins' murder! Mother Des-Pins has been killed, and they think I did it!

Inspector Leduc kept staring at the young man with great interest. He saw Nicolas's consternation! He also recognized the accent of truth in his whole demeanor. For a moment, his convictions were shaken, but he soon recovered from his doubt by telling himself: "He plays his role well, the young man!"

Inspector Leduc had his culprit! He was the answer he had been waiting for, everything pointed to him. First, he had motive for the crime; eliminating a woman who was threatening to denounce him. Second, he was the last one to have seen her alive. More, he had reasons to hate her openly and to want revenge for her interference. Finally, like the Father Chaplain, he possessed keys to the house. Inspector Leduc told himself that he could not assume his innocence just on intuition. He had the murderer in his hands; he was not going to let him go! And from this moment, the Investigator concentrated only on the certainty that he was the culprit. He began his questionings;

"Tell me what happened last Sunday night in the boiler room where you worked?"

'Well, that night, Colette, hem, Sister Marie-Marthe came to see me like every Sunday night."

"At what time did she arrive?"

"Around midnight."

"Was this her usual time?"

"No, she usually came around eleven, after everyone was asleep."

"Why was she late that night?"

"She told me she had met Mother Des-Pins on the staircase of the second floor, and that she had to wait till she was asleep before coming down from her room where she had returned as not to arouse suspicion."

"When she arrived, what did you do?"

"I took her in my arms, and I kissed her."

"And after?"

"Well, we laid down on the camp bed."

"And you were making love when Mother Guardian surprised you?"

"Yes."

"What did she say then?"

"She said to Colette: You have found your rosary, Sister?"

"Why did she say that under those circumstances?" asked the Inspector, puzzled.

"Probably because it was the excuse Colette had given her when she had surprised her, the first time, going down the stairs toward the kitchen. She had told her she was looking for her beads."

"I guess Mother Notre-Dame-Des-Pins didn't start to recite the rosary with you when she discovered the two of you together?" mocked the policeman.

"Not really, she threw me outside with my clothes."

"And then, what happened? You went home and toward the end of the night you came back. You entered the Convent. You took a tool from your box, and you came up to kill Mother Guardian?" concluded the Officer in a triumphant tone.

"No! It's impossible, I couldn't have gotten back in. The door was locked from inside. Plus, I have never been upstairs, I wouldn't have been able to locate Mother Des-Pins's room."

"That's exactly what all the criminals say when they want to exonerate themselves: they know nothing, they saw nothing, they didn't do anything!" said the Inspector, putting an end to the interrogation.

Nicolas S. was brought to the county jail to be detained while waiting for the Coroner's report.

Nicolas's Family

Nicolas's arrest had caused quite a stir in the little community of R. The immediate neighbors had quickly spread the news throughout the town. They were the first line of witnesses. They were called, they were asked for their opinion and they felt important! For many days now, the gossip had started alerting the population to the strange things happening around the Convent. Those two events were soon connected.

It had all begun that villainous Monday morning when Mother Notre-Dame-Des-Pins had been found murdered. The people who lived nearby had observed the police cars going to and fro the entire day. Then, at the end of the afternoon, the arrival of an ambulance and the carrying out of a body on a stretcher, completely covered by a white sheet, had given the signal that someone had died in abnormal circumstances.

From that moment, these amateur detectives started tattlers. Every morning now, Inspector Leduc's white Pontiac was parked in front of the Convent at seven o'clock. One soon understood that its owner was a police Officer since patrolmen were seen talking to him at the end of the day,

At twelve o'clock on the dot, Mr. Leduc would take his vehicle and leave for an hour. Neighbors were spurred on by curiosity. Why was he going out? Where was he going? The enigma was resolved when they learned that the man had his dinner at the village's hotel.

The employees of the restaurant where Mr. Leduc went to eat also became significant individuals. They were questioned over and over again. They described a very nice man who came every day to dine at their place. The man talked about the weather and always left a generous tip. He drove a white Pontiac. It was the person they were looking for.

The curious busybodies would have liked to uncover spicy details that would have given them celebrity status. They were disappointed, for nothing particular was ever said during those meals: no secret hypothesis, no suspicious phone call. In fact, his presence had become so familiar that it was often forgotten that he was a commissioned police Officer in their city.

However, Nicolas's arrest had revived the inquisitorial minds. They now had fresh material to bite into. They followed every minute of his arrest with avid interest. They parked themselves in front of their window to see what would happen next. They had watched the young man in handcuffs get into the patrol car and brought to the Convent. Those who persevered had witnessed, hours later, him being brought back to the police car and taken to an unknown location. The day after, the whole city knew Nicolas S was in prison.

In the young man's house, consternation was at its highest point. The two other occupants, Nicola's mother, Aurore V, and his uncle, Édouard V, were very distressed. Since last Monday, they were sure something serious had happened. That morning, Nicolas, faithful to his duty for four years, had come back from the Convent telling them that he had been fired by the nuns. His mother had pestered him with questions, but he had answered evasively before locking himself in his room. She couldn't learn anything more. Uncle Édouard, Aurore's brother, had been her lodger since her husband's sudden death four years earlier. Mr. V was a retired former Provincial Police Agent. He had remained in contact with many of the friends he had made throughout his career.

Since the beginning of the week, when the rumor machine began running full time about the Convent's incidents, the uncle had been worried by his nephew's attitude. He hadn't gone to work for several days. Locked in his room, he didn't even leave to have his meals with them.

Uncle Édouard decided to try and learn more about all the stories diffusing through the air. He feared Nicolas was mixed up with some unexpected events at his place of work, which could explain his expulsion from there. So, he had learned about Mother Notre-Dame-Des-Pins's murder. On the other hand, even by turning and turning the facts in his head, he couldn't see the link between this death and Nicolas's dismissal. However, he was sure there was a connection between the two facts, but what was it?

Nicolas's arrest had confirmed his suspicions. His nephew was implicated in this sordid murder affair and had been arrested as an important witness.

Aurore, Nicolas's mother, was a fragile woman. Her super sensitivity had even affected her health. When she was still very young, she had contracted tuberculosis and had been sick for many years. The family V, like many French Canadian's families at the time, had plenty of children, but little money. Édouard was the eldest and Aurore, the youngest. When the big brother had learnt that his little sister was so gravely ill, he decided to send her to the best sanatorium at his expense. He was a young Policeman at the time. His salary was not high, but he had decided Aurore should be a priority.

The child's heath had eventually improved, and it was a blossoming young girl whom Édouard had picked up at the hospital some years later. She was pretty, men would notice her, and soon she would be married.

For his part, Édouard had not yet married because his financial situation was precarious from all the hospital fees he had accrued. Realizing that very few young ladies would have been ready to see their husband sacrifice a part of his revenue to aid his sister, he had decided to postpone plans for a family.

Before he had time to think about his own future, he was asked once again to be involved in that of his sister's. Aurore had been married for only a few months when, one night, she called her brother for help. On his arrival, she explained that her husband was still not back from work in spite of the late hour.

"Where is Philibert? Did he call to explain why he was going to be late?"

"No, but I know where he is," said Aurore sadly.

"Where is he?"

"He's at the tavern, drinking with his friends."

"Ah! Yes? Does he go there often?"

"Two or three times a week."

"When will he be back?"

"Quite soon, said the young woman, that's why I called you. I'm afraid!"

"You are afraid? Does he beat you?"

"Yes, when he comes in. He doesn't know what he is doing and he takes it out on me!"

"And you didn't tell this to me before?" remarked her brother.

"I didn't want to worry you; you've already done enough, sacrificing a part of your life to pay for my health. You deserve a chance to think about yourself."

"I want you to be happy, not beaten by a drunkard for the rest of your life!"

"Be careful! I think he is coming!" worried Aurore.

"Go in your room, I'll take care of him!" ordered Édouard.

The young man was really drunk; he could hardly stand on his legs.

"Hi, brother-in-law, you came to see your little sister!"

"No, I came to talk to you!" said Édouard, hardly able to contain his madness.

"Come on! Sit down; we'll have a beer together," he said, even though he could barely speak.

"No! I've come to warn you that if you ever hurt my sister again, you'll have news from me!".

"She told you that! That blasted woman! Wait till I have a talk with her!" shouted Philibert, going straight to his room where he knew his wife was.

Meanwhile, Édouard called his friends in the police. He identified himself and asked for a car to be sent to arrest a man for assaulting on his wife. Then, he went to rescue his sister from her husband, who had already begun striking her. He soon punched him out and was reassuring his dear Aurore when the Policemen arrived.

"Hi guys! Thanks for coming so quickly! This man hit my sister. If you don't mind, take him to the station till tomorrow when he'll have regained his senses."

"No problem, right away!"

After a night spent in prison, Philibert had learnt not to hurt a Policeman's sister.

Aurore's husband continued drinking, but he never beat his wife again. Édouard couldn't do any more for the young woman. She was married to an impossible man for the rest of her life. Nicolas was born the following year. As a result of his alcoholic excursions, Philibert didn't have much time for his son. Édouard kept his eye on Nicolas and had been there for all through his childhood and later on as well.

Philibert had the good idea to die young. At forty-five, a heart attack had taken him away. Édouard thought his sister would finally have a little peace. Unfortunately, he soon realized that all those years of worry and sadness had ruined her nerves, and she was in a deep depression. Her tears continued to flow from morning to night. Édouard was convinced she couldn't be left alone. She needed someone constantly at her side. He even feared for her life. That's why her big brother had decided to come himself and look after "the little one" as he still called her. Moreover, he had taken early retirement to be even more present. Aurore's health returned, but she remained an extremely fragile and vulnerable creature on whom two men, her brother and her son, watched constantly.

Nicolas's arrest deeply troubled Édouard. Moreover, he was intensely worried about the repercussions on his sister's health. He fussed over her, assuring her it was only a mistake. His long career had taught him what a criminal was, and Nicolas was certainly not one, and he, his uncle, would prove it without a doubt. Finally, Aurore calmed down. Édouard waited till she was sleeping soundly to call a friend in charge of the Valleyfield's prison. When he had the man on the end of the line, he said:

"Hi, old brother! It's Édouard V calling you."

"What a nice surprise! It has been so long since we've talked! I wanted to invite you to a fishing party I'm having at my summerhouse with some friends…"

"We'll talk about that later if you don't mind. For the moment, I have bigger problems on my shoulders. I absolutely need your help!"

"Sure! If I can do something for you, it'll be a pleasure. Tell me what it's all about!"

"Were you there this afternoon when a certain Nicolas S was brought in?"

"Nicolas S? Wait a minute; he arrived toward the end of the afternoon, didn't he?" remembered the man.

"Yes, that's it", answered the uncle sadly.

"Do you know him?"

"He's my nephew, Nicolas."

"It's impossible! I don't believe you!"

"But yes, he's my sister's son. I'm living with them now."

"But I know this kid! You brought him once to my little Philippe's birthday party?"

"Yes, it's true, I remember. But he is no longer a child and his position is rather bad!"

"I've been looking at his file. He's only being detained until the Corner's review if I'm right? He is not yet charged. He's only an important witness"

"Yes, but what I want to know, is why has he been arrested? What is the accusation against him?"

"Well, there has been a murder of a nun of a certain age at the Convent of R. He's a suspect."

"But what was his interest in killing this woman?"

"There is something else, a bit more complicated, which could be the key to unlocking the puzzle."

"What?" asked the uncle, feeling he was finally going to get some answers.

"There was a suicide of a young nun two days after the murder.

"How old was she?"

"About twenty, she hanged herself."

"Is there a relation between the two events?"

"It's what Inspector Leduc is trying to prove."

"Do I know him?"

"No, he came from Lac St-Jean. He arrived just after you left. To come back to your nephew, I wouldn't worry if I were you! Nothing has been proved against him yet! He's just a suspect..."

"You can't imagine how stressed I am! I couldn't even talk to him when they took him out! Everything happened so fast!"

"Listen, Édouard, why don't you come and see him tomorrow. You can talk with him and ask him all the questions you want. Would that help you?"

"Of course! I'm so glad! I knew I could count on you!" said the uncle, touched.

"O.K. then, we will see each other early tomorrow morning, I guess?"

"I'll be there at eight o'clock!"

"That's it! See you tomorrow!"

Édouard went to bed a little relieved. He was determined to get to the bottom of the matter.

Uncle Édouard Wants to Know.

Very early the next morning, Édouard woke his sister, explaining that he would be away all day. Above all, he sought to reassure her about the reason behind his journey: to go see Nicolas and try to learn more about the "affair". Then, he planned to conduct his own personal inquest.

She was worried:

"Are you sure they'll let you meet with him?"

"Yes, I know the director of the prison very well. He's a friend of mine. I called him last night when you were asleep. He assured me that if I go, he'll let me talk to Nicolas for as long as I want."

"Will he be willing to talk with you? For two days, he has hardly said a word to either of us."

"Don't worry, little sister, what he went through yesterday and, where he woke up this morning will be troubling enough that he'll be ready to talk to anyone promising to get him out of there!"

"You believe it?" said Aurore, a little sceptical.

"I don't believe it, I'm sure of it! I've seen a lot of tougher guys than him, in the same condition, feeling like lost children."

"Poor little one," said the mother as she started to cry.

"That's the reason I have to go now and gather the fruit while it's ripe, if I may say."

"Dear Édouard, what would I do if you weren't here! I know you're going to get us out of this nasty business. I trust you so much!"

Aurore put her two arms around her brother's neck and rested her head on his shoulder like a little girl.

"I'm placing in your hands the most precious thing in the world to me: my Nicolas, our Nicolas, I mean, because I know you love him as much as I do."

"You're right, little sister, said the man touched. Now, I have to leave if I want to come back. I have a long drive ahead."

"When will you return?"

"Towards the end of the afternoon probably. I cannot give you the precise hour. If something unexpected should happen, I'll call you, promise. Do you intend to go out today?"

"No, I don't feel like it as you may have guessed."

"I understand you, but don't be sad. Keep telling yourself that your big brother is there, and that you're not alone." said Édouard leaving.

"Good-bye, drive safe and especially good luck! Don't forget to kiss the little one for me!" said Aurore, who couldn't hold back her tears.

Édouard was very emotional as well, but he put on a brave face for his sister, not sure how the day would turn out.

Édouard had a good car, a new Buick, just recently bought. It was a rare luxury he had done for himself. The uncle had judged the purchase indispensable as it would serve the whole family.

At around seven o'clock on a sunny November morning, Uncle Édouard left the small town of R. This insignificant country village with only a few streets pompously called itself a city. No industry assured the living of its inhabitants. The only interesting attraction was the mountain where a Sanctuary dedicated to the Holy Virgin lured some tourists and pilgrims during the summer. The place was lovely, but not very well known, and in spite of the incessant demands from the parish, no Chapel had ever been built to receive visitors. Every ceremony took place outside, and bad weather would often scatter the pious gatherings.

The car left the town in the direction of the expressway 40. This highway, newly constructed, allowed one to leave the metropolitan of Montreal and 400 kilometres later reach another big Metropolis in Canada, Toronto, located in the neighbouring

Province. Another branch of this highway led to Ottawa, Canada's Capital, where the Federal Government was situated. And one could leave R. and arrive in Valleyfield, where Nicolas was detained, an hour later.

Édouard was driving at a good speed now and had almost arrived at his destination. The surrounding landscape was fields as far as the eye could see. The long ribbon of the road unfolded through the endless countryside, or so it seemed, but in reality, a simple flashing light could take one to a nearby city, only a few kilometres away. Nicolas's uncle took exit 12, also called *Pont Monseigneur Langlois*. It led directly to the two viaducts which linked together the twin banks of St-François Lake, now separated only by a narrow piece of land. The structure served as a dam, controlling the water flow to the St Laurence River from which a seaway to the United States had just been built. All these infrastructures were new in the landscape. They facilitated traveling, but they had cost the people of the Province a fortune in taxes and fees. All had been realized on the eve of the Provincial Election of Maurice Duplessis, Premier of the Province of Québec. This person of eminent authority was always very generous towards the government's friends. Thus, those people were thanked for their past support and solicited for a future mandate at the same time.

At this time, Church and State held hands in Québec. However, certain alliances were more obvious than others, and the friendship between Prime Minister Duplessis and the Bishop of Valleyfield, Monseigneur Langlois, was to remain famous for generations to come. It had taken years to build this very costly route, but no one would question the prelate's influence in obtaining this governmental gift for the bridge was named after the Bishop himself, Monseigneur Langlois.

These thoughts made Uncle Édouard smile. Before he retired, as an employee of the government, he had never meddled in politics, but certain abuses were hard not to notice. However, he had to keep his opinions secret as long as he was in service for the Provincial Police of Québec. Maurice Duplessis was a tyrant who did not tolerate any criticism. The

Premier had a long memory and a far-reaching arm. Certain individuals could still remember what it had cost them to dare express disapproval of his power: they had simply lost their jobs, without any explanation.

Édouard was driving along Lake St-François on his way to the center of the city. He had lived there for many years and knew exactly where he was going. It was a charming little city built around a wonderful lake. The town seemed to be holding back this body of water, but at a certain moment, it suddenly escaped and opened up to meet the horizon. Far away, it joined Lake St-Pierre which emptied into the St Laurence river. A part of the city had developed on the *left* side of the lake where the less fortunate lived. Symbolically, on the *right* side of the lake, stood the magnificent Cathedral adjacent to the residence of the presiding Bishop. The courthouse and the prison were also located on this side. After traveling the length of the Beauharnois Canal, along Victoria Street, Édouard turned right onto Salaberry Street to arrive at his destination.

It was seven forty-five, which left time to park the car, to enter and present himself to the Officer at the reception area. Then, uncle Édouard was sitting in front of his old friend Alfred. They had a polite, but short conversation as Édouard was anxious to meet with his nephew.

His arrest the day before, the Police accusation, and his night in prison had completely devastated Nicolas. It was as if everything was set against him. He was not the first young man to transgress the Rules for a love affair, but he could never have guessed that he would be accused of murder as a result. He felt the sensation of having committed a crime, but not for the one of which he was accused. Nicolas had lost his way. He couldn't understand how he had become fatally caught up in the system. He knew he was guilty of accepting the love of a young woman instead of pushing her away because of her religious commitment. For his part, he was convinced he had seduced this nun; (was it not rather the contrary which had happened?) But who would believe him? And would he also be held responsible for the death of the wicked woman who had thrown him outside, completely nude? But why were they accusing him? And Colette, what was she thinking about all of this? Did she at least believe he was innocent? Nicolas had never felt so alone in his life.

When the door of his cell opened to let his Uncle Édouard in, Nicolas had thrown himself into his arms, crying like a little boy. The man waited until his nephew's emotion passed and then had him sit down, telling him affectionately:

"Dear Nicolas, you've put yourself in a bad position. I have come to help you get out of it. You must trust me. You must tell me absolutely everything that happened. I won't judge you. I know too much about human weaknesses, including my own, to condemn anyone. It is imperative that you confide in me. You know, your preliminary inquest will take place on Monday, I only have a short time as to prove your innocence in front of the Coroner; it is the only way to avoid a trial."

"I'll tell you everything, Uncle. You have to know the truth from the beginning." And Nicolas started his narration:

"Everything started when a young nun from the kitchen came on an errand to the furnace room. There had been a break in the current, and they wanted me to repair it, so they could continue preparing the meal."

"If I understand you, the electricity didn't pass only through the wires?"

"You are right; it passed between Colette and me as well."

"You call her Colette, but what is her religious name?" asked the uncle, suddenly very interested.

"It's Sister Marie-Marthe," replied Nicola simply.

At this moment, Édouard understood that Nicolas did not yet know what had happened to the young girl. He realized that he would eventually have to tell him the horrible news of her suicide, but he had to know everything before his nephew fell into despair.

"And then, did you ask her to come and see you again?"

"Not directly, I just said jokingly that I hoped another shortage would happen, so I'd have the pleasure of seeing her again."

"That's all; you didn't try to kiss her or grab her in a corner?"

"Uncle!" said Nicolas, shocked. "I respect the nuns too much to do such things!"

"But how did you see each other then?"

"One afternoon, she came back. It was a month later, I believe. She was ill at ease, but she confessed that since the day we had first met, she hadn't stop thinking of me and had come in spite of herself because my image obsessed her."

"That's called love at first sight! How did you answer her?"

"What did you want me to answer? I felt troubled too, you understand. So, I didn't say anything, I just took her hand in mine. I didn't want her to think I was judging or rejecting her. I'll confess to you that I had often thought of her too. But, under the circumstances, I wouldn't have tempted anything. For me, it was forbidden, that's all! But she was there; she was telling me she loved me. I had feelings for her, too! It was hard to resist at that moment!"

"For sure, I understand! And it was your first love?"

"Yes, it was so strong! I couldn't understand what was happening to me! Then, she came almost every week after that. Nothing happened, we just sat there, talking, holdings hands, and when she was leaving, I'd take her in my arms and kiss her. But I never went farther than that; I respected her too much to try anything else."

"And nothing more happened?"

"Wait, you're going too fast! Sure, something more happened, but later on. A month later, if I remember well, she asked me if I could come back later during the evening. I didn't need a drawing to understand that she wanted us to go further. I have to be honest, I was thinking of it for a long time, but I didn't want to frighten her, so I restrained myself. However, if she was ready, I was too, and for a long while!"

"And you had a rendezvous for the next Sunday at eleven o'clock?"

"How did you know?"

"I knew since I always sleep with one eye open because of your mother. Her nerves are so frail. I'm always worrying. I notice all the unusual noises in the house. That's why when you left your room at ten forty-five, I woke up every time. I kept listening to make sure it was you, then, I recognized your step and the outside door closing. I knew you had left.

To be sure, I'd go into your room; the bed was empty. Afterwards, I'd check if your mother was sleeping. She would be snoring away. With all the medication she takes, she falls soundly asleep as soon as she goes to bed."

"You knew everything, and you'd never talked to me about it!"

"Listen, Nicolas, you are no longer a little boy. At twenty-two, you have a right to your private life. And you were never late, and the day after, you woke up punctually to go to work. I felt I didn't have to concern myself about it and harass you with questions. Now, on the contrary, under the circumstances, I'll have to intrude on your privacy and ask you for more details. How did things go that first night?"

"When she arrived, she wasn't wearing her religious attire. She was wearing just a nightgown with a cape on her shoulders and only a small veil on her hair."

"And you lost your head?"

"We both lost our heads! She wanted it as much as me! It was even her who asked me to lie on the bed because she was so impatient!"

"If I understand, everything was going well between you up to this infamous Sunday?"

"Yes, that's it. That evening she was an hour late. I even thought about leaving."

"Why was she late?"

"She had met Mother Guardian coming down the stairs. She had gone back to her room and waited an hour to be sure everyone was sleeping. That's what she told me when she arrived. Then, we laid down as usual, and a little later, Mother Des-Pins surprised us."

"Wow! Things must have become hot!"

"Yes, Mother Des-Pins was outraged! She picked up my clothes and threw them outside. Then, she ordered me to get out! You can guess how embarrassed I was to walk naked in front of her".

"Did you obey her?"

"What else could I do? I was so ashamed! I got out of the bed and ran outside, hiding my sex with my two hands."

"And then, you dressed and came back home?"

"Sure! I was so unhappy. I had only one idea in my head, to go and hide in my room."

"Later on, did you leave again?"

"You ask strange questions! Why would have I gone back out? I had no interest in returning after what had happened."

Édouard had asked the question, only to ease his conscience, because he knew that after Nicolas had returned, no one had left the house that night!

"The day after, you woke up to go to work? I heard you as usual."

"Yes, at seven o'clock, I was at the Convent's door like every morning for the past four years."

"Why did you come back ten minutes later?"

"Because I couldn't unlock the door to get in!"

"Did you still have your keys with you, or had you lost them when your clothes were thrown out?"

"Yes, I had them, for I always put them in my shirt pocket that closes with a button. Otherwise, you'd be right! At the speed my clothes landed on the grass, I would have lost them for sure."

"Why couldn't you get in then?"

"Because the door was locked from the inside""

"Had it ever happened before?"

"Never! This bolt can be put in place only from the inside. I didn't understand, for I had been warned to never use it because of the insurance. What I usually did was lock the door from the outside when I left, so I could open it the next day."

"Someone had bolted the door after you left?"

"That had to be it! Otherwise, it's impossible."

"Is your key the master of the whole house?"

"Yes, it is."

"Why didn't you take the main entrance?" Ill at ease, the young man didn't answer.

"After that, you came back home because you thought your presence was no longer welcomed there."

"Exactly! And then, you know the rest: I was arrested, questioned, and imprisoned, said the young man, wiping tears from his face."

"Don't cry Nicolas, keep your tears, you'll need them. Tell me instead, what Inspector Leduc said to you?"

"He accused me of murdering Mother Des Pins."

Uncle Édouard had learnt a lot about the circumstances surrounding the sad incident, and he was eager to start his own investigation. He had only a few days left to prove his nephew's innocence.

Otherwise, uncle Édouard still had a painful obligation to fulfill:

"Listen, Nicolas, I know you're telling the truth. You've convinced me. I'll do everything I can to get you out of here! Before, I have something difficult to say.

"Did something happen to mum?" asked the young man anxiously.

"No, not your mum," hesitated the man.

"About Colette?"

"Yes, about Colette, she took her own life a few days ago."

"No! No! Not that! It's too unfair! She was only twenty, and I loved her more than anything else in the world!"

Édouard stayed a long time beside Nicolas. First, he cried, then he just stayed there without moving, weighed down with sadness. Édouard became afraid for him. He left without the young man even noticing. Édouard went to his friend's Office. Seeing the look of worry on his face, Alfred asked:

"What's going on? Things didn't go as you planned with your nephew?"

"No, on the contrary, everything went perfectly. It's something else that happened. I just told him about the little nun's suicide. He took it very badly. I didn't like his reaction. I would like to stay with him, but I have to go…

"I understand, said his friend. Leave in peace, I promise to take care of him. I'll even call the Chaplain of the prison to come and pay him a little visit. He's an experienced man. He'll find the words to comfort him."

"I thank you very much, Alfred! answered Édouard relieved. I knew I could count on you. Oh! I still have something else to ask of you. I have to find a lawyer for Nicolas. Does Mr. T still have his practice?"

"Yes, but his son Jean-François T. has taken it over."

"Do you think he'd accept a case like ours at the last minute?"

"I don't know, I'll have to ask him, but I can tell you we're very good friend if you understand what I mean…"

"You mean he owes you one."

"That's it! So, let's say it's nearly done. I'll ask him to come and see Nicolas this afternoon. As for you, if you want to meet him, I'll ask him to convene with you tomorrow. What do you think of it?"

"If you can arrange it like that, it'll be perfect for me! I'm very pleased, but I'm a little uncomfortable asking so much of you…"

"Oh! It's nothing! I'm sure under the same circumstance you'd do the same for me! Otherwise, on a side note, it looks as if you're going back into service. Private practice, I suppose though."

"One cannot hide anything from you, sly old fox", answered Édouard leaving.

Inspector Leduc Exults

The police Investigator Leduc was very satisfied with the events of the last hour. He had expected one of the most difficult inquests of his career, but after only a few days, he already had an important suspect. It was more than he had dared to hope for. Moreover, it was the perfect crime scenario; a great hidden and passionate love affair in a Convent, uncovered by a person in authority who was a merciless woman ready to destroy the life of the two lovebirds, followed by the murder of this same person. All was in place for a violent defensive reaction from the young man.

Mr. Leduc remembered a psychiatrist saying: "One must fear a man who feels threatened, he can be dangerous." Nicolas had everything against him, or nearly everything, thought the Policeman trying to temper himself: In addition, since Sister Marie-Marthe was dead, anything could be said against her, including that she was an accomplice to the young man's plot, guiding him through the house in order to kill Mother Notre-Dame-Des-Pins, reflected the man, cynically.

Mr. Leduc was dreaming of his success when Canon R knocked at his door. He looked fresh and calm.

"Good afternoon, Father, you have benefited from your little nap, if I may say. You're not the same man I saw this morning."

"How are you, Inspector Leduc? You're right, I feel better. I was really tired. I am not looking at life in the same way as I did this morning either."

What the priest didn't mention was that the feeling of despair had left his soul since he had prayed to God for help. He had asked for peace, and serenity had fallen on him during his sleep.

151

"I have good news for you, for us, I should say, said the Inspector. The young man in question is now in prison."

"The one whom Mother Notre-Dame-Des-Pins surprised with the little nun on the eve of the murder?"

"Yes, it's him, Nicolas S."

"Did he confess to you? asked Canon R naïvely."

"No, not yet, it'll happen at the right moment, believe me. Anyway, he's the culprit! I have no doubt about it! He'll have to plead guilty one day!"

"It's nice to also be a clairvoyant!" said the Canon admiringly.

Mr. Leduc doubted the sincerity of this declaration. He perceived a touch of irony. He didn't pay attention! He wanted to stay positive.

"Of course, I still have to work out some details before I can show sufficient incriminating evidence."

"What's missing?" the Canon wanted to know.

"I already have the motive and the circumstance as he is the last one who saw Mother Guardian alive, but I still don't have the murder weapon or another specific piece of evidence that is beyond reasonable doubt which would allow us to accuse him formally."

"What kind of a proof would be conclusive?"

"If I could certify that the young man had come back during the night. Then, it would be easy to prove that Sister Marie-Marthe had waited for him and guided him to Mother Notre-Dame-Des-Pins' room."

"She's an accomplice according to you?" questioned the Canon.

"Yes, probably. In my opinion and from my deductions, there's no doubt. Did the nun confide to you about it?"

"She assured me that she hadn't killed Mother Guardian. As for the young man..." The Canon's accusing silence was suggesting many things...

At this moment, the priest was experiencing a great dilemma in his conscience. He had heard Sister Marie-Marthe in Confession. She had clearly said she had not killed Mother Guardian, nor had she helped her lover do so. However, this Nicolas was the perfect culprit. With him as the offender, he could clear Father Jean, who the Bishop had sent him to save, from all accusations. In addition, he reasoned: "She told me she hadn't killed her herself, but maybe, she didn't want to denounce the one she loved. Or, this guy may have acted by himself? In brief, Father R didn't reveal all he knew about the affair. "God will forgive me if I am doing wrong, but it seems to me, it's the best solution," he thought as he tried to find excuses for himself.

From time immemorial, scapegoats have always been sacrificed for the good of humanity, and with the help of obscure opportunists like the little Canon, *Justice* would once again undoubtedly be ridiculed blissfully.

All of a sudden, Inspector Leduc remembered that he still had some things to settle.

"I beg you to excuse me, Father Canon, but I must go and meet Mother Superior. I need her to verify something very important."

"I'll leave you to your work, but tell me if something new happens."

"I won't forget, Father Canon."

Mr. Leduc asked the doorkeeper Sister to go and find Mother Marie-Des-Saints-Anges.

When she was standing in front of him, the Investigator noticed that pain had distorted her facial features. She had aged ten years in a few days. The Inspector thought she was going through a great torment, made worst by bad company, as he saw the face of Mother Provincial in his mind.

"Sister, please, could you lead me to where Nicolas S. worked?"

"You mean the furnace room in the basement?"

"Yes, Sister."

Mother Marie-Des-Saints-Anges guided the man through the house, went across the kitchen and took the stairs down with him. In the darkness, the two steered themselves toward the far away light as Colette had done so often. At the end of the room, a middle age man was sitting in Nicolas' chair. He greeted the two visitors as he rose from his chair.

"Don't bother, my friend, we're here only to check the door," said Inspector Leduc coldly.

It was a solid steel door. There was a locking mechanism, which allowed a key to open and close it, but only from the exterior. Inside the door, the Investigator noted a latch which could be put down to close the door from the inside.

"What is this latch for, Sister?"

"I don't really know. I think it has always been there. On the other hand, we never use it for the Insurance company warned us. This latch should never be on they said, for if something serious should happen to the furnace, the firemen couldn't enter quickly enough, resulting in great damage to the house. Otherwise, a rapid intervention could make a big difference."

"I understand, said Inspector Leduc. Do all the nuns know about it?"

"Certainly, I even had to insist because the nuns have the habit of locking everything twice."

"So, you can testify to me that nobody, as far as you know, has ever disobeyed this obligation?"

"Yes, Sir, I'm positive."

The new employee had returned to his seat as no one seemed to need him. Inspector Leduc and Mother Superior left without even glancing at him.

When he returned to his office, a man was waiting for him. He was sitting on a chair beside the Detective's office door. Uncle Édouard rose up and held out his hand.

"How do you do? You are Inspector Leduc if I am not mistaken. I am Édouard V, former member of the Provincial Police, now retired, and also uncle of Nicolas S. I would like to speak with you if you don't mind."

Inspector Leduc was annoyed. He ignored the extended hand. He didn't like people who took this kind of initiative. He wanted to remain in control of the situation. Plus, he didn't like this man's face. It was said that former Policemen always thought they knew more than anyone else. If this one imagined teaching him his job, he had the wrong address!

These thoughts were rolling around in his head as he led Mister V. into his office. Inspector Leduc sat behind his desk and designated a chair in front of him for Uncle Édouard.

"What can I do for you?" the Investigator asked coldly.

"I visited my nephew this morning," began the visitor.

"Oh! Yes? On whose authority?" growled Mr. Leduc

"I had the permission of the Valleyfield prison's Director. My nephew is detained only in view of the Coroner's inquest. He was in no way Incommunicado" protested Uncle Édouard.

Inspector Leduc was even more irritated since the man was right.

"What have you learnt that is so important to tell me! My time is limited, you know!"

"Your time should not be limited when you are looking for justice! This is a murder case! I bring you facts which could facilitate you in your investigation. I don't understand your hostility!"

"I run this inquest as it pleases me! If I need to hear a witness, I call for him. No one imposes his way of thinking on me!"

Édouard held his tongue. He was not in a strong position, and if he wanted to be heard, he had to be diplomatic.

"It was not my intention to force you in any way! On the other hand, you must understand that my nephew's fate concerns me a lot. He is now imprisoned and can be accused of murder at any time. I'm coming here to tell you that he couldn't have killed this nun!"

"Oh! Yes? And why not?' asked the policeman sarcastically.

"Because he didn't leave his room."

"How do you know?"

"I have lived with him for four years. My sister, Nicolas's mother, is in fragile health; I came to stay with her after her husband's death. My nephew's bedroom is just next to mine. I know all his coming and goings because I sleep very lightly."

"Did you know he had a love affair with a young nun, and that on the night of the murder he had come to meet her, and that the two lovers had been surprised and threatened by Mother

Notre-Dame-Des-Pins, and that this woman was murdered a few hours later?"

"I knew Nicolas left at ten fort-five every Sunday night and that he came back two hours later. He was as punctual as a clock. I heard him go away and then come back.".

"Did you know where he was going?"

"I never asked him. Nicolas is twenty-two years old; he has a right to his private life. I kept telling myself that one day he would tell us everything, and if he didn't, he had his reasons."

"Quite fishy reasons, don't you think Mister V?" ... Then he added "If I understand you well, you want me to have confidence in the testimony of a close relative who, even while asleep at night, can assure that his nephew didn't leave his room? Come on! Be serious, it's certainly not the kind of proof that would convince a jury! said Inspector Leduc meanly."

"So, you are granting me no credibility as a witness bringing an alibi for the accused!"

"No Sir! None! For three reasons. First, you're too near the victim to be impartial ... and I am being polite. Second, you were in bed. How can you swear you didn't fall sleep for a few minutes, which may have disturbed your watch? Third, your nephew may have gone out by another door and not heard by anyone? This possibility seems the most logical to me. In fact, is there another door in your house?"

"Yes, the emergency door behind the house." Uncle Édouard was very frustrated by the Officer's arrogance.

Inspector Leduc went on:

"You see how right I am! You admit yourself; he could have gone out without you noticing him! No, trust me, if I find evidence to exonerate Nicolas S, I will not hesitate to disclose it. For the moment, we're only in the preliminary inquest. No trial is yet to be held yet. If it was the case, then, it would be necessary to submit very indisputable evidence."

"If I interpret you correctly, I'm a liar who has come to build a story in order to save his nephew!" resumed uncle Édouard angrily.

Mr. Leduc didn't answer. The man had taken the words right out of his mouth.

Mr. V was outraged, he added drily:

"You are displaying too much confident to be a real professional. A true Investigator always keeps a reasonable doubt about the culprit's guilt. You seemed to have already condemned him after a three-day inquest! You met with Nicolas only once, and for a few minutes! Your amateurism frightens me, Mister Leduc," said Mr. V as he rose to leave. "I promise you, we'll see each other again, and on that day, you will be a lot less jubilant."

This interview had been very difficult for the retired police Officer, Uncle Édouard. He knew all the mechanics of the system. He had perfectly assessed the Investigator's abuse of power in refusing to hear the testimony of an alibi for someone who was accused of murder. Nevertheless, he was completely powerless in confronting this injustice.

However, Uncle Édouard was not the kind of man to be discouraged when faced with difficulty. On contrary, it only provoked his fighting spirit.

Uncle Édouard Is
Looking for Evidence

É douard V. had little time in front of him. Within a few hours, he had to find rock-solid conclusive evidence that attested to Nicolas's innocence.

After so many years in criminal investigations, the man had developed his own method. He was said to have police intuition. When asked for his recipe, he would just smile. How could he explain, without being teased by his fellow Officers, that sometimes when the situation became tangled up in a confused knot, he would just pray? He did not recite any made-up formulas. He just retreated inside himself and asked the Spirit of Truth to enlighten him toward a solution. Amazingly, from that moment, things would begin to move.

Today, he was facing the most important case in his life. His sister's happiness, his nephew's liberty and his own peace of mind, depended on his rapid intervention. Many paths were before him. With such little time left, he was obliged to choose the right one. He addressed his interior voice with ardor.

Édouard V had lived in the little city of R. for only four years, but since he was very sociable, and now retired, he had plenty of leisure time and had already developed a circle of friends. He was a pleasant man, jovial, always ready to help.

The unofficial men's social club in R was a restaurant with billiard tables. It allowed them to meet and exchange views over a cup of coffee, before challenging each other to a game of pool.

Édouard also knew the whole population was looking in his direction since his nephew's arrest. He was a little uncomfortable to show himself publicly.

On the other hand, he knew too the only way to stop the rumors was to give his own version of the facts. Moreover, his intuition was telling him his inquest would start right there. Mustering all his courage, he walked into the restaurant where some people were already seated. As soon as he entered, everything became quiet. "Well, I guess they were just talking about us!" thought Édouard, amused. He called out happily:

"Hi, fellows! How are you? I know you're going to tell me you feel sorry for what's happening to my family, but I want to reassure you right away that it is a mistake, and my nephew will be released by the weekend."

Seeing Édouard V, so optimistic and sure of himself, the atmosphere relaxed. They all wanted to know more. He was bombarded with questions.

"Can you tell us exactly what happened over there?"

"A nun was murdered."

"Why was your nephew arrested? Do the police think he is the murderer?".

Uncle Édouard answered loudly, as to cover the question:

"He was the only able-bodied man in the house. It was certain he would be the first on the list of suspects."

"And what about Father Jean, the Chaplain?"

"Do you think Father Jean is a real man?" They all roared with laughter. Then he added more seriously;

"You know, in this kind of case, especially in a Convent of women, one always looks at the stranger, all the more if he is a male. As everyone knows, only a male can be guilty of murder! Women are known to be absolutely unable to commit a violent act of any kind? Doesn't everyone know that?" Édouard ended his sentence in such a mocking tone that all the laughter's was on his side.

Then he added "Now, if you don't mind, I'd like to have a little fun. I want to have a re-match with Jean-Paul who beat me last week in pool. I want to take my revenge.".

Choosing Jean-Paul was not accidental. Édouard thought the city's blabbermouth might give him some precious information. Édouard played badly as his mind was preoccupied. When it was over, he congratulated his opponent:

"O.K. Jean-Paul, you're still the best! Come and sit with me, I'll pay you a coffee."

Jean-Paul Lemieux, bitten with curiosity, welcomed the invitation. He wanted to learn everything about the situation. As soon as the two men were seated, the questioning began:

"You know, I never believed your nephew was guilty! Such a good guy! He doesn't even have a girlfriend, hey?"

"No, my nephew spends all his time between his work and his family. His mother is in weak health; he looks after her a lot!"

"Now, he'll have even more time, since he doesn't work at the Convent anymore."

"Who told you he didn't work there anymore?" asked the uncle, curious

"You didn't know? Ovide Ladouceur replaced him in the boiler room at the convent?"

"Since when?"

"He began on Tuesday, late in the afternoon, I think. That's what he told me anyway."

"Ovide Ladouceur? This name doesn't mean anything to me. Do I know him?"

"Sure! You remember the skittle tournament held last year?"

"In Vaudreuil?"

"Exactly! He was the winner!"

"I'm not sure I know him. I just remember seeing his picture in the paper. Does he live in R?"

"Yes, his house faces the church. It's white with blue gables."

Édouard had just learned something quite interesting! He looked at his watch: "Oh! It's already five o'clock, and I promised my sister I'd bring her back some meat for supper. I have to go before the store closes! Goodbye, Jean-Paul! I'll keep waiting for my revenge!"

Édouard had tried to hide how anxious he was to leave as he now had an interesting lead to follow.

A few minutes later, he was parking his car in front of a white house with blue gables. The church was just on the other side of the street! He rang the doorbell. A middle-aged woman answered.

"How do you do, madam? May I see Mr. Ladouceur?"

The woman turned and cried;

"Ovide! It's for you!"

A tall man came. He was in his fifties and had bright blue and intelligent eyes.

"Yes, can I do something for you?"

"How do you do Mr. Ladouceur? I am Édouard V., Nicolas S's uncle." Since the man didn't seem to understand, he clarified:

"Nicolas is the one you replaced a few days ago in the Convent's boiler room?"

"Oh! Yes! I didn't know his whole name!"

"I would like to talk with you!" said Uncle Édouard.

Like the whole city, Ovide Ladouceur had learned about Nicolas S's arrest. He felt sorry for him. He was a good man who found no pleasure in the pain of others. On the contrary, he was prone to sympathize with those who suffered. He understood how Uncle Édouard would be worried about his nephew.

"Come in and have a seat, Sir."

Édouard sat in the designated chair and without losing one minute, he started.

"Listen Mr. Ladouceur, I'll get straight to the point. First, let me say that I am a retired Provincial Police Agent. I'm trying to conduct my own little inquest to help Nicolas out of his predicament. As he was working at the Convent the very evening of the murder, he is now imprisoned as an important witness in this affair. I met him this morning, and there're some details I would like to check with you."

"If I can help you in any way, I'll be a pleasure" answered the man.

***

Mr. V. parked his car in the driveway. He didn't have to open the door as Aurore was waiting for him at the door. She threw herself in his arms crying:

"Have you news of Nicolas? How is he? Has he any chance to get out of there?"

She was plying her brother with questions. Her nerves were on the edge, for she had spent her whole day thinking the worst.

"Calm yourself, Aurore. I'm bringing you good news. We'll get him out of there, our Nicolas!" said her brother. He played the optimistic card to reassure her.

"I prepared your supper! Do you want to eat now?"

"No, later on, I'll start by telling you everything."

Seated at the kitchen table, Édouard gave a detailed account of his day. Facing him, Nicola's mother literally drank his words. The more he advanced in his story, the more the mother's face lightened.

"Do you think your arguments will convince them of Nicolas's innocence?"

"I'll need more proof because Inspector Leduc will try everything to have him convicted. He's convinced of his guilt."

"What other proof will you need?"

"I have to show them without a shadow of a doubt that Nicolas couldn't have left the house to go to the Convent without me noticing it.

"But I know you sleep with one eye open. For four years now, I've never got up during night without you coming and asking me if everything was all right. I could go and tell them!"

Suddenly, Édouard became lost in thought. Aurore noticed it.

"What's going on? Is there another problem?"

"Yes, Inspector Leduc argued that Nicolas could have gone out the house by the emergency door. As it's on the other side of the house, he said I wouldn't have heard him."

"The stairs we never use?"

"Yes, but it's there anyway. While you finish preparing supper, I'll have a look at this stairs."

"That's a good idea! If you could find something, they would have nothing against Nicolas!"

Uncle Édouard unlocked the emergency door and went down the iron stairs, which spiraled down to the ground.

Nicolas's family lived on the second floor of the building. When Mr. V. arrived on the first floor, a stout police dog started

162

to bark at him fiercely as he jumped at the patio door. Édouard wanted to learn more about this dog. He returned to the kitchen and told his sister: "I have to go and talk to the neighbor about his dog. Wait for me, I won't be long."

Édouard V. went down the front stairs and knocked at an identical door to theirs, but on the floor below. A strong muscled man wearing a white sweatshirt opened the door.

"What is it?" he asked brusquely.

"I'm your upstairs neighbor. Do you recognize me?" answered Édouard with the greatest politeness.

"Oh! Yes! Come in. I beg your pardon, I was rude, but I hate peddlers and Jehovah 's Witnesses," he added laughing. "What can I do for you?"

Diane Gourd's Secret Life

I t is sometimes said that certain people are born, "with a silver spoon in their mouth." As soon as they enter life, everything is easy for them. Mother Notre-Dame-Des-Pins, born Diane Gourd, was one of them.

Her parents were wealthy people. Alphonse Gourd had inherited some very attractive capital from his father. He had never tried to know the source of all this money as the story seemed rather vague and complicated. If he had dug deeper, he may have uncovered certain shady dealings or even perhaps some significant fraud. Diane's father, Alphonse, had preferred to think that fortune smiles on the courageous and everyone makes his own luck in life. It was easier that way. With this approach, he could represent his ancestors as pioneers in the new world who created their own destiny by climbing the social ladder on the strength of their character. The truth was certainly less glorifying, but there is no one as ignorant as the one who pretends he doesn't know. Alphonse had even invented a story about members of his family who had made their fortune in the Klondike gold rush during the past century.

These easy circumstances had allowed him to study at the best Colleges and Universities. He had become a lawyer, but with his political contacts, he had soon been appointed as a judge. Then, he had met Antoinette Vallières, who was from modest means, but who had received a good education from a Convent. He had married her.

When Diane, his daughter, was born, Alphonse had been the happiest man in the word! He loved children and this little one was so much like his mother, who had died some years earlier, and whom her son had idealized immensely. In fact, Diane was effectively the image of her grandmother, physically as well as

164

in her personality. The father was immediately attached to her and became her protector. A great deal of patience was required to raise this quick-tempered and difficult child. Antoinette, her mother, couldn't control her fiery temperament. As soon as she was contradicted, baby Diane fell into an uncontrollable rage. She would throw herself on the floor, shout and struggle like the very devil, till she was out of breath, had turned crimson red, and on the edge of having a stroke. These outbursts left her mother powerless. She knew only one-way to discipline: repression. However, with Diane, this approach just amplified her unreasonable reactions to the point of fearing for the child's life. So, on those occasions, Antoinette called to the father for help.

"Your daughter is still possessed!" she shouted.

"Let me do it, I'll take care of her."

There seemed to be no limit to Alphonse's patience. He would approach Diane, softly calling her name, and then he'd recount the tale about a nice little girl whose father loved her very much. He would add that the little girl was going to stop crying because her father was sad to watch her tiring herself out like that! Slowly, the agitation calmed down, her shrieks became less shrilled, and she let herself be touched, and finally ended in her father's arms. However, Alphonse didn't want to spoil Diane. He'd always agree with Antoinette and continued to expect the same things as the mother. He'd never give into the child's blackmail, but he knew how to calm her down by diverting her attention.

As time passed by, their relationship became even closer. The child's insatiable curiosity charmed her father who spent hours answering her questions, and creating extraordinary stories for her.

Alphonse was equally proud of the birth of his first son to whom his mother, Antoinette, had completely appropriated for herself. It was her own baby, this one! Alphonse could only look at him from a distance, waiting for permission to come closer.

Parenthood is often a thankless task, but it brings great rewards in another way. When a child arrives, a new order happens in the family. Two people who, up to then have lived for themselves, see the arrival of a new entity, their baby, who lives only for himself and asks the whole world to do the same. It is very difficult to be selfish while being a parent. Inversely, the endless affection and the need to protect his vulnerability creates, for the authors of his days, an instinctive attachment toward the little being born from their own flesh.

When her brother was born, Diane was three-years-old. She was a very beautiful child, she had a nice little face, adorned with wonderful curly hair. Everywhere she went she was her parents' pride. Endowed with a bright intelligence, people marveled on hearing the clarity and precision of her language. She was a little queen who wore exquisite clothes made from the best dressmakers in town. Surrounded by the love of her parents, Diane was living a life of happiness that she believed would never end.

When Antoinette became pregnant, she tried to prepare her daughter for the arrival of a little brother or sister. Whenever her mother talked about the upcoming event, Diane didn't listen. She became completely deaf on those occasions. In truth, she was refusing to accept the reality that her reign as an only child was coming to an end. All children are more or less egocentric, but there was no kindness in Diane Gourd's heart. She never showed any tenderness towards other children and had the unfortunate tendency to meanly hurt anyone whom she saw as a potential rival. Alphonse was not concerned by this behavior. Contrary to his wife, he was convinced everything would fall into place once the baby arrived.

When Antoinette came back from hospital, she presented the fragile babe-in-arms to Diane, who scarcely looked at him and tried to interest her parents with something else. On the other hand, she was continuously watching her mother from the corner of her eye while she took care of her little brother. Many times, Antoinette had surprised her daughter watching Charles as he slept. Antoinette was moved by the sight.

Alphonse wanted to create a bond with his male heir. He insisted on taking him in his arms. Antoinette let him hold the baby while giving him his bottle, a long and monotonous task, for a mother who had a hundred other things to do. Diane stood silently, right beside her father, feeling dispossessed of his affection by this newcomer.

Diane was as deceitful as she was bright. She knew that each afternoon when Charles was sleeping, her mother called her friends. Deprived of social interactions as a result of her two young children, Antoinette liked to keep contact with the outside world. It also allowed her a chance to change her ideas.

One afternoon, while her mother was chatting with her best friend, Diane went into her brother's room with a big pair of scissors in her hands. The baby was sleeping on his back. The little girl passed her hands between the bars of the crib and succeeded in lowering her brother's diaper. She took his tiny penis in her hand and tried to cut it off. The little boy uttered such a yell that the mother dashed into the room as fast as lightening. In one glance, she had understood the situation. In a fury, she grabbed her daughter and threw her against the opposite wall. Antoinette cried and shrieked like a mad woman on seeing the surging blood. She was sure her boy had lost his sex.

"My baby! My baby!"

Charles was crying so loudly that the cook rushed in. She fetched a cotton cloth and sponged the wound. When the blood finally coagulated, the two women realized that only a part of the skin had been cut.

A terrible wrath against Diane rose in Antoinette's soul. She looked everywhere to find her daughter, but without any result. Meanwhile, Alphonse had returned from work.

His wife was out of her mind. He had never seen her like that. He looked after her, and finally, she succeeded in saying something. She did not mention the drama though, for she was still too upset to talk about it calmly.

"I don't know where Diane is. We can't find her anywhere! We've been looking for an hour!"

"Calm yourself, darling, I'll find her. She must be somewhere. Could she be outside?"

"I don't think so. All the doors are locked, and she can't open them by herself."

"It'll be easier like that!"

Alphonse called his daughter's name softly while wandering everywhere. Nothing in the basement, nothing on the first floor either. The father looked in every corner. On the second floor, at the end of the hall, he heard a noise coming from a wardrobe. Diane was hiding in the back, curled up in a ball. When he had gathered her in his arms, she began to cry desperately.

"Darling, what happened? Why are you hiding? What are you afraid of?"

Suddenly, the child stopped crying and declared in cold determination:

"Mummy was very mean to me; she hurt me very much."

"Where did mummy hurt you?"

"All over, all over! I don't want to see her anymore! Take me with you, far away!"

Alphonse felt heartbroken. He could feel his daughter's distress, and he had to assume the terrible reality. Was his wife a cruel mother who tortured his children while he was away?

He went down to the main floor. With a devastated look on his face and holding his daughter in his arms, he entered his son's room. Antoinette was sitting in a chair with the baby on her lap. Diane had a terrible fit like she had never had:

"No! Daddy, take me away! She's bad! She'll hurt me!"

Alphonse put his daughter in her room, cautiously closed her door, and then came back to his wife with a solemn and determined look on his face.

"What did you do to our daughter? She told me you hit her?"

"Yes, it's true, I lost my head when I saw what she was doing."

"But what was she doing that was so terrible?"

"She tried to cut off Charles's penis with scissors!"

"Did she succeed?" asked Alphonse, greatly alarmed.

"She just tore off a bit of the flesh without any serious damage. I temporarily dressed the wound, but we'll have to call the doctor in any case, so he can examine it and prevent any infection from occurring!"

"I'll call him immediately!" said Alphonse hastily.

An hour later, the doctor came. He disinfected the wound and gave the baby an injection. Then, no one spoke of it anymore.

From this day, the relationship between father and daughter would never be the same.

Diane began school at the age of six. She attended a private school in the district of Westmont. Right from the start, she did very well in school.

She was first in her class and always a winner! She was extremely polite with the nuns, but she treated her fellow classmates with contempt. Her arrogance and rudeness distanced her from the other little girls. She was always alone.

Diane had, however, noticed one of them. Not very pretty, a little skinny, she was isolated from the others. One day, Diane, tired of always being alone, had asked Patricia to play with her. She had accepted joyfully. They had a lot of fun together during recess. The friendship lasted a week. Then, Diane's true nature showed itself. When she lost a game, or if her friend did not agree with her, Diane would hit and bite Patricia. The little girl would cry and go away, refusing to keep playing with this cruel girl. The day after, she would come back as if she had forgotten everything. One day though, she had enough of being treated badly and refused to play with Diane anymore. Besides, she had made a new friend.

Diane was furious. She swore she would have her revenge. After recess, when everyone was seated, Diane left her seat to whisper something in the teacher's ear. This one frowned and went directly to Patricia's desk.

"Open your desk, Miss!" ordered the woman with authority.

Very surprised, Patricia obeyed. On top of her books was Diane 's pencil box.

"Miss Patricia, a thief has no place in this institution! Take your things and go to the Director's office, I'll be there in a minute."

It's the way Patricia D. was expelled from Diane Gourd's school. Diane congratulated and prided herself on her success.

Diane Gourd Spreads Terror

Diane reached the age of wisdom without reaping its fruits. It is said that from the age of seven, the child enters a transitory period of calm between the disorder of childhood and the turmoil of adolescence. So, between seven and twelve-years-old, socialization takes place. The child becomes more aware of others. He realizes his true place in the social order of the family. He is then ready to make concessions in order to keep and merit his parents' affection.

Diane, with her insatiable need to dominate, had not developed any characteristic which could please those around her. She now had two brothers and behaved like a real tyrant toward them. In no way could they enter the princess's room without unleashing a terrible revengeful rage, but she was not shy in stealing her brothers' small treasures.

The family had two bathrooms. One was reserved for the parents; the other, Diane had appropriated for herself. She was in there early in the morning and would only come out at the last minute, just before the school bus stopped in front of their door.

Her brothers, angry and frustrated by her dictator's attitude, couldn't do anything to have their turn in the bathroom. They had to be content with hurrying to the school's washroom when they arrived.

Antoinette was an accomplished woman who was a master in supervising her household. With a refined taste, she had decorated their wonderful house on the mountain. Located on Côte-Ste-Catherine Road, it clung to the hillside of Mont-Royal It had been built by a wealthy merchant at the beginning of the century and bought by Alphonse Gourd some years later. It was a sumptuous house whose turrets on each side highlighted the massive gray stones walls. In the interior of the house, vast rooms with dark wooden paneling and vaulted ceilings were managed with warmth and furnished in good taste.

Servants inhabited a part of the house. They helped Antoinette with the upkeep of the house as well as in the kitchen or garden. The mother directed them in a fair and respectful manner. On the contrary, they were Diane's personal slaves. She knew that in spite of their adult status, they were at her service. She was perfecting her malicious tyranny on them. Every time Antoinette witnessed her being impolite toward the people in her service, she intervened and severely scolded her daughter. Diane mocked her openly. Antoinette felt powerless in front of the rebellious and insensible nature of her daughter. She did not know how to relate to her. She would have liked to interest her in light woman work, such as knitting or crochet, but Diane hated it. She deeply despised the role of her mother in the house. She was convinced that her mother was but another servant. In no way, did she want her future life to be like hers.

Angelina, the family's cook, had been employed by the Gourd's before Diane's birth. She had watched her grow up. The woman felt affection for this hardheaded girl, but she wasn't shy to put her in her proper place when necessary. The employee, in her fifties, came from a big family. She had lived through some difficult times in her youth and had acquired the wisdom to rule her life with dignity.

Diane was divided in her relationship, with the one she had known for so long. She couldn't help but respect such a good and clever person. This feeling bothered Diane. She imagined such a high place for herself in the future; how could she lower herself to esteem someone in such a humble position? Diane was twelve-years-old and very intelligent. She had just become interested about things in life.

One day, when she was in the kitchen tasting fresh-from-the-oven homemade cookies, Diane had decided to settle once and for all her rapport with Miss Angelina. With the intuition of such a young person for perceiving the vulnerability of others, she attacked the woman bluntly:

171

"And you, Angelina, why aren't you married? Is it because you're so big and ugly, no man has ever wanted to marry you?"

When their own integrity is attacked, few people find enough strength not to take it personally. Angelina was offended, but she didn't want to show it. She didn't answer the insult, but instead concentrated all her energy into finding the right response. Facing her silence, Diane took the opportunity to add:

"If you don't answer, it's because I'm right!"

"You know, Diane, you are seeing me when I'm fifty; you've no idea how I looked when I was twenty- five. Then, I was neither big, nor ugly, as you say in such a wicked way, I've had boyfriends who wanted to marry me. It's me who refused them. Ask your mother about the suitors who once came here to visit me on my days off." The woman went on:

"The body's outside envelope is perhaps noticed first, but it becomes secondary when you want to know someone's soul. Take you, for example, you have a nice face and a fine body, but if what's in your heart should appear on your face, you'd see yourself so ugly, you'd hide your face under a pillow case."

"Why are you being so mean with me?"

"I said that, Diane, because I know you very well. Don't forget, I was there when you were born. I have watched you grow up, and what I've seen was not always very nice! Far from it! And when you say I'm mean to you, I'm happy you realize what others may feel when you hurt them as you just did me."

Diane was hurt to the quick by Angelina's comments; she left the kitchen with dignity, but ran to her room to check her face in the mirror. She feared the woman's words might have had a magical effect, imprinting nasty traits on her beautiful face. What she ignored was that as the years would pass by, life was to print her soul on her flesh. Sometimes, a young beauty of twenty can find herself made ugly over time by her bad thoughts and her ill deeds having become kneaded into her features mercilessly."

Diane was only in the learning stage of life. However, she thought she knew everything and wanted to inform everyone else of their ignorance. Her grades at school were high, but her schoolmates fled from her bad temper. She had a few friends though. In fact, two faithful supporters, Pierrots and Beatrice, were always at her side. They were weak individuals completely subjected to the will of their leader, Diane. As high-class young women, they wouldn't do anything which could tarnish their public image. However, when they were alone, they could do anything they liked. On these occasions, Diane would use them as her puppets, ready to satisfy her every whim.

In their class, there was a girl named Rose Fontaine who had joined them lately. She was from a poor family who lived in the lower part of the town. One of her teachers had noticed how gifted she was and had recommended her for a student's grant given by a generous donor who, each year, paid for the education of the school's district best candidate. Rose Fontaine had been chosen and registered in this private school of Westmount. She was a serious challenge to Diane's academic success, occasionally stealing her first place. In the beginning, nobody knew of her modest background. One day, the teacher had circulated a sheet on which each student had to write down her parents' name and address. When it came to Diane's desk, she noted all the details concerning Rose Fontaine in a notebook before inscribing her own.

That evening, she asked her father:

"Daddy, where is Hochelaga Street?"

"Hochelaga Street? Why are you talking about that street? Did somebody asked you to go there?" inquired the father, suspicious. "It's not a good place" he added.

"I's the address of one of my classmates!"

"Your classmate's address? It's highly improbable a girl from over there is coming to school here."

"Maybe, but it's like that! I took down her address this morning when I had the list of all our addresses in my hand. Let me show you!"

Alphonse checked. Diane was right. He was shocked by such a mixing of the social classes: "Those people don't have the same upbringing as ours. They shouldn't be allowed to come here and dishonor us with their vulgarity." The father was very mad.

He was a member of the school board which presided over the schools in the district. When the association met the following Monday, he asked how such a transfer was possible? He was explained that every year students on scholarships from every corner of the city were admitted to their schools. However, they had to be recommended by their school's principal and proven to be exceptionally gifted. Alphonse had tried to explain, that in spite of their talent, the moral values of those people could badly influence their own children. Other members of the board, however, felt that the presence of these young people only stimulated the other students.

Alphonse was alone in his opposition, and it was rejected by the group. For him, it was a serious issue. He asked Diane many questions about the young girl. When he learned that Rose Fontaine often took Diane's first place in the class, he was furious.

Diane understood that this girl was not part of their world, and consequently, she had no place in their school. If her father couldn't succeed in reestablishing the right order, she would do it.

One day, during recess, Diane interrogated Rose right in front of a group of young girls,

"Hey! Rose, can you tell us where you live? From what part of the city you are from?"

Rose hadn't foreseen this question about her humble beginnings. Now, she had two choices in front of her: to fabricate a lie and become entrapped in some vague explanation, or to tell the truth and risk lowering herself in the eyes of her peers. With courage, she chose the second.

"I leave on Hochelaga Street downtown."

"How come you're her at a school in Westmount?"

"I have a scholarship."

"A scholarship? What's that? Explain yourself!"

"It means that since I had the highest marks in my school, someone offered to pay for my studies here.""

"In reality, what you are saying is that your parents are too poor to send you to a school like ours!"

When Diane mentioned her parents' poverty, Rose felt her heart tighten. It was true, her parents had no money. Sometimes, there was not even enough to properly feed their children every day. Rose thought of her sick father, unable to work, and her mother, working as a cleaning woman in other people's homes. Rose deeply loved her parents, but at that moment, she was ashamed of them. She was humiliated by their wretchedness, mortified by her own misery in front of those arrogant girls who were so proud of their parents' wealth as if they had earned the right to be born into privilege.

From this day, Rose was pushed aside, judged unworthy to associate with the pretentious girls of Westmount's elite.

Despite Diane's efforts, Rose had, from then on, always held first place in the class.

Rose Fontaine's Life

Rose Fontaine was the personification of faithfulness to her principles. Before anything, she was a woman of duty. Once settled on a course of action, she would not wander from it. At the same time, she was a complex individual. It was as if she had two personalities. As much as she was guided by strong ethics, she could descend to the basest scheme in order not to deviate from her path. Rose was not a supple person.

Despite her excellent results, she had been unable to finish her studies. At home, her mother, worn down by her work as a domestic, had fallen ill. She was no longer able to provide for the upkeep of the household. Someone had to replace her. Rose's father had already died some years before. Four younger brothers and sisters were still in school.

Claude, her eldest brother, offered to support the family financially. Surprisingly, he had found a lucrative job in those depressed economic times. No one ever bothered to ask where his good fortune came from.

However, a maternal presence was needed in the house to take care of the children and their sick mother. This ungrateful task fell onto Rose who had to interrupt her brilliant education made possible by a generous donor. The disappointment of the young girl was huge as she had been living only for her scholarly achievements. There, she had found self-validation and interesting prospects for the future. However, her sense of loyalty had silenced her selfishness. So, Rose had renounced her future ambitions.

On the other hand, she had not forgotten the wealthy young women she had once known, and whom she still envied. As Rose read the papers, she was always interested in the news about the prosperous quarters of the great metropolis of Montreal. It was while reading the obituaries that she had learnt about the death of Diane Gourd's mother. It included the address of the funeral home as well as the hours for viewing. Rose couldn't resist the temptation to make a visit.

Diane was only eighteen when her mother had died from a sudden heart attack. Mother and daughter had quarreled frequently, but Diane had never realized the important place her mother had occupied in her life. She was devastated by grief. Her passionate nature was afflicted with an almost immeasurable pain.

As result of her bad temperament, Diane had created a void around her. The few friends, who were still with her for their own self-interest, were absent on this sad occasion.

When Diane saw Rose enter the funeral home, she ran towards her and wept in her arms. Rose had developed a motherly attitude with her younger brothers and sisters. She spent the whole afternoon with Diane, pushing aside all the hurt she had experienced at the hand of this same girl. She was also there for the funeral. Her friendship was a crucial support for the orphan, Diane. A new link was developing between the two young girls. Ravaged by pain, Diane lost her arrogant attitude. She desperately needed a confidant to sustain her in her grief. Rose was there. She offered herself freely and with competency.

On the express demand of Diane, Rose often paid her a visit. However, as a result of her household responsibilities, Rose could only come in the evenings. She traveled by bus, or her brother, Claude Fontaine, would come and drive her back home in his car. When he arrived at the end of the evening and rang the bell of the imposing building, a servant would invite him in.

Claude Fontaine was twenty-five years old. He was a very handsome man. He was tall and slim with shiny curly dark hair and amazing green eyes. His sensual lips opened to reveal white sharp teeth. He was a young wolf, who flirted with the underworld, enjoying its benefits. He was also an admirer of beautiful women. Coming from a poor downtown neighborhood, his regular visits to this prosperous area of Montréal impressed him very much. For her part, Diane had become a beautiful woman. "The face of an angel on the body of a goddess" as Claude had described the young girl's picture. Poor Rose, stout and plump, with her masculine features was the exact opposite of Diane delicate attributes.

Claude did not miss any opportunity to come and pick up his sister after her visits with Diane, who had become her best friend.

It's in this way that Rose had introduced her brother to Diane Gourd. On each encounter, he became more acquainted with the young girl. He knew, better than anyone else, how to pay her a compliment. Claude was so charming; Diane would invite Rose more often, just to have another opportunity to see her brother.

On their way back home, one night, Rose had told her brother:

"You know, Claude, I believe Diane likes you."

"Why do you say that?" asked the young man, suddenly very interested.

"She's not the same when you're there."

"You're not being clear! Explain yourself! How is she different?"

"She's more cheerful, more exuberant! She does all she can to attract your attention. Sometimes, when we are all together, it seems to me that I'm in the way. I don't mean to say that you're not nice to me, but it's like there is just the two of you, alone!"

Claude didn't answer, he was thinking. He, too, had noticed the power he appeared to have on Miss Diane. However, he wasn't completely sure of himself. He had gone out with many young girls in his district. He knew how to deal with them, but now, he was facing a new category of women, one he was unfamiliar with. He felt as if he was walking on eggs shells.

Nevertheless, the challenges only increased his desire to win. Claude was born a Don Juan. He no longer kept count of his amorous conquests. However, even if he had gone around with many young women, he had never become emotionally involved with any of them. His freedom was much too precious to him! He would say jokingly "Why be a prisoner to a single woman, when you can have all of them at your feet?"

With Diane, it was different! It was not only about the desire to conquer a woman. He also wanted to be accepted into her milieu as never a little gangster like him could have even dreamed of. He knew his siste, Rose could be very useful to him. He had to know more to determine a plan of action.

"What does Diane's father do?"

"He is a judge at the Superior Court, but his fortune doesn't come from there."

"No? From where does it come?"

When he heard the word *fortune*, Claude Fontaine felt his interest in the Gourd family's wealthy heiress, grow considerably.

"Her grandfather was a very rich man. When he died, he left everything to his son. So, by your age, Diane's father was already a millionaire."

The young man thought that the way prosperity was distributed on earth was very unfair. When he was a kid, he had known hunger and had been deprived of everything he would have liked to possess. Even in his immediate surrounding, he had many friends who enjoyed a more comfortable life with their parents. They ate every day and even had a little money to spend. Claude had never said anything though, for he often profited from his friends' generosity. They would pay his way when they went out together. He was ashamed of his own situation and angry about it.

With age, his knowledge had evolved, and he came to understand that, those he had considered riches when he was young, were absolutely nothing compared to true wealthy people. Claude had also realized that considering his modest background, his chance of becoming prosperous was practically non-existent. Perhaps by working like a mad man and with a lot of ambition, he could hope to live decently. However, this rascal wanted the power of money right away! He didn't have the patience to wait forty years till his dreams come true.

He was associated with the local underworld. The benefits were immediate without much effort. The young man was completely unscrupulous. He wanted to be rich and climb the social ladder by any means. Claude Fontaine was ready to do everything necessary to accomplish his plan. He tried to arrange with his sister, so he could meet with Diane more intimately. One day, he proposed to his sister:

"Hey, sis, could you invite your friend for a little road trip. I could take you somewhere in the country. I know a wonderful place on the edge of the water. If the weather's nice, we could have a picnic lunch there!"

"There he is, showing his hands now! I'm not sure I'll be able to keep my friend for very long! I'm convinced I'll lose the competition if you enter it. But tell me brother, are you interested in Diane or in her social position?"

"With both, my dear! A beautiful woman who is rich, it doesn't take away from her charm, on the contrary."

"Wouldn't it be special if it ended in marriage?"

"Don't dream too much, Rose. You know me, I'm a great lover of nice women, but I prefer renting, not buying. It's less engaging! I've learnt too that there is no difference between a ring on one's finger and a ring in one's nose! Anyway, those marriages always end badly. But before a lifetime commitment, it's not forbidden to have a little fun while waiting. And you'll be with us, my dear Rose!

"Yes, but for how long?" she asked laughing.

Rose loved her big brother very much, and she couldn't refuse him anything. It had been easy to convince Diane to come with her for a little trip in the country with her brother Claude.

It was a wonderful summer day in July. The sun was shining, the air was fresh and warm. The young people had decided to leave early in the morning, so they could enjoy the whole day.

To impress the two women, Claude had arranged for a little paradise. Otherwise, they were in 1935; neither the roads nor the cars were very adequate. However, Claude had decided to go far up north in the Laurentians to St-Emilie-de-l'Énergie.

The route was long, but the landscape was extraordinary. The route, bordered by deciduous trees and conifers, was surrounded on one side by the rounded mountains of the Laurentide. On the other side, the outstanding scenery was a raging river, La Noire, which twisted through the green forest. They left the car on the side of the road since they wanted to get closer to the tumultuous water. It was wild and they fell under its spell. The waves crashed tirelessly against the rocks, and then calmed a bit before rushing again, forming frightening little whirlpools. Fascinated, they followed its turbulent course through the woods. Suddenly, a clearing completely changed the scenery. The river seemed to lose its speed and was now flowing in narrow rivulets, leaving large rocky spaces to explore. They decided to stop there, spreading their blankets on the stones and taking out a picnic basket full of good food: there were sandwiches, cheeses, cold cuts, fresh fruits, wine as well as many other good things. All had been prepared by Diane's cook. Claude and Rose ate with relish, realizing that all these delicacies could certainly not have come from their place.

Rose was not used to drinking wine, and it had a calming effect on her. After eating, she had soon fallen asleep on a blanket.

Left alone, Diane and Claude were a little shy in the beginning. They talked about the weather and especially the extraordinary landscape surrounding them. However, Don Juan soon started playing his game.

"You know, Diane, in my whole life, I have never met such a beautiful woman as you. Since the first time I saw you, I haven't stopped thinking about you!"

Diane, who was listening to her first testament of love, was in seventh heaven. She thought she was in Paradise! This handsome man was the Prince Charming whom she had waited so long for. Diane was convinced he was as good as he was attractive! And he had feelings for her! She was in another world.

To hide her troubled mind, the young girl didn't answer, but had rose up to approach the dark water flowing below. Sitting down, she took off her shoes and plunged her feet into the frozen water. A minute later, Claude sat down beside her and put his arm around her shoulders. Diane didn't move, hypnotized by the warmth of his touch. Slowly, his fingers started moving down her back and along her arm. She thought she would die from the pleasure.

"The water is not too cold, Diane?"

Rose's voice had called her seductive brother to order. The three spent the rest of the afternoon walking and playing in water. Finally, it was time to return. Diane had lived one of the most fabulous days in her life.

Diane and Claude Meet More Often

The death of Antoinette had greatly affected her husband, Alphonse. They had been married for more than twenty years. A kind of symbiosis had developed between the two. With the disappearance of his wife, Alphonse literally felt he had lost a part of himself. He was absent minded, haggard, as if waiting for someone to come. It required all his energy just to stand up. It explains, why this family man, usually so vigilant, didn't see his oldest daughter going down a very troubling path: the discovery of love.

The little trip in the country had inflamed Diane's heart and Claude's senses. Deep down in their souls, they both wanted to meet again.

The young woman was not prepared for the shock of love at first sight. She hadn't been warned of its devastating effects. From the moment she had met Claude, Diane no longer considered love as an abstract concept, but as a reality burning into her flesh and weakening her self-control. Her critical mind, usually so alert, had been silenced. How could she understand this flame which had ignited inside her, dazzling and blinding her at the same time? Diane saw Claude through a glow that endowed him with all the virtues. He was the man of her dreams who had come to carry away his beloved.

For Claude, it was not his first adventure, far from it. However, each adventure presented a new challenge. The greater the obstacle between him and his conquest, the greater the predator's thrill. Diane was a choice morsel. Her social rank as the daughter of a man who was a judge in the Superior

Court excited him very much. Moreover, Diane was a beautiful woman whose charms were unquestionable.

Claude imagined telling his adventure to his friends who wouldn't believe him until he brought them tangible proof. This kind of victory was not to be celebrated alone. It ought to be proclaimed publicly.

However, the young man knew he shouldn't announce his victory too soon; the slightest mistake could spoil everything. The days following that wonderful Sunday, Claude was thoughtful and rather quiet.

Since that day in the country, Rose had been invited to Diane's place many times without Claude showing the least interest in the big Westmount house. His sister questioned him and was answered that: "Fruits have to ripen before being collected." This unexplainable language made her laugh, and she didn't inquire further, knowing her brother knew how to handle his own business. She suspected that he was preparing to make a clever move.

In reality, experience had taught him that love should never be hurried and that it was better to let a woman languished in love than to rush her. Diane, who was wildly in love, would have liked to see the young man the next day.

The first few moments decide how an amorous relationship will develop. The partner who keeps a cool head calculates each move, and thus can easily leave any liaison with the opposite sex, unscathed and as a winner. On the contrary, the unhappy victim who, in the impetuosity of passion, offers herself in a generous but foolish gesture to a calculating and selfish partner risk losing everything in the disastrous adventure.

After a week of complete silence, Diane was going out of her mind. Finally, one night, Claude came to get his sister. The young woman was both happy and furious with the young man. She didn't know what to think exactly. Fortunately, a little pride was left in her, and she succeeded in hiding her emotions under a false indifference.

It was at this moment that Claude played the great card of a tearful romantic. When Rose went to another room to collect her things, the young man took the occasion to declare:

"Diane, for a whole week, I've been dying from my love for you. However, I restrained myself from running to you. My conscience stopped me."

"Oh! Yes? Why?" answered Diane happy, but surprised.

"Haven't you realized how everything separates us? I'm not worthy to be in a relationship with a woman like you!" said the man, feigning a deep humility.

"Explain yourself! I don't understand what you mean, Claude?"

"Diane, you're beautiful, wealthy and educated. I'm nothing in comparison!"

"Claude, don't talk like that! If you knew how highly I appreciate you!"

"You said, *Appreciate*? Poor me! It's the last thing I would have hoped to hear! I'm burning with love for you,"

In a surge of love, Diane came near the young man, taking his hands in hers, and whispered while looking into his eyes:

"Claude, I feel a lot more than appreciation for you! But how can I confess my love for you! That's not the way a well-mannered lady behaves!"

Diane spoke enthusiastically, showing how intense her passion was! She hadn't calculated anything. She was as sincere as one could be. Claude told himself, his plan was unfolding well, and that the fish was firmly hooked.

"Oh! Darling, don't say anything else! I'm weak with emotion! whispered Claude, surprising himself with his acting talent. May I hope that you'll accept an invitation to come and dine with me?"

"Anytime you wish, Claude!" replied Diane fervently.

"Let say I'll come and get you tomorrow afternoon."

"Shall Rose come with us?" asked Diane hesitantly. "I think it'll be better with only the two of us. What do you think? We've so many things to tell each other!" insisted the young man.

"Oh! I agree! It's not that I don't like Rose, but there's a time for some privacy!"

"You're right!"

Just at this moment, Rose came back with her coat, ready to leave. At the sight of their confused faces, she understood something had happened between the two. Tactful, she didn't say anything. But once in the car and dying from curiosity, she questioned her brother:

"How is your affair with the beautiful Diane?"

"She accepted an invitation to come to a restaurant with me." declared Claude proudly.

"Oh! Yes? That fast! You're very clever! I'd have never thought she'd accept so quickly!"

"That's it, sister! You've understood everything!" laughed Claude.

"Well, anyhow, be careful. You're her first love, you know! Try not to hurt her too much!"

"Her first? You're sure of it?"

"Yes, I'm sure of it! Why is it so important?"

Claude looked at his sister condescendingly. He told himself she didn't know much about matters in life. At the same time, he felt Rose was not ready to learn about such low things. She was above them.

The young man didn't answer his sister's question. How could he dare confess that the idea of a young virgin, sacrificing herself on the altar of his manhood was filling him with unmentionable pride?

As for Diane, she explained to her father that she was finding the ambiance of the house depressing and, being young, she needed some distraction. That Sunday spent with her friends had been so good for her moral! Alphonse listened attentively, understanding that his daughter needed to go out more often. All the more, she was in the company of a former classmate- he didn't recall that she was the one he had despised so much some years ago- who was frequently coming over and in whom he had confidence. Anyway, the poor man was unable at the moment to oppose his daughter in anything. He was still struggling through his pain. Diane arranged things wisely, for she was not obliged to ask for permission every time she wanted to leave. Having argued in defense of her mental health, she had obtained them all in advance.

The day after, when Claude rang the bell. Diane was ready and wopened the door herself. She had told her father that she was going out with Rose, and that her brother was taking them in his car. However, if Alphonse had looked carefully, he would have seen only two seated in the vehicle, and not three.

For their first date together, Claude had carefully selected his clothes. He wore a pin-striped black suit with fine gray lines; a little vest, with a gold chain for a pocket watch, worn over a white shirt and tie. A nice raincoat, and a wide brimmed hat tacked down in the front, completed the outfit. He looked like a gentleman. Diane was also very elegant in her cloche hat and a long coat with a fur collar, over a pretty low-cut dress They were a smart looking couple.

The young man knew some chic places in the city. He had made reservation for two at a stylish restaurant in old Montréal.

Having not gone out often in high class society, Diane enjoyed the luxury and wealth of the place. In fact, it was a highly rated dining room. Candles had been lighted on the tables that were adorned with white tablecloths. A huge fire was burning in the chimney. The white wine, bubbling in her glass, put a sparkle in Diane's eyes. She had never been so happy in her life!

Every week now, Claude came to take Diane out for a lover's dinner.

The young girl was treated like a princess. She didn't doubt for a minute that all the gifts and attention had a price and, sooner or later, she would have to pay the bill. After a month of investment, Claude decided it was time to collect the benefits.

That night, the meal had gone down very well; the two lovers having consumed two bottles of wine. Diane was joyful, and Claude took the occasion to propose a visit to the upper floor. Without being aware of the trap she was entering. the young woman followed the man into a superb suite of two rooms on the second floor. The first was a nice living room, richly adorned, where little lamps on finely sculpted low tables diffused a soft light. Claude offered a drink to Diane who accepted with confidence. The man had taken the opportunity to double the alcohol in her glass. He told himself tha with a lot of ice, she won't notice the difference. He was right, but the body of the young girl more or less absorbed the blow. Momentarily a little confused, she lost her usual points of reference. In another way, she felt so well, so confident with Claude! When he sat beside her on the couch and placed his arm around her shoulders, she let go of her inhibitions.

First, he kissed her tenderly for a long time. Then, he lowered his hand to her chest. She offered no resistance. He slowly unbuttoned her dress, exposing her wonderful round and white breasts. Taking his time, Claude caressed and kissed them slowly. Diane was crazy with excitement. Groaning with pleasure, she was like a volcano on the verge of erupting. When Claude gathered her in his arms to put her on the bed, she voiced no objections. She let the young man undress her completely. That night, Claude didn't want to consummate his own pleasure, for he knew he had a lot of time. He just caressed and kissed Diane's clitoris, giving her intense pleasure. Then, she seemed to come back to reality, saying that it was late, and that she had to go home. Claude, docile, let her dress and drove her back to her father's place. He knew that Diane, having had a taste of sex, she was his now, and that she would easily return. The most important is yet to come, but it will happen "only when she will be ready for it"" the young man promised himself.

The following week, after their meal, Claude did not have to insist. Diane followed him into the room. The first time, the man had not completely undressed, as not to frighten the young virgin. "But this time, someone will have to take care of me," Claude thought.

When Diane was completely naked, he undressed himself. She opened her eyes wide on seeing the sex of the young man erected. She didn't dare say a word and show her ignorance. After having caressed Diane for a long time, when Claude thought she was warm enough, he slowly introduced his penis into her dripping vagina which seemed to invite him. She was torn and it hunted, but she liked this kind of pain that was mixed with pleasure.

During the following months, the only occupation of the couple was to share a meal at the same hotel table and then, enjoy having sex together. The two young people waited for those moments with anticipation.

Consequences

These love encounters lasted for about three months. Diane was happy. She was on a little cloud away from reality. The weekly excursions gave her the illusion of escaping into another dimension where there was only tenderness, words of love and sexual pleasure.

However, she felt slightly sick every morning. Otherwise, since the feeling disappeared as soon as she had eaten something, she was not concerned. It will pass, she told herself. However, when other symptoms arrived, and she no longer had her monthly periods, Diane realized she was sicker that she had thought.

Even if it seems incredible, her ignorance of the facts of life was such that the young woman never suspected the truth, at least not consciously. However, the precautions she had taken to avoid her father realizing something was wrong, and especially the secret with which she made the doctor's appointment, bring doubt to her flawless innocence about what was going on.

When Diane entered the old building on Sherbrooke Street, memories from her childhood rushed into her mind. She must have been five-years-old the first time her mother had taken her there. She had had a bad case of tonsillitis. The young doctor, with whom her father had gone to school, had been so kind to her, that a bond of trust had developed between them.

Today, once again, she was coming to see Doctor Latulippe with the same confidence of that little girl from another time.

The professional was glad to see the daughter of his friend, Alphonse. He could hardly believe that the little chrysalides, he had known long ago, had transformed into the beautiful butterfly that stood before him. After inquiring about her father and the rest of the family, he asked:

"What brings you here, dear Diane? You cannot be very sick, for you are the picture of health."

"My troubles are only in the morning when I awake. It is as if I digest badly at night, for when I wake up, I have a bit of nausea."

"And what about your period, when did you have it last?" worried the man.

"Well, it's not right either. It seems to have stopped about a month ago."

"O.K. Come into the other room and I'll have a look at you."

Doctor Latulippe gave her a meticulous examination. He would have liked so much to find another explanation, but the truth was inexorably there. Diane Gourd, a young single, nineteen-year-old woman, was pregnant. On hearing the news, Diane panicked. It was as if her whole word had collapsed around her.

"Are you sure, Doctor?"

"Alas! There is no doubt, dear Diane. Is the man from a good family? Maybe everything can be worked out?"

"It's exactly what I have to check. I'm not sure of anything on that side."

"You mean this man would flee from his responsibility?"

"I don't know how he will react when I tell him the news. No matter, depending on his response, I'll know what kind of man he really is."

"Diane, you should talk with your lover and tell him about the situation. If he is an honorable young man, he won't let you go through it alone. After all, it is his child! Maybe he'll be full of joy?"

In front of her expression, Doctor Latulippe doubted things would be that easy. The man added, trying to reassure her:

"If he abandons you, come back and see me. We'll discuss what would be the best solution for you."

That week, Claude came to get Diane as usual. Before arriving at the hotel, Diane asked him to park the car on a small side street.

"What's the mystery?" asked the young man.

"I have something important to tell you!" answered Diane, becoming very serious.

"I hope it won't spoil our evening?"

"It depends on you, Claude. I'll come straight to the point. I went to the doctor this week, and he told me I was pregnant."

The man was stunned. A storm rose in his head. He didn't expect this news at all! In all his adventures, he had never encountered this reality. He was angry with Diane for bringing him back to earth. According to his own philosophy, women were there to give men pleasure, not to place them in trouble!

For a short instant, he thought of marrying Diane. After all, there would be money to assure a good living. Then, he imagined how bizarre the union of their two families would be. Moreover, he saw the loss of his precious liberty, plunging him into a life of conformity. He would be encaged; a rich cage, but a cage nevertheless. His whole being was revolted. No! Not that! He couldn't imagine being a prisoner for the rest of his life! He was not ready! He was too young! He looked at Diane, so nice and so soft now, but in a glance, he could foresee the demanding mother and the pitiless wife she would become.

He knew their relationship had to end now before it is too late. All these thoughts had passed through his head as fast as lightening. Claude realized he had compromised himself enough. He did not give another thought to the girl sitting beside him, who was only an object of pleasure, a lust of the flesh.

Waiting, Diane looked impassible.

"Well, Diane, I'm very sorry to hear what has happen to you, but I think you didn't take enough preventive measures. You know, it's a woman's responsibility to be careful. As for us men, we don't know anything about it... I cannot help you; you'll have to make arrangements with your doctor."

The young girl was deeply disillusioned. For the first time, she was seeing Claude for whom he really was. He was nothing, but a coward and a profiteer. He had never loved her. He had just taken advantage of her and now that she needed him, he was running away! She hated him with all her strength. She found him intensely disgusting. How could she have been mistaken so much! She had taken someone for a prince, who was, in fact, only a vulgar thief. No! She would not lower herself and beg for his pity! He didn't even deserve a word of explanation!

Diane opened the car door and left without saying a word. She told herself that under the circumstances, her pride was the only thing she had left. She was not going to lose it. She had sacrificed enough to that vile man.

That afternoon, when Doctor Latulippe saw Diane enter his office, he uunderstood that the young girl had a long road of suffering before her. Abortion was not even thinkable. It was forbidden both by the clergy and the medical profession. No! Diane had to go ahead and carry her pregnancy to full term while trying to avoid a scandal! However, it was not always possible. The man talked softly to the young girl:

"Diane, I know you've lost your mother last year... On hearing those words, the tears, which Diane had restrained for many days, erupted. Doctor Latulippe, who was also a fine psychologist, had intentionally caused this outburst, having found Diane too far from her emotions. This attitude had to be changed. It was imperative to empty a little of her excess emotions that, otherwise, could provoke a reaction, even more treacherous.

"I assume your father doesn't know what has happen to you?"

"He doesn't even know I was seeing someone."

"He has to be told about the situation. He's the one responsible for you. It would be very bad to hide the truth from him. What do you think, Diane?"

"I must confess, Doctor that I am at the point where I don't know what to think. All that's happening to me was so unexpected! I never experienced such a thing in my life! I'm totally relying on your judgment. I'll do whatever you think is best!"

"I'll begin by calling your father to tell him I'm coming for a visit. Then, during our conversation, I'll tell him the truth about what has happened. Does this sound all right to you, Diane?"

"Yes, certainly, Doctor, you're very nice to take care of me like this!"

"It's my pleasure! We have to be present when our friends need us the most, don't you think?" Diane felt relieved that someone was sharing her burden. She felt as if a steamroller had crushed her and a benevolent hand had reached in to lift a bit of the weight off her back.

A few days later, Alphonse told Diane that his old friend Louis Latulippe was coming to pay him a visit.

"He said that he wanted to see me about you. I wonder what he has to say? Do you know anything about it, Diane?" questioned Alphonse.

"Be patient, Daddy, you'll know it when he tells you. Why are you in such a hurry?"

Diane wanted to enjoy the few hours of impunity left to her. She feared her father's reaction. She only knew the nice and good man he usually was. But facing these unexpected circumstances, who could foresee his response? What secret mechanism would be unleashed in his head? What tenacious prejudice would darken his judgment? All these thoughts had not stopped turning in the young woman's mind till the doctor, faithful to his promise, arrived on time.

Alphonse and Louis were seating by the fireplace in the living room. Diane took her place a little apart in silence. The two friends spoke about the weather, and then, Alphonse confided his grief over Antoinette's death, mentioning how empty his life seemed to him now. Skillfully, Doctor Latulippe brought up the subject of children, most specifically about Diane. Delicately, from one sentence to another, he directed the conversation towards a parents' responsibility when their children fall into trouble.

Alphonse understood his friend wanted to tell him something, but he still could not figure out what it was about.

"Listen, Louis, stop walking around the bush and tell me what's happening with Diane. It's true, she's been often going out the past little while, and I don't really know where she goes. I hope nothing serious has happened though?"

"Alas! Yes! My poor friend, our Diane is pregnant."

If the house had fallen on top of his head, Alphonse couldn't have reacted more vehemently. He opened his mouth without any sound coming out. He became as pale as death, then as red as a geranium. The doctor was afraid for his immediate health. A terrible explosion of angry saved the father from having a stroke. In a brutal and uncivil manner, he chased away his friend, accusing him of being an accomplice with Diane. A little further, he would have accused him of having raped his daughter!

Humiliated, his head low, Louis Latulippe left, but not without a last look at the victim whom he was leaving in the hands of her implacable father.

As soon as they were alone, Alphonse screamed at Diane:

"Go up to your room. I don't want to see you anymore! I forbid you to come down, even for meals. They'll be taken to you upstairs."

Diane obeyed without uttering a word. She threw herself onto her bed and cried a part of the night.

During this time, Alphonse made some phone calls before taking a decision. It was irrevocable.

If Antoinette had been there, she would have tempered his fury. Alone, he was blinded by his indignation.

There are faults that a man can understand. He had been tempted by them himself and had maybe even succumbed to them. But for Alphonse, as for many men of his generation, the faults of women were unacceptable. According to his values, there were two categories of woman; the good ones were wives and mothers while the others were loose women or prostitutes. Unhappily, his daughter now belonged to the latter. Alphonse saw himself as the good gardener who doesn't hesitate to cut off a rotten branch that is harmful to the rest of the tree. He had to keep his daughter far away from her brothers before she contaminated them.

A few days later, he asked Diane to come down to the living room.

"Prepare a suitcase, you're leaving the house this afternoon."

"Where am I going?" asked Diane frightened.

"You're going where women like you go to have their babies!"

"Not to the Miséricorde's Hospital?" cried Diane

She had shouted the damned name which was terror to all the women of that time. They talked about it as if it was hell.

"Yes, girl, your name has already been registered, and I'll assure myself that you'll be there this very afternoon."

"And after?"

Diane gave her father such a pleading look that a stone would have been moved, but Alphonse, having closed his heart, did not even notice.

"After? You'll go to hell! I don't want to see you ever again! I forbid you from trying to contact your brothers as well. From now on, you're no longer a member of this family!"

On these words, Alphonse had left without turning around.

In the afternoon, a car came to the luxurious residence. Two nuns rang the bell and Diane accompanied them without even saying good-bye to her father.

Rose, for her part, noticed that her brother's routine had changed. On Tuesday, he no longer left towards the end of the afternoon to only return late at night. Curious, she decided to call Diane. She was answered that her friend didn't live there anymore. When she tried to inquire further, the line had been disconnected. She really began to worry. What had happened to her friend? What had her brother done to her? When Claude returned that night, she pressed him with questions. He confessed everything.

Rose was consternated. Diane's life was ruin! She felt awfully guilty about it! She thought for a long time about what could have happened to Diane? Finally, she came to a conclusion, but it had to be verified. She gave herself the task to try and repair, at least a little, the harm her brother had done to her friend. She went to the Miséricorde Hospital and asked if a certain Diane Gourd was registered. On receiving a positive response, she asked to see her.

Rose would never forget that day, or the scene that unfolded before her eyes. A tiny shape in a gray uniform came towards her. With her belly protuberant, Diane was now emaciated and ugly. Her beautiful hair, looking tousled and unkempt, it was loosely tied behind the back of her neck. When Diane saw Rose, she rushed toward her shouting:

"You, bloody bitch, I cannot believe you had the guts to come and see me here! You've ruined my life! I know you set the whole thing up with your brother to destroy me! You've always been jealous of me! You must be happy; I've lost everything now! No! I've gained this!"

Thumping her belly with her fists, she continued, "I curse it, just like I curse you! Don't forget that one day I'll have my revenge, and you're going to pay for everything I am suffering now!" And Diane spat in Rose's face before turning her back to return from where she had come.

Big Decisions

The solitude of her confinement matured Diane. In a short period of time, she had passed through several significant stages of life.

Newly orphaned, she had been separated from someone dear to her, whose very presence had been carrying her through the last years of adolescence. Then, a few months after the death of her mother, Diane had experienced the first great love of her life, an unwanted pregnancy, her lover's betrayal, and the worst of all, rejection from her father and her family.

Diane thought she was alone in the world. At first, she denied her condition and rejected her baby's existence, but as he was continuously reminding her of his presence, demanding her attention, she came to realize that they were two in this miserable business: he and she. On the other hand, he was a symbol of Claude's presence inside her, and she hated this extension of the man. Later, she was compelled to acknowledge her own responsibility in abandoning herself to the affair without thinking. She recalled the joy those encounters brought her. To be honest, she had to admit that she had wanted them and nobody had forced her. Claude had been a wonderful dream for her, even if she hated him now. And this innocent little thing, conceived in love, should not have to pay for her ignorance? She pitied this child she had brought into existence, but whom she didn't want to recognize.

The nuns had approached Diane many times. They wanted her to sign the adoption papers for her baby. By doing so, she would be giving her child away and renouncing him forever. Diane had always refused in an attempt to procrastinate the decision.

Then, the labor pains started. The mothers-to-be did not receive any moral support during those difficult hours. Parked in the labor rooms, they were practically left alone. The nuns in charge of these unmarried mothers were warned against those sinners. They felt only contempt for them. This sentiment was encouraged by the superiors who believed that as a result of their vows they were above the dregs of the female population. It was when their labor started that this hatred manifested itself more openly. The "spouses of Christ", as they called themselves, thought they were immediate witnesses to God's divine punition over these guilty women.

Being in labor, and still not having signed the adoption's papers, Diane was pressed hard. They were fierce and unrelentingly: "You have to sign. You will not be able to take care of that child. He'll starve and you too! Be reasonable. We have a good family who is waiting to adopt him. He'll be better off with them than with you!"

The purpose of this stubborn insistence was to help them take charge of the baby once it arrived, and thus avoids useless displays of affection from the mother. Often, after the baby's birth, nature spoke strongly to the new mother. As the mother cat knows instinctively how to protect her little ones against predators, the young girls wanted to take possession of their baby whom the nuns coveted for themselves since they were generously rewarded for it.

To the great annoyance of the nuns, Diane kept refusing to sign. Against all logic, she was still hoping for a miracle.

She had made an agreement with a girl who had become her friend while in the hospital. Diane had asked her to call Doctor Louis Latulippe when she was ready to give birth. Very aware of the importance of her mission, Lucette had tried to contact him several times. It was a delicate operation since all outside communication was monitored. However, like all places of detention, the prisoners developed effective ways around it.

Finally, she succeeded in reaching him. She explained that she was calling on the part of Diane Gourd who was soon to deliver her baby.

"Where are you now?" asked a blunt voice on the telephone.

"I'm at the Miséricorde's Hospital."

"And you're telling me Diane Gourd is going to have her baby?"

"That's right Sir, and she wants you to come and see her!"

"I'm coming!" answered the man with determination.

Louis Latulippe knew he was looking for trouble in going there. He also understood that he should act as a friend, rather than a doctor, otherwise, his presence would be misinterpreted. On the other hand, he just couldn't say no to such a call of distress.

When he arrived, Diane had not yet been taken into the delivery room. She was in the last stages though as the unbearable pains were now constant.

When she saw Doctor Latulippe, she smiled, holding out her arms.

"You came! How good you are!"

"My little girl, how are you? Are you suffering a lot? When did the pain start?"

"Since yesterday at noon", she answered with difficulty.

"That's twenty-six hours! It shouldn't be long now!"

At this moment a nun came into the room. She looked severely toward the man.

"Get out, Sir. Men are not allowed in here!"

"Calm yourself, Sister. I'm a doctor, and I have permission from the doctor in charge of the delivery. I am Diane's uncle."

Since she didn't believe him, she went to verify his claim. Knowing she only had a few minutes, Diane hurried to tell the man:

"They want me to sign the papers to give my baby up for adoption. I have refused. What do you think I should do?"

"Let me take care of that. I'll try to settle everything for the best. You concentrate on yourself. It's going to be hard, but you have to go through it!"

The nurse came back and asked Doctor Latulippe to leave the room for a few moments. Her tone had changed; she was now more polite, as if she was accepting that he could be with Diane. It seemed her verifications had been positive.

She soon exited and told the Doctor Latulippe:

"It's time to bring her to the delivery room."

She entered the room with a stretcher pushed by another nun. When Diane was rolled out into the corridor, Louis Latulippe squeezed her hands and talked to her as if she was still a little girl.

"Be courageous Princess! I'll see you soon!"

The young woman was no longer alone. Another human being had taken her burden on his shoulders for a few minutes. She cried with relief. Otherwise, she was preparing to live through one of the most difficult challenges of her life!

While Diane was giving birth to her child, Doctor Louis Latulippe concerned himself to the child's future.

The nuns of the Religious Order who were the wealthy owner of the hospital, had measures in place to keep strangers from interfering in their affairs. Even the doctors were completely at their service and had absolutely no say in how they managed the institution.

Doctor Latulippe knew the rules, and under usual circumstances, he couldn't have done anything for Diane and her baby. Fortunately, the young woman had not signed the adoption papers. It was her last hope for salvation. The mother's signature was a legal obligation in adoption cases. It was the reason the nuns applied urgent pressure on the young mothers to do so. Afterwards, they could do whatever they wanted with the child without being accountable to anyone! In addition, it allowed for absolute secrecy as to what happened to the child.

Louis Latulippe went to the director's office. He greeted the Superior and identified himself. She had already been informed that a stranger was in their house, inquiring about one of the residents. She asked him dryly:

"What do you want, Sir?"

"I wish to look after the adoption of Diane's Gourd's baby into a family of my choice. Since she hasn't yet signed her papers, I will promise to obtain it!"

The woman reflected in silence. The man guessed her thoughts.

"The family I'll chose will be very grateful towards you. They're wealthy people!"

"In that case, you'll sign a discharge for me, attesting that you are taking full responsibly for the case."

"No problem, Sister, I will do it anytime!" answered the man with satisfaction.

What the doctor wanted above all was to be certain of the people the baby was to be given to. He sought at the same time to be assured that in the long-term Diane's baby would always to be well treated and would lack nothing. He was thus naming himself the child's godfather.

Louis Latulippe had only one phone call to make. One of his friends and his wife had been desperately looking to adopt a child for two years. He called them and asked if they were ready to take John home? –Like a great magician, he had guessed the sex and name of the baby- His friends didn't have a minute of hesitation;

"Where is this child right now?" asked the future father.

"He is being born right at this moment!"

"Oh! My Lord!" answered a failing voice

"Come on, you'll not faint out! You've wanted a child so long! Tell your wife to get ready, and both of you come to the Miséricorde as soon as possible."

It is under these circumstances that Diane had learnt about the future parents of her son, John, already baptized by a kind-hearted sorcerer, Doctor Latulippe.

While she was recuperating at the hospital, Diane made a big decision. Even if she tried to look at the question on every angle, her future was completely obstructed. There was no solution on the horizon, now or in the distance. She had not completed her education, and without the financial support of father, what could she hope for?

The young girl decided to knock at the door of a Missionary Convent. Diane introduced herself to one of their houses in Montréal, but had been informed that she had to apply in Québec City. They had given her a form to fill.

Later on, she went to Doctor Latulippe's office on Sherbrooke Street once again.

"My poor Diane, how are you? I was just thinking of you. My friend called me yesterday to tell me how happy they are with our little John. They find him so lovely. The mother is really in love with him!"

"I'm also very happy to know my child has good parents, said the young mother with emotion. However, I don't think I will be able to have news of him often!"

"Oh! No? Why do you say that dear child?"

"Because I'm entering a Convent, Doctor Latulippe."

"I think it's a very wise decision under the circumstances."

"I have a little problem though. I must have my father's signature if I want to be accepted.".

"Since our last encounter, I have tried to call him, but he refuses to talk to me."

"I went to the house, and I was told he wasn't there, even if his car was in the garage."

"Well, I think we've only one solution left. I will declare myself responsible for you and hope the nuns will accept the signature of your new guardian, said the doctor laughing. Let's have a look at those papers. Oh! They don't ask for a cent! Good! So, I'll have only your bus ticket to pay."

So, on this nice spring afternoon, Diane Gourd had entered the missionary Convent in Québec.

Diane had chosen this missionary Community because some years ago in her Westmont school, two nuns had come to speak about their mission throughout the world. They had been invited to promote their Orders.

They had talked about their lives in far-away countries, explaining how their Community had houses on nearly every continent: Asia, Europe, Africa, and in America, of course. They had also related the exemplary life of one of their Sisters who had accomplished miracles since her death, and whom the Pope thought to canonize: Sister Maria Assunta.

The adventurous tales and the great accomplishments of the Community had ignited the children's imagination. They had dreamt of this extraordinary life!

A year later, Rose's mother died. There was only one of her brothers left, and he was adopted by an uncle who loved him deeply.

Rose tried to insert herself back into society, but having no training or experience, she had to go to work in a factory. The noise was awful, and Rose found the people so vulgar. She realized that her place was not there. She wanted to fulfill her secret dream: to enter the Missionary Convent in Québec.

The Two Enemies Face Off

Since her birth, Diane Gourd's imperious nature had always dominated the people around her. As a Postulant, her pride was still alive despite the humiliation she had to endure.

In devoting themselves to religious life, those women were making a commitment for the rest of their existence: thus, engaging themselves to fight the most difficult struggle, the one against their own self according to their three vows: Poverty, Chastity and Obedience.

The first human instinct is life itself; to feed oneself, to stock up provisions, to be wealthy with what one possesses. A vow of Poverty hinders this need as the nuns abandons their survival into the hands of someone else.

The second instinct is reproduction which translates itself into the amorous desire to be united with another of the opposite sex. This other great impulse of life is programmed by nature to ensure the continuation of the human race. It is as strong as life itself. One cannot separate it from the human entity. The Chastity vow contradicts nature and condemns the body to a life of solitude.

The third, the more difficult by far for man, the king of creation, is to renounce its intelligence, abdicating it completely to others who themselves must submit to an even higher authority. The Obedience vow is so strict that a mere explanation, a pertinent remark, or even a simple personal thought is considered unlawful behavior according to the Rule.

This was the reason why the young Postulants had to be put to the test in order to ensure their capacity to pass through the adversity of their interior battles. The immediate superior, the

Postulant's Mistress, whose intuition was like a powerful radar that could swiftly ascertain the weakness of each.

Diane had a dominant character. Many times, she had to humiliate herself, to constrain herself in silence, as she burned with the desire to defend herself.

One day, her group was assigned to clean the dormitory. When it was finished, Diane had been given the task of collecting everyone's dust cloth and bring them downstairs to shake each one outside before putting them back in their place upstairs. She had to do all of this alone while the others were free to head towards the Chapel. She ran like a mad fool to finish everything, so she wouldn't be late, the most inadmissible of behaviors. She succeeded and was proud of herself. During the meal that followed, the Postulant's Mistress interrupted the reader to show a cloth which Diane recognized too well. It was one she had accidentally dropped in her race against the clock.

"Who left this in the stairs?" the nun asked severely.

"It was me, Mother," answered Diane in a little voice.

"Stand up, so everyone will see the irresponsible fool who scatters things around. In the future, you will work on your sense of duty."

The young Postulant was not guilty, logic was on her side; the extra task had been unreasonable. However, pride was a hidden trap, denounced by the sacred Rule. A single word to justify herself, and Diane would have been lost, for dismissal was hanging above her head like the sword of Damocles. The Obedience vow obliged her to keep quiet.

However, submitting at any rate the individual to a strict observance of the Rule, neglects the essential aim of Religion.

Alas, the Catholic Church which presents itself as the foundation of Christianity, and the first successors of Jesus Christ, had forgotten the message of *Love* from the *Master.* She preferred to brandish the threat of mortal sin and the spectrum of Eternal Damnation to better control her subjects.

So, Love was written anywhere in the Rule.

Diane was working hard to attain saintliness. One day, her path to perfection was seriously compromised. The Mother in charge of the Postulants presented a newcomer to the community: her name was Rose Fontaine.

The rage in the heart of Diane Gourd was far from being subdued. She felt it rising in her soul like an impetuous torrent. She used all her willpower not to shout:

"No! Chase her away! She is a traitor! She has no right to be one of us! I'll unmask her right here in front of all of you! I'll expose all her faults!"

Fortunately, she managed to control herself. Instead, she decided to take her own revenge.

Soon, Rose recognized the one who had spat hatred into her face. She was hoping her enemy's wrath had calmed down with time. Rose had worked very hard to be admitted into the Community of her dreams. She did not want to renounce it because of the bad blood between them.

Later on, it happened that the two young nuns were left alone for a few minutes. Breaking the Rule of silence, Diane Gourd, future Mother Notre-Dame-Des-Pins, said:

"Rose Fontaine, I haven't forgotten anything! You're going to pay for all! Take nothing for granted! I am going to wait for the right moment, day and night, but I will have my revenge for all the suffering you caused me. Never sleep in peace; I vow that I'll ruin your life!"

Rose was deeply troubled by these words of warning. She understood that no matter how she tried to explain, it would be a waste of time. Diane had nourished her hatred with care; its maintenance had kept her alive.

Despite everything, those two years as a Postulate were almost happy ones for Rose. Naturally humble and submissive, she didn't have to be broken by the Rule. She was not discouraged by the hard work assigned to her neither. It was nothing compared to that which she had endured during her life of poverty with her family.

On Diane's part, she worked hard to be equal to the challenge. Though somewhat crushed, her strong personality survived, but it was kept hidden from others. Otherwise, her attitude conformed to the Rule.

Finally, the day everyone was dreaming of arrived: the taking of the veil. This ceremony had kept in expectation these young women, who, up to then, had not dressed in religious garments. They were made to prove the sincerity of their vocation during the two trial years as a Postulate.

Rose Fontaine's new name was Sister Thérèse–De-Lima, and Diane, Mother Notre-Dame-Des-Pins. The two were accepted and asked to pronounce their temporary vows for their three years as a Novice.

The Franciscans-Missionaries- of- Mary were above all a missionary Congregation. As soon as the young nuns were ready, they were sent to far away countries.

There were six newcomers on this occasion, and three were assigned to Cameroon in Africa. Counted among them were Diane Gourd and Rose Fontaine. They were going to replace a group of fellow Sisters, aged and tired, who had been operating in this country for years.

A boat took them to another continent, but once in Africa, they had to endure a long trip by cart for many days, before arriving at their destination. The mission's house was located back of the beyond. There, the missionaries had a dispensary and a classroom to teach religion to the children.

The comfort of modern life was unknown at that place. It was hundreds of miles away from all civilization.

The Sisters' house, built for some years, was a low one-floor construction. It had been made from bricks the villagers had fabricated themselves from sand and water. The two ingredients were mixed and formed into a kind of cake which was let to dry under the sun. The next day, they had hardened enough to build a row or two of a wall. The process had taken weeks. When everything was finished, the walls had been whitewashed. The roof was made of straw. It protected them from the rays of the hot summer and also of the heavy rains of the winter monsoons.

Nearby, a tumultuous river offered a little beach where water could be drawn and clothes washed. One had to be very careful though, because a hundred feet further, there was a dangerous waterfall.

Diane Gourd, Mother Notre-Dame-Des-Pins, was appointed as a teacher while Rose Fontaine, Sister Thérèse-De-Lima, was assigned to the laundry. Every day, Rose took a basket with all the dirty clothes and linen from the previous day, and went down to the edge of the river to rub it all with crude soap on the stones, before rinsing everything in clear water. Finally, she wrung each piece of washing and then, hung it up to dry on a long cord provided for this purpose.

Large trees bordered the river. One day, while Sister Thérèse was doing the laundry, a massive branch dropped off hitting her in the back, and literally pushed her into the river. Surprised, she was immediately carried away by the strong current towards the falls. Passing beside a low limb, she grabbed it in desperation. With all her force, she shouted: "Help! Help!" Some Sisters ran from the house, they threw her a rope she grabbed and they pulled her back to shore. Not far, up in a tree, a boy, who worked for the mission, had watched the entire scene from his perch.

That same night, hidden in the tall grass, far away from the house, Boba, a young employee of the mission, was having a discussion with Mother Notre-Dame-Des-Pins.

"No! You're just clumsy! You'll not have what I promised. You failed your task. She is still alive. If you really want your gift, you'll start over and succeed next time."

On her arrival, a month ago, Mother Notre-Dame-Des-Pins had surprised the young boy playing with a flashlight which belonged to the Community. About fourteen-years of age, he was a clever and thorough fellow. The nun had scolded him, grabbing the flashlight from his hands. A minute later, she seemed to change her mind:

"Would you like to have this thing?"

"Yes, for sure! I'd have a lot of fun with my friend! We could catch some big fish with it at night!"

"All right, I promise to give you one, but you'll have to do something for me first!"

"Anything you want "missu" answered the boy with bright eyes."

"You know the Sister who washes the clothes by the river?".

"Yes, Sister."

"I would like that someone or something to accidentally push her into the river, so she'll go over the falls. Can you do that?"

"Yes, it won't be difficult. I'll take a long branch just above the water and I'll tie it back. When the Sister arrives, I'll undo the rope, and the branch will push her into the river!"

"Very well! When everything is done, you'll have your reward."

Boba had put his plan in action. If it wasn't for that unfortunate branch she had grabbed onto, he would have had his flashlight! Now, everything had to be started over!

Everybody presumed it was an accident, and poor Rose had just been terribly frightened! However, she was convinced that something had pushed her. No one believed her. It was said she was distracted, or worst, just careless.

A few days later, Sister Thérèse-De-Lima was awakened by a whistling sound as she slept in her small cell. Sensing she was in immediate danger; she opened her eyes to face a boa constrictor whose hideous head was directed toward hers. In a survival reaction, she jumped to the other side of the bed and ran out of her room yelling:

"A snake! There's a snake in my room! Help!" The beast was found and killed.

The two incidents, happening within days of each other, had greatly disturbed the young woman. She suffered from attacks of panic that she could not overcome. Just the sight of a spider would trigger a crisis. She was unable to stay alone neither! In a word, she became hysterical.

Her nerves were so shaken she had to be brought bac home.

And it was to the peace of R. that Rose Fontaine came to rebuild her health.

Sister Thérèse-De-Lima Recovers Her Mental Sanity

U p until her encounter with death in Africa, the young woman's life had been relatively unscathed. Certainly, Rose had known poverty, deceptions and renunciations, but never had she faced an *evil leading directly to death.*

When a soul is confronted with this somber reality, it retreats into the solitude of terror. It's a world where God's mercy has vanished. Its isolation is entirely left to the forces of darkness. There is no light, no warmth and no comfort. The Divine Father seems to have abandoned his creature into the hands of the Devil. The Evil Spirit completely possesses his prey, convincing it of its guilt, with no possibility of relief from its pain:

In this world of sufferings, what allows a man to continue when everything overwhelms him? How can a man go on breathing when he has just learnt that death is close? Why does someone consent to live after hearing that his child has died? *Hope* is the grace that binds us to life; it is a gift from heaven. The ultimate test comes when this also is taken away, leaving only a dying broken puppet that is slowly fading away; it is called Depression.

Rose went through this hardship of her soul and it almost destroyed her.

The tranquil atmosphere of the Juvenate, the beauty of the countryside nature, the mountains and the surrounding woods helped to calm the torment in Sister Thérèse-De-Lima's soul.

The doctor had recommended walks in the fresh air. Every time she went for her stroll, Sister Rose-De-Lina had met with the aging nun who was in charge of the garden.

211

Rose asked about the crops. Sometimes, she helped the old woman lift a heavy weight or carry a cumbersome load. As they gardened together, a friendship developed between the two women. Sister Thérèse became closer and closer to Sister Geneviève-Marie.

One day, Rose had asked to be assigned the gardening and poultry task with her friend. The Superior, Mother Marie-Des-Saints-Anges, had accepted, happy to see the young Novice rediscovering her interest for life. Besides, Sister Geneviève-Marie was getting old and needed help. The younger nuns were not often interested in this heavy outdoor work. No one ever wanted to do it, so it seemed that Sister Thérèse-De-Lima had arrived just in time. Her companion received her with open arms. She was eager to teach her all the secrets of an accomplished gardener.

For five years, the two women worked in harmony, transforming and improving their surroundings. Rose was alert and vigilant, wanting everything to be perfect.

Below the garden, there was a large henhouse. Though still in use, it had been built many years ago. One day, Sister Thérèse–De- Lima had remarked to Sister Geneviève-Marie that the roof was leaking. The holes were clearly visible.

"Poor child, it's been like that a long time. It started before you were here. In the beginning, it was only a drop here and there, now it's almost a flood."

"But all this falling water will rot the floorboards too! As for the roof, it's already finished. Sooner or later, the henhouse will be useless! We have to tell someone!"

"Oh! You know, that is not really my business!"

The old Sister saw the crumbling structure as natural, for her own body was deteriorating a little more each day. She had a fatalistic philosophy when it came to the passing of time.

Rose was a young woman with her whole life in front of her. She couldn't imagine the Convent without its henhouse. In fact, it was an important source of food for the community. She had gone to Mother Superior with her concerns. Mother Marie-Des-

Saints-Anges had approved her initiative since she understood that routine maintenance spares costly repairs.

One day, when it was pouring rain, the Mother Superior had gone down there under a big umbrella. She wanted to check the extent of the damage herself. She had judged the situation urgent. However, as those women led a secluded life, they had little contact with the outside world. Mother Marie-Des-Saints-Anges didn't know who to contact to repair the roof. She had discussed it with Nicolas, the man in charge of the furnace. She asked him if he knew anyone who would do the job without asking a fortune. After thinking it over, Nicolas had answered:

"Yes, I think I know someone! He does things like that in his spare time. He is retired and has always been good at handiwork. If I remember well, he built his own house with some of his friends. I believe his price would be reasonable."

"He is exactly the person I'm looking for! Who is he?"

"It's my Uncle Édouard. He lives with us. I'll talk to him about it tonight, and I'll give you his answer tomorrow."

Uncle Édouard was pleased to do this favor for the Convent. The next day he was there as to check everything.

Mother Superior showed him the henhouse. After having gone up on the roof, he announced that it had to be completely redone. Even the wood under the shingles was decaying and would have to be replaced. He calculated the material needed and showed the numbers to the Superior who looked worried:

"It's expensive! I'd never thought we'd have to pay that much!"

The uncle understood her embarrassment and proposed a solution:

"I think you haven't bought construction material for a long time, Sister. Prices have gone up, but I'll make you an offer: I won't charge you for my time if you'll provide someone to help. This person won't have to go up there, but she'll have to fill a basket that I will hoist up on the roof with a pulley."

Mother Marie-Des-Saints-Anges was very interested in such savings. She immediately thought of Sister Thérèse-De-Lima as the best person for the job.

"This agreement is very attractive, Mister V. Wait a minute, and I'll see if I can find the person to help you."

Uncle Édouard watched as the Superior climbed up the slope and headed towards someone bending over the garden. After a few minutes, she came back with Sister Thérèse-De-Lima.

"Mister V. I would like you to meet one of our gardeners, Sister Thérèse-De-Lima. She is willing to be your assistant."

"It's a pleasure to meet you, Sister. I'm sure we'll make a good team!"

"How do you do, Sir" answered Sister Thérèse, a bit reserved.

Sister Thérèse-De-Lima's attitude was modest, but Uncle Édouard noticed that her eyes shone with pleasure.

"Well, said Mother Superior, all is settled, Mister V. Please order the material; we have an open account at the general store. Ask them to deliver it here and whenever you're ready, Sister Thérèse will be at your service. Isn't that so, Sister?"

"Yes, Sister, as you like!"

It was in this way that Uncle Édouard and Sister Thérèse-De-Lima had met. The young woman had completely recovered from the bad depression which had inflicted her a few years earlier. She was now happy and radiant. She imagined she would finish her days here in the peace of nature.

During those few weeks they worked together, the two became friends. The uncle worked slowly and methodically. When he arrived in the morning, he would take the time to explain the work planned for that day, so she would understand what she had to do. At noon, they were brought a big wicker basket with their lunch. The Superior had considered it fair to feed a man who was working for free. Besides, it saved time, and the work would be finished sooner. As the days passed, a trust developed between Uncle Édouard and Sister Thérèse-De-Lima, and as they ate together, they began to confide in each other.

Uncle Édouard, as many laities, often wondered how a young woman, or a young man, could renounce all worldly pleasures for a life of solitude and sacrifice.

Sister Thérèse tried to explain:

"It's not the right way to look at things, Mister V. If you consider our way of living from the outside, it may appear like a life of denial, but it is not true. On the contrary, it is a life of joy! However, it's true we don't have the same freedom other people have. But what's the use of freedom when someone is poor without any options as I was? Here, I am confident as I am protected from outside difficulties. I don't have to worry about work, it is assured. When I'll be no longer able to accomplish it, I'll be given another one. If I become sick, I'll be looked after. I'll never be left alone like so many of the elderly in society."

"What about your family? You can never visit them!"

"It's true that I cannot go and see them at their home, but they can come and see me here. In fact, every time there's a new baby, they come to show it to me. So, as the years pass, I see my nieces and nephews grow up. And you know, I'm very near to them in prayer. When a member of the family has a problem, they write and ask me to pray for them. So, I'm always with them in my thoughts."

"Do you usually obtain what you ask four iin your prayers?" teased Uncle Édouard

"Not always as we would wish. At least, we're given the strength and courage to overcome the ordeals we have to endure for our spiritual growth."

"In brief, if I understand you well, here, in this Convent, you feel you're completely secured and protected from all dangers of this world?" assessed Uncle Édouard.

Rose's face suddenly turned serious. Memories of the past were coming back in waves of anguish. "No, not from everything, not always...." The nun didn't finish her sentence. Instead, she suggested they start back to work right away, for she did not want the man to see her growing discomfort. However, Uncle Édouard was an acute observer who noticed everything.

As the afternoon went by, the work progressed as well. Sister Thérèse-De-Lima was placing things in the basket, and Uncle Édouard was pulling them up on the roof.

It was nearly the end of the day, when suddenly, the man on the roof heard a terrible shriek like he had never heard before. He thought the nun was seriously hurt and in great danger, as she didn't stop screaming. Her cries sounded as if they would continue forever. Uncle Édouard climbed down the ladder as fast as he could. He saw that Sister Thérèse was completely hysterical by something which she was staring at in horror at her feet. Édouard V looked down and saw a small snake its head raised. It appeared as surprised as the woman. At the sound of the man steps, the tiny black reptile with yellow stripes disappeared into the tall grass. It was a grass snake.

The nun was trembling all over. Her teeth were chattering in her mouth. Uncle Édouard made her sit on a rock. She cried for a long time without a word, shuddering huge sobs. The man stayed beside her, knowing his presence was reassuring her. After a while, she calmed down.

"You must think I'm completely crazy. I know it's not reasonable, but I really thought I was going to die!"

"I have seen plenty of people who were afraid of snakes, but they didn't think they were going to die when they met them! No, yours was more than a mere fright reflex! It was a lot more serious than that!"

"You are right, Mister V. When I was in Africa, in Cameroon, a serpent had crawled into my bed. It woke me up; it was an enormous beast, a cobra.".

"Oh! I'm beginning to understand! You were reliving that terror!"

"Yes, but it's more than that! In the same week, I nearly drowned. I fell into a torrent that was carrying me towards the falls. I had been pushed... and then a few days later a serpent was put in my room!"

"Do you think somebody wanted to kill you?"

"Yes, I'm quite sure of it!"

"How can you be so sure?"

"I had been warned. A Sister had threatened me. She told me she would have her revenge no matter what."

"Another nun?"

"Yes, someone I knew before entering the Convent. She believed I had ruined her life. She was furious with me!"

"Was she right?"

"No! I did absolutely nothing against her. Certain things happened because she had encouraged them! But she couldn't accept her own responsibility in the matter and preferred to blame someone else."

"Do you still see this person?"

"No! Fortunately, she's still in Cameroon"

. "And you're here in Canada, safe!"

"Yes! Thank God!"

Preparing for Trial

nspector Leduc had been busy as well. He wanted to
establish an indisputable case in which the evidence was
overwhelming against Nicolas S. He had already checked
his alibi. He was convinced he could quickly discredit his
uncle's statement. It would be easy to prove that the testimony
of a person, lying in bed at night, was not a hundred percent
reliable. He had also ascertained the flaw behind Nicolas's
assertion that "he couldn't have come back in, since the door
was locked from the inside." He could rely on the testimony of
the Mother Superior to contradict him.

He was now waiting for the lab results about the evidence
left at the scene of crime. Most important was the autopsy
reports, identifying the weapon of the crime, and the way it had
been utilized by the murderer.

Coroner Ryan came to the Convent himself this Friday
afternoon. The doorkeeper's Sister led him to Inspector Leduc's
office. The Inspector immediately stood up on seeing him;

"Don't disturbed yourself, Mr. Leduc, I think we have many
things to discuss."

"How do you do, Coroner Ryan, I'm glad to see you! I guess
you're bringing me new information?"

"Yes, indeed. However, I need to make something clear first.
The young man you've put in custody, Nicolas S. If I remember
correctly, he is being illegally detained."

"Why do you say that?"

"At this stage of an investigation, no accusation can be held
against someone without evidence, is that not so?"

"I've asked you for a warrant against him because I
presumed, he was an important witness in view of the Public
Inquiry conducted by yourself, Doctor!"

"I guessed you had good reasons to think so, but this kind of detention cannot last for more than forty-height hours. Unless you are certain that this man is dangerous for society, and, if you don't, as we are on Friday. you have to know how to count, and release him soon!"

Doctor Ryan, Coroner and skilled physician, was the government representative in the incident. He was a man of principles, zealous and meticulous. One of his grand leitmotifs was: "Work well done is work perfectly done" He scrutinized every detail, and nothing seemed to escape his attention. So, when it was time to bring a charge against someone, he was incredibly rigorous. He couldn't tolerate questionable evidence or slapdash jobs. He was feared and admired because of his detailed method of working.

"If I understand you well, it means that I should have him released today?"

"No, you can wait until tomorrow and take the time to advise the detention center."

Inspector Leduc looked at the man in front of him: he had a predatory nose, the eyes of an eagle and a mouth without any lips, making his face a repulsive mask of a dangerous monster that frightens children. Mr. Leduc had to admit he hated Coroner Ryan a little more than was permitted. He pushed away this unpleasant thought to ask:

"Do you have the autopsy report?"

"Yes, the forensic surgeon is positive: two strikes of a triangular, sharp edged object. Someone calm and strong committed the act. This person would be accustomed to acting with a lot of precision.

"How can he make such a detailed conclusion?"

"Because the intended target, the jugulars, were severed by a single stroke each time. Imagine! the person had to strike only two times to directly meet his objective."

"Did it require the strength of a man?"

"Not strength as much as precision, a certain physical vigor too, but nothing above the average. I suppose it's more a question of accuracy."

"Would a woman have been able to do this?"

"It depends on the size of the lady and her physical fitness. But, she could if she was a strong and intensely determined person."

"You've mentioned a triangular and sharp object? What could it be?"

"There lies the mystery. We have been unable to identify it. It must be used for a specific task, but we don't know which one."

"Did the murderer leave clues behind?"

"The lifted prints belonged to the victim. There was no sign of a break in, neither of a struggle. The murderer came from inside the house. As for you, why did you arrest this Nicolas S?"

"He was the lover of the young nun who committed suicide. They were together that Sunday night; Mother Notre-Dame-Des-Pins had surprised them!"

"At what time did that happen?"

"Between one and two in the morning."

"The pathologist cited the death at five in the morning. Three hours passed between the two events. Would the man have stayed inside to commit his crime later?"

"It's highly improbable! After what she had seen, the Guardian must have thrown him outside immediately."

"But he may have come back during the night?"

"That's what I believe."

"Do you think he knew the house well enough to find the nun's room and kill her while she slept?"

"I don't know. Even though no lay person is ever allowed to circulate freely inside the Convent, maybe the young man was asked to do some repairs, thus saving the expense of hiring an outside worker. Yes, he could know the place well enough. Or his lover, the young nun, could have led him..."

"It's an excellent deduction although the nun knew that five o'clock was the moment everybody wakes up in the house. The danger of detection was high. However, in the three hours preceding, they could have acted freely. More, if, as you claim, Sister Des-Pins had thrown the man outside and most probably sent the young religious to her bed, when did the two of them communicate to co-ordinate the precise hour to meet and go to the victim's room?"

In a few sentences, Coroner Ryan had considerably reduced the evidence Inspector Leduc had built with so much pleasure the previous hours, and that he had judged irrefutable. He felt a strong resentment against this overly clever man, who was turning more and more detestable in his eyes. He wanted to mislead the doctor in his own fashion.

"And for you, Coroner, who is the culprit?"

"I don't have the slightest idea! That's your problem. I know you have questioned many people suspected of being connected in one way or another to this story, and that you have not retained any of them, except this young man?"

"No! You're forgetting the young nun and her child lover. The two had a very interesting motive; their survival within these walls, not to mention avoiding the scandal that would erupt. And the Chaplin is not to be forgotten either, though he is sensitive man if I may say. His religious reputation was also at risk. However, I must confess that the young man's case particularly intrigued me, I'm anxious to hear his testimony on Monday when the Crown attorney will press him with questions. Some interesting details may be revealed."

"Evidently, it's the classical scenario of the castoff lover who looks for revenge, though it's too simple for me. My intuition tells me the answer is a little more complicated than that!"

For a second time, Inspector Leduc was greatly annoyed. Not a single good word! No encouragement! Only negative comments aimed at undermining his efforts to resolve the case! That man really deserved his sour reputation, thought Mr. Leduc.

As for Uncle Édouard, he hadn't wasted any of his time. This Friday, he had met with the lawyer who was to represent Nicolas.

It was not an easy matter to find someone competent for a last-minute case such as Nicolas's. As a result of the intervention from his friend, Alfred, Valleyfield's chief of Police, he had found this young specialist in criminal law, Jean-François T., who had accepted to do a favor for the Officer. The lawyer had already met Nicolas on Thursday; Uncle Édouard had been scheduled for the day after in Valleyfield.

Jean-François T was a young man in his thirties who had not yet lost his enthusiasm for justice. The man listened with a lot of attention to everything uncle Édouard told him.

"Are you telling me you have witnesses?"

"Yes, three people, two to corroborate his alibi, and the other to verify that my nephew couldn't have come back to the Convent that night."

"Could you give me their names and addresses? I'll have a subpoena sent to them as soon as possible. It's two o'clock, we're lucky, the bailiff works till five today!"

Édouard, who had anticipated everything, gave the names and the addresses required. The lawyer told him he had met with Nicolas the day before to prepare the case with him. He was satisfied with this encounter, for his client had appeared to be a very credible young man.

Édouard was very pleased with the way things were unfolding. Before leaving the city, he wanted to visit a very special place to him and all the inhabitants of the city: The Chapel of the Sisters Clarisse.

The man had told himself it was on his way home. As he drove along the lake on Boulevard du Havre, he crossed Monastery Street on the right which led him directly to this place of prayer.

Those Cloistered nuns never went out. They did not engage in any activity other than pray day and night at the Holy Office's rhythm. They lived exclusively on the charity of the community. Since their arrival in Valleyfield, many years ago, these women, without even asking, had never been deprived of anything.

A long gray cement wall surrounded the Convent. At the entrance, nothing indicated that, in that place, the nuns were making a bridge between Heaven and Earth.

When the visitor entered the little Chapel opened to the public, a celestial presence could be felt. A discreet murmur seemed to continually resound around the ribbed vaults of the gothic ceiling. Those diffused voices brought attention to the main altar where the sanctuary lamp shone as if the tiny flame signaled Divine Presence. If the person was still conscious of his body at this point, it was lost as soon as he knelt down on one of the few benches situated on each side of the central aisle where lovely stained windows in the form of praying hands let the daylight in.

Uncle Édouard thanked God for the helpful circumstances placed in his path by Providence. He confided to Him the fate of Nicolas who still had to pass through the terrible ordeal of the Preliminary Inquest with Coroner Ryan.

Having regained his serenity, Uncle Édouard resumed his journey home. His heart was at peace since he had placed his whole family into the hands of God.

The next day at noon, Nicolas's mother answered the phone. She was speechless with joy when she heard the voice on the other end:" Can my uncle come and bring me home! Édouard, seeing his sister ready to faint, took the phone from her hands and on recognizing Nicolas's voice, had cried joyfully: "I'm on my way!"

Scarcely two hours later, Aurore was shedding tears as she pressed her son into her chest. Nicolas was visibly happy as well. However, his uncle noticed his nephew had the ravaged face of someone who had cried too much. Everyone seemed so cheerful, Édouard didn't want to recall sad memories.

Early Monday morning, the whole family left in the direction of Valleyfield. The young lawyer had asked to meet with Nicolas to settle a few details before the hearing in front of the Coroner.

The courtroom was small, without any windows. Benches reserved for the public were facing a large tribunal where the Coroner would take his place behind the desk, now empty. To his right, the Crown Attorney, a tall man, who looked stubborn and aggressive, was waiting somberly. At his side, Inspector Leduc looked like someone who wanted to win at any cost. On the left-hand side, a clerk was assigned to record the minutes of the proceedings. In the chamber, facing the Coroner, the main witness, Nicolas and his lawyer were sitting at a table. Nicolas was deathly pale; he seemed absent as if his mind was completely taken over by fear. At his side, his lawyer presented a calm and steady demeanor. Serious, he possessed the serenity of one who was confident in defending a just cause.

Several peoples occupied the benches behind: Édouard and Aurore were in the first row, as near as possible to Nicolas. On the other side, to the left, five men, looking stiff in their Sunday best, had been chosen as jurors. Later on, they would have to decide the fate of the potential suspects. They would have to judge if the evidences presented had convinced them to send the accused to trial or if there was enough doubt to dismiss the suspects.

At the rear of the room, on the left, asking themselves what they were doing there, stood Mr. Ovide Ladouceur, who was in charge of the Convent's furnace, as well as the family's downstairs' neighbor, owner of a German Shepherd.

On the other side, to the right, hidden near the wall, as if they were forgettable, sat the delegation sent straight from the Convent: Father Jean, Mother Marie-Des-Saints-Anges, Mother E, the little Marie-Céline and the big Germaine. Other individuals, accompanied by their children, were looking reproachfully at Father's Jean whose carelessness had placed them in this embarrassing situation. It was easy to guess it was the little altar boy, his friend, and their parents. In a remote corner, hardly noticeable as he was well concealed in his black garments from which emerged only a rounded furry hat, sat the Bishop inquisitor, Canon R.

Before Coroner Ryan entered, a loud voice announced: "Everyone stand in the court!

The Public Hearing

The first person called by the bailiff was the forensic pathologist who had conducted the autopsy on the victim. The man identified himself and responded to the following question: "Do you swear to tell the truth, the whole truth, and nothing but the truth? Raise your right hand and say: I swear it"

"I swear it!"

The Crown Attorney began his interrogation:

"Doctor Mongeau, are you the individual who did the post mortem examination on the body of the murdered nun, known as Mother-Notre-Dame-Des-Pins, of the Convent of R.?"

"Yes, I did, Mister Attorney."

"Could you tell us what you observed on the victim's body?"

"The person was about forty-five years of age and had two lesions on her neck. They corresponded to the jugular veins which had been sliced on both sides of the throat, the right and the left one."

"Were they the only wounds observed on the body?"

"Yes, Sir."

"According to you, were those incisions the cause of death?"

"Yes, the instrument used had been plunged into the flesh more than one inch deep, at two different places, causing a massive hemorrhage. Death would have been almost immediate, within a few seconds."

"After your observations, have you been able to identify the murder weapon?"

"Here, Sir, I have to confess that we have been unable to solve that mystery. Every tool which could have caused this kind of perforation has been examined, and even after consulting with several specialists, it has been impossible to come to any positive conclusion."

"Would you explain yourself, Doctor Mongeau?"

"At first, we believed it was an ordinary screwdriver. However, its sharp triangular point, measuring close to a quarter of an inch sideways, left us perplexed. No tool known corresponded to that specification. We concluded that it was probably an instrument designed for a very specific task, but we did not know for what"

"At what time did you set as the hour of the death?"

"At around five o'clock in the morning."

"That will be all, Doctor. Thank you."

"I call the crime technician, Mr. Langlois." The man walked to the front on hearing his name. "Would you identify yourself and take the oath please?" After he did, he was asked:

"It is written in your report that on Monday, the16th of November 195… you were summoned early in the morning to the scene of a crime which had been committed during the preceding night at the Convent of R?"

"Yes, Mr. Attorney."

"According to your drawing, there was no sign of a break-in or altercation. You sketched the body of a woman lying in her bed, probably killed in her sleep. Have I interpreted your thinking correctly?"

"Yes, Mr. Attorney."

"Did you discover any suspicious fingerprints at the scene?"

"None. The only prints found were those of the victim."

"Could you show us the photos you took at the crime scene?"

"Certainly." Then, the man took out several snapshots from a folder. The Crown Attorney gave them a quick glance before presenting them to the Coroner who examined them attentively before nodding his head to continue."

The Crown Attorney was conducting his interrogations briskly. Tall, stout shouldered, nearly a giant, he was acting with a lot of zeal as if he had been given the mission to track down the criminals and bring them to justice. In a serious voice, he announced:

"I would like to question, Inspector Leduc!"

The Policeman stood up and entered the witness box. He identified himself and was then sworn in.

"Inspector Leduc, you were called to the scene of a crime on Monday, November the sixteenth of the present year?"

"Yes, Mr. Attorney."

"What did you notice when you entered the room of the murder?"

"The victim was covered with blood. It seemed to have spurted all over on her clothes."

"According to you, was the position of the body consistent with the information presented by the crime technician? After examining the crime photos, he nodded, and then declared:

"Absolutely, Sir!"

"You set up an office in the Convent to begin your inquest?"

"Yes, Mister"

"From Monday the 16th to Friday the 20th, you've interviewed several witnesses who were potentially connected to the murder?"

"Yes, the Chaplain and the Mother Superior, the Sister who had discovered the body, another Sister and a young girl. In addition, I received the Canon Investigator sent by the Bishop. He was sent because the Bishop had learnt that a priest had been questioned. This Canon informed me about a very interesting fact he had uncovered. Finally, I questioned the main witness, Mr. Nicolas S."

"Which testimony were you particularly interested in?"

"The one from the Canon sent by the Bishop."

"Why?"

"Of everything I had learnt up to that moment, none seemed directly related to the murder. On Tuesday, toward the end of the day, an unexpected incident happened: a young nun hanged herself. The day after, the Canon was very upset. He came and told me some troubling facts. The day before, he had heard the young religious in Confession. She had revealed something astonishing before she committed suicide. After her death, the priest considered himself free from his religious obligations, and he came to tell me what he knew."

"What were those revelations?"

"If the court permits, I think the Canon should explain himself about everything.".

"I asked for Father Canon representative of the Bishop" Shouted the lawyer.

After those words, a deep silence fell over the courtroom. No one moved. There was a moment of uncertainty as if someone was absent. The Canon was not supposed to be called, because it was believed he would not be present. The Bishop had made an imperative call to that effect.

As the attorney searched the crowd with his eyes, a small dark package stirred and a figure emerged.

The little man came forward and took the oath. He seemed ill at ease, even contrite. When he had told the Bishop of his discovery, and especially when he had mentioned the violation of the Confession's confidentiality, his Superior had severely reproached him. Canon R had endured the reprimand in silence, for he knew it was the only solution to remove the Church from this impasse. Once again, the Canon had realized the ingratitude his task entailed: he had to play in the dirt without ever becoming soiled. However, he had reasoned that everything had been very discreet between him and Inspector Leduc. On the contrary, all was to become public now! The attorney began his questioning:

"What brought you to the Convent of R on Tuesday, the seventeenth of November 195...?"

"The Bishop had received a phone call advising him that a member of the clergy was being questioned in the case of a murder committed at the Convent of R. I was dispatched as an observer."

"How did you intervene in the affair?"

"I asked to hear everyone in Confession."

"Mister Canon, what did you learn during this exercise that was so interesting?"

"I learnt that a nun, Sister Marie-Marthe, who is now deceased, had sexual relations with an employee of the house, and that on the eve of her death, Mother Notre-Dame-Des-Pins had surprised them when they were together."

"And you communicated this to Inspector Leduc?"

"Yes, Sir."

"Did you give him any more details?"

"Yes, I told him the name of her lover."

"What was that name?"

"It was the man working in the furnace room of the Convent, Nicolas S, who is sitting here in front of me."

"That will be all Father. I'd like to recall Inspector Leduc again! shouted the attorney."

"Mr. Leduc, could you tell us more about Father Canon's revelation? What exactly happened in the minutes following Mother Notre-Dame-Des-Pins unexpected arrival?"

"The young man was thrown outside, and the nun sent back to her bed."

"From whom did you learn these details?".

"From the mouth of Nicolas S. in the minutes following his arrest."

"What was this man doing at the Convent?"

"He was responsible for the steam heating system of the house."

"You immediately had him arrested and detained as an important witness?"

"Yes, Sir."

"For what reasons?"

"Three reasons brought me to this decision: First, Nicolas S had a serious motive to eliminate this woman who was going to denounce him and cause him to lose the job he had occupied for the last four years. Second, he was the last person to have seen the victim alive. Third, even if he had been chased away from the place, he still had his key to the house, so he could have come back any time to committed the murder."

Investigator Leduc had assessed his reasons with authority as someone convinced of the truth. He even noticed that he had impressed the merciless Crown Attorney

"I thank you for your testimony, Inspector Leduc. It will be all."

Right at this moment, Nicolas's lawyer rose up and asked permission to question Mr. Leduc. The Corner Ryan granted it to him. The young lawyer, Mr. Jean-François T., seemed calm and confident as he asked the Policeman:

"Inspector Leduc, when you questioned my client about his eventual return to his place of employment, how did he answer you?"

"He told me it was impossible because the next morning when he had come to work at seven o'clock, he had not been able to open the door with his key. He said that it was locked from the inside, so he had been obliged to go back home."

"Did you check his assertion with a person of authority in the house?"

"Yes, I went to the furnace room with the Mother Superior. We looked at the door. There was indeed a latch which could be employed from the inside, preventing anyone from entering. However, this person of authority in the house told me that the Insurance Company had given strict orders to never use this latch. in case of a fire, because immediate intervention could be delayed. She further explained that all the nuns knew of this ordinance and followed it scrupulously."

"Did you verify the young man's alibi as to how he had spent the rest of his time that night?"

"Yes, I heard the testimony of his uncle, Mr. Édouard V. He lives with the witness. He was in bed that night. He came to inform me that he had noticed his nephew's return around one o'clock in the morning and that he hadn't heard him leave afterwards. I doubted the testimony of a person who was sleeping. Besides, there is an emergency door at the rear of the house which could allow someone to leave without being noticed."

"Thank you, Inspector Leduc. That will be all. "

Coroner Ryan addressed the two lawyers, one who represented the Crown while the other defended the accused Nicolas S, "Sirs, do you have any other witnesses you want to present?

The Crown Attorney answered in the negative while M. Jean-François T said he still had a few more. The Coroner gave him permission. The young man asked for Nicolas's mother, Aurore

V. As she came towards the front, Nicolas turned to watch her and barely recognized her. Usually so shy and possessing a manner devoid of energy, she was crossing the room at a bold pace. Nicolas could read the determination in her eyes as he had never seen it before! She was the lioness coming to defend her little one against the enemy who was attacking him.

Her son's lawyer indicated her place. She was asked to identify herself, and then vowed to tell the truth by placing her hand on the Bible. Jean-Francois T. began:

"Mrs. V, we would like to question you about your brother, Mr. Édouard V. Investigator Leduc has just testified that he couldn't believe his testimony. Your brother claims he is aware of everything that happens in the house while he is sleeping. Inspector Leduc thinks this is highly improbable. What's your opinion on the subject?"

"Contrary to Inspector Leduc, I can assure that what my brother said is true. He is a man who sleeps with one eye open. He has lived at our place for four years, ever since my husband died. During all that time, never once did I get up without him coming to check if everything was all right. One time, there was some birthday cake left over from supper. I had a sugar craving during the night and wanted another piece. I was ashamed of myself and didn't want anyone to see my gluttony. I left my bed, trying to make as little noise as possible. I was sure I had succeeded. I was enjoying my forbidden fruit when suddenly I heard my brother behind me saying: "I would like a taste too if you don't mind?" Also, I would like to add this. Let us suppose that in the unlikely event, that my brother had not heard Nicolas leave the house and his usual vigilance was flawed. It is impossible that it could have happened twice! He would certainly have heard him return!"

Aurore testified with calm and dignity, making a convincing argument.

"That will be all Mrs. V. You may go."

Aurore returned to her seat, but not before throwing a glance at her "little one".

"I call Mr. Louis Robitaille!"

The large man, who was the downstairs' neighbor of the V's family, came to the stand. After the usual formalities, Mr. T questioned him:

"You live downstairs from the V's family?"

"Yes, Sir, for six years."

"Is there an emergency stairway at the back of your house?"

"Yes, there is one just in front of my back door."

"Is it possible that someone could have gone down those stairs without you noticing it?"

"No, it is absolutely impossible!"

"Why do you say that?"

"Because of my dog: a German Shepherd who would have barked, giving the alarm! It sleeps just beside the door where the stairs are located. It has been trained so that nothing escapes its attention."

"But if the noise stopped, the dog would have stopped barking, and if you were sleeping soundly, you could have missed it!"

"No! This dog has been trained to keep barking until I go beside it and tell it to shut up."

"Did you have to get out of bed and go tell your dog to calm down on the night of November, the sixteenth 195.....?"

"No, Sir."

"Thank you, that will be all!" The man left.

"I wish to hear Mr. Ovide Ladouceur.

The furnace man, recently employed at the Convent, walked to the front. Nicolas turned his head to see the one who had taken over his job. He was surprised to read kindness on the man's face. He was satisfied with his replacement.

Nicolas's lawyer, Mr. Jean-François T, appeared very conscious of every gesture, for he realized Mr. Ladouceur was his key-witness. All of Nicolas's future depended on this man's testimony. After asking him to identify himself, the bailiff asked him slowly: Do you swear to tell the truth, the whole truth, and nothing but the truth?

"I swear it!"

The young lawyer began: "Mr. Ladouceur, how long have you worked for the Convent of R?"

"Since last Tuesday, the 17th of November."

"Is it accurate to say that you took the place of the accused, Nicolas S, who is sitting here?"

"Yes, Sir, I did. No one was looking after the furnace from that Sunday night when he left till the Tuesday when I arrived."

"How can you affirm that, Sir?"

"Because the door, where the furnace man is supposed to enter had not been opened since the last employee's left. It was locked from the inside."

Then, after the Lawyer turned toward the Coroner and glance at the jury, he said, emphasizing each syllable:

"Mr. Coroner, I would like to point out the significance of Mr. Ladouceur's statement. I'll pose my question in another way. Be careful how you answer. According to you, is Mr. Nicolas S telling the truth when he claims that on Monday morning, the 16th of November, when he tried to open the door to enter the furnace room, as he had done for the past four years, he couldn't because the door was locked from the inside?"

"He is telling the truth because the day after, my first day of work at this place, on Tuesday, the doorkeeper Sister gave me the keys to the side entrance of the furnace room. I was unable to open the door. I had to come back and ask this Sister to send someone to check the door from the inside to see what was blocking it.

A few minutes later, when I tried again, the door magically opened.

Later on, she came to excuse herself explaining me the door had accidentally been locked from the inside."

"It is very well, Mr. Ladouceur. You may go."

The young man turned toward the Coroner and said: "It will be all, Mr. President, I have no more witnesses."

Once again, Father Jean's innocence had been easily proved by the parents who testified that at no moment had their children mentioned any kind of sexual abuse, and no complaint had ever been lodged against him.

Time was the element that saved Mother E and the little Marie-Céline. There was no possible way that Germaine could know exactly what time it was since there was no clock in the dormitory and watches were prohibited in the Convent. As a result, her testimony had been nullified.

The Coroner explained to the five men, called as jurors, that they had to go into another room to discuss their verdict. "Your decision will have to be unanimous, and beyond any reasonable doubt to whether the evidences presented in this room against the principal witness and the other suspects are sufficient enough to hold them criminally responsible for the death of Mother Notre-Dame-Des-Pins and justifies bringing them to trial for murder before the Court of Assizes.

A half hour later, the jurors returned to claim that the evidence against Nicolas S. was not insufficient to convict him, nor for any of the other suspects, they had added.

Uncle Édouard, his sister Aurore and his nephew, Nicolas, now knew that the tempest was behind them, and that it had passed without causing irreversible damages.

With the end of the Coroner's inquest, Inspector Leduc was told that he was being removed from the case. The probability of finding the murderer was now considered too slim. Moreover, the religious authorities had specifically asked that he leaves the Convent immediately. The file was to remain opened, but it was better for the Inspector to pass onto something else. Mr. Leduc felt a profound resentment which was to grow over time.

As for Uncle Édouard, he invited his friend, Alfred, chief of Police of the Detention Center in Valleyfield, to a grand restaurant for a fine meal. He wanted to thank him for all he had done for him and his family.

For Alfred's part, he had requested that Édouard, unofficially, keep an eye on the Convent and its surroundings.

"You understand we cannot afford to have men working on this file for months. Also, we've already had political and religious pressure to let the matter drop. However, our position is quite different. A crapulous murder has been committed in this Convent, and the investigation is still opened since we didn't find the culprit. You know how the press is always eager to judge our incompetence in these matters. Nothing would make me happier than to find this murderer. That's why, my dear Édouard, I am going to give you, under the greatest of secrecy naturally, a copy of the file, so you'll have all the information necessary. As you are living near the place, you can advise us if ever you notice something or someone suspicious. May I count on you?"

"Listen Alfred, after what you've done for us, it is the least I can do. Besides, it will remind me of the old times and add a little diversion into my life. However, I cannot promise you any results as I can only investigate on the grounds, but with a little luck, one can never know.".

The Nightmare Returns

O n the other side of the world, in fa-away Africa, Diane Gourd, Mother Notre-Dame-Des-Pins, was not happy. Her heart was not at peace. She still dreamt of revenge, and it tortured her spirit. She was convinced that only the fulfillment of her dark ambitions would calm her soul from that devouring passion. For five years, nothing had been erased from her memory. Time, the great pacifier, had only revived her profound wounds. The thought which tormented her the most, was that she had nearly succeeded in eliminating from the face of the earth the one by whom all her pains had started. She repeated to herself constantly, "As long as she is breathing, I will not be happy!"

When a new comer arrived from Canada, Diane Gourd would inquire about Rose Fontaine, Sister Thérèse-De-Lima. She was told that since she had returned to Canada, her health had improved significantly.

If anyone could have read Mother Notre-Dame-Des-Pin's thoughts on hearing those words, they would have been frightened. Hidden under a nice smile, venom was ready to assail her victim.

After spending several years in mission, every nun could ask to be sent back to their own country. When her turn came, Mother-Notre-Dame-Des-Pins asked to be repatriated. On the pretext of needing to rest in nature, she made a special demand to go to R.

Before leaving, she renewed her pact of alliance with Boba, promising him all he wished if he succeeded in the mission he had never finished.

- But how can I kill Sister Thérèse–De-Lima if she is in Canada?

- Don't worry, I'll send her to you, Mother Notre-Dame-Des-Pins had assured him before leaving. If you don't forget me, I won't forget you. You can be certain of it!

It was a Mother Guardian for the Juvenists that was precisely needed at the Convent of R. As Mother Notre-Dame-Des-Pins had taught the children in Cameroon for many years, her experience was judged sufficient to assume her competence with the young women in Québec. Overnight, without any preparation, Mother Notre-Dame-Des-Pins became the Guardian of the Juvenists at R. Her Superior had insisted that she maintained a severe discipline without fault.

In Africa, children came to catechism voluntarily. The Sisters would try to please them in order to incite them to return. Gentleness and good humor were a necessity. Mother Notre-Dame-Des-Pins was told that it would be totally different at the Juvenate where a rigid and harsh discipline was required. This state of mind perfectly suited her personal disposition.

When Sister Thérèse-De-Lima discovered the presence of her enemy in the Convent, she understood that her happiness had come to an end. Their first encounter was an exact replica as the one in Québec many years earlier. The two women were young Postulants then, and Diane Gourd had declared her hatred to Rose Fontaine. At R, Mother Notre-Dame-Des-Pins had laughed malevolently when she had met Sister Thérèse-De-Lima on the stairs:

"How do you do, Sister? You seem in good health, but mark my word, it'll be different when I'm finished with you! Watch yourself day and night, I'm preparing my revenge, and it will be terrible!"

Rose had not answered, but had simply lowered her head. The weight of anguish once again seized her. She developed the fear of a tracked animal, alone to face its fate. Her peaceful environment seemed hostile to her now. From that damned day, she saw danger everywhere. Sister Thérèse-De-Lima's health began to deteriorate. She had the same symptoms of emotional instability as she had on her arrival five years previously. Mother Notre-Dame-Des-Saints-Anges wanted her to be healed, but she could not have realized that it was the very atmosphere of the Convent that was harming her. On the contrary, she thought that if the fresh country air had cured her the first time, it could have the same beneficial effects once again. All the more, the nun had asked to keep her outdoor responsibilities. The contact with the earth and the hens calmed her immensely.

Mother Notre-Dame-Des-Pins was clever. Even if she had just arrived in the house, she immediately understood where the real authority laid. Mother Notre-Dame-Des-Saints-Anges was a good and honest person. She wouldn't tolerate the least derogation from her moral values of justice and charity. She didn't covet honor or personal glory. She was incorruptible. The Guardian could hope for nothing from her.

However, on her first encounter with Mother De-La-Purification, the Provincial of all the Orders in Canada, she knew she had found the one she was waiting for. The Provincial, arrogant, scheming and hypocritical, represented all that Mother Notre-Dame-Des-Pins was searching for. The two made a connection right away. The Father Chaplain's problem had occurred, and the two women had sworn the priest's downfall in their common hatred of men. Mother Marie-Des--Anges, Superior of the Convent, had seen her authority ridiculed as everything had been played behind her back by the Provincial and the Guardian. Those two malicious women shared the same moral values.

They understood and complemented each other. Mother Notre-Dame-Des-Pins fawned upon the Provincial's vanity who, in return, bestowed upon her the authority which belonged to the Superior. Thus, on her visits, the Provincial first consulted Mother Notre-Dame-Des-Pins on the smooth operation of the house, even though her only jurisdiction was the Juvenate. However, Mother Notre-Dame-Des-Pins was very perceptive and knew everything. She had all the answers which often placed Mother Marie-Des-Saint-Anges in an awkward position. These small intestinal battles within her Convent made the Superior unhappy, for she only dreamt of peace and harmony.

Mother Provincial's visits were rare, and it takes time to weave bonds of real trust. However, Mother Notre-Dame-Des-Pins was patient and able to wait for the right moment.

She had begun talking about Sister Thérèse-De-Lima's case to the Provincial who had the authority to transfer nuns at her discretion. Mother Notre-Dame-Des-Pins had assured that she knew Sister Thérèse-De-Lima very well, having accompanied her on mission. She strongly recommended sending her back to Cameroon to improve her health.

On hearing this, the Mother Superior had jumped:

"I don't know who told you that being on mission was beneficial to Sister Thérèse-De-Lima. On the contrary, she encountered certain perils in this foreign country. She was in a miserable state on arriving here. Her nerves were finished, and she was afraid of her own shadow. She had been greatly traumatized over there. And you are thinking of sending her back there for her mental health? I can't believe my ears! You have been ill informed. When you return to the Mother House in Québec, question the Sisters working in the infirmary. They'll tell you that they were even considering sending her to the psychiatric ward, so fearful they were of her mental condition. Thank God, she recovered on coming here! However, it's true, she's not doing that well right now, but I'm sure that with a little patience, everything will fall back into place. I talk with her often, and every time, she assures me that she is trying to get better, and she seems very determined. For me, that is a sign of a sure recovery!"

In front of such certitude, the Provincial went back to discuss it with Mother Notre-Dame-Des-Pins;

"You have to understand that if the Mother Superior is very opposed to the transfer, and if the person doesn't make a request... More, if her health seems unsuitable for such a trip, I would have to have a very convincing argument to order her departure."

Mother Notre-Dame-Des-Pins had received badly this second rebuff to her destiny. So close to her goal, she couldn't renounce all that she had so patiently built.

Facing this important difficulty, the woman decided to play her hand. She informed Rose Fontaine that due to her recommendations, her departure for Cameroon had been arranged, and that on her next visit, Mother Provincial would announce the news. She had added viciously: "There's someone waiting for you over there, you know!"

Mother Notre-Dame-Des-Pins was convinced that when confronted with the force of authority, Sister Thérèse-De-Lima would submit to the will of Mother Provincial and ask herself to leave.

Sister Thérèse- De-Lima knew death was waiting for her if she was sent back to Cameroon. Panic began to weigh down on her. She went to the henhouse to hide and was not seen for the whole day. Her mind came to a heavy decision.

In nature, animals instinctively know this law of survival: the best defense is to attack. Fear paralyses. It weakens the one who is assailed. On the contrary, if the victim shifts into reverse, turning the negative energy back towards his opponent, he is saved.

By the end of the afternoon, when the Chapel bell had rung, Sister Thérèse-De-Lima was finishing the final details of her plan. She had come in for the evening meal. Her calm air and confident attitude were in sharp contrast to the fear one could usually read in her eyes. The evening recess had passed without a hitch. Sister Thérèse-De-Lima appeared very relaxed and serene.

At ten o'clock, everybody went to bed. That night, Rose Fontaine didn't sleep. She spent it fortifying her decision. At four forty-five, in charge of waking several nuns, she had gone to Diane Gourd's room, wearing her big apron, her boots and her gloves of slaughter.

When Sister Thérèse-De-Lima slit the chicken's throats, the spurting blood could soil her hands and her white robe. She would put on protective garments, always covered in blood, to shield herself from the splatters. Used to darkness, her eyes had easily located her victim's neck. The instrument, which normally pierced the palate of poultry, easily went through the exposed neck of Mother Notre-Dame-Des-Pins. Sister Thérèse-De-Lima had then taken off her apron, boots and gloves, she had carefully folding them into a jute bag. She had concealed the package behind the big fern located in the hallway, so she could come back and retrieve it later. After that, she began shouting, "Help! Help!" with all her heart.

Epilogue

S ome months later, Uncle Édouard was taking a walk in front of the Convent when he had the idea to have a look at the roof, he had repaired the year before.

The man had not been on the premises since last summer. The garden was full of beautiful vegetables and adorned with flowers. His pace was slow as he admired the magnificent landscape. The sun was low in the horizon, lighting the sky with wonderful colors.

He was now beyond the garden and was descending the slope which led to the henhouse. From far, he noticed that the door was closed. The place seemed completely deserted. When he arrived at the henhouse's entrance, he saw something moving in front of the small glass window. He came closer, putting his two hands on either side of his face to better see inside.

He found the sight before his eyes fascinating: Sister Thérèse-De-Lima had suspended some chickens by their feet. She passed from one to the other and, in a single precise movement, plunged the instrument of death into each beak that she held open. The blood soon gushed forth. The nun was bleeding hens for the kitchen.

Uncle Édouard knocked on the glass. Sister Thérèse jumped nervously. The bloody tool slipped from her hands. The uncle opened the door. The woman seemed paralyzed. Her face was livid.

Uncle Édouard picked up the fallen object. He examined it meticulously. Its triangle edges were very sharp. He recalled the technician's words: "At first glance, it appeared to be a screwdriver, but in reality, it must have been a very specialized instrument used for a specific task, though we were unable to ascertain for what."

Uncle Édouard looked at the woman, petrified with fear, and he said calmly:

"I read in the police report that Mother Notre-Dame-Des-Pins was back from Cameroon for a few months. As soon as she was here, she threatened you directly, did she not?

A heavy silence followed and the man continued:

"You know, Sister Thérèse-De-Lima, certain people will talk about murder, but they are wrong. Myself, I'd call it acting in self-defense. What do you think, Sister? As for me, I promise to forget what I've just seen. You can rest in peace, Sister," concluded Uncle Édouard affectionately.

Review Requested:
We'd like to know if you enjoyed the book. Please consider leaving a review on the platform from which you purchased the book.

Lightning Source UK Ltd.
Milton Keynes UK
UKHW040014060620
364507UK00001B/122